LOST ON MARS

For the Clarkes and the Lakes

LOST ON MARS

PAUL MAGRS

Firefly

First published in 2015
by Firefly Press
25 Gabalfa Road, Llandaff North, Cardiff, CF14 2JJ
www.fireflypress.co.uk

Print ISBN 9781910080221
epub ISBN 9781910080238

*This book has been published with the support of the
Welsh Books Council.*

Typeset by: Elaine Sharples

Printed and bound by: Bell and Bain, Glasgow

1

Dawn was coming over the edges of the plain. It was so early that we could hardly see each other. We were half asleep, all except Da, who was always up early and worked the land every day. That day we joined him at earliest light. We had about a day's work ahead of us, he said. The dust storm would hit that very night. And in just a few hours all the crops would be gone. They'd be laid waste, he said.

So we were all out there. Ma, my little sister, my brother Al, Da and me. We took the beasts from their pen and rode out to the furthest edge of our land.

Grandma was up early too. But she wouldn't come with us. She stood on the veranda of our Homestead and yelled at us, hollering fit to burst, her nightgown all stained and greasy. It was hard to pick out what she was yammering about. Ma always said that Grandma was just an old lady, and we didn't have to pay her any heed…

Ma and Da explained to me when I was old enough to understand the truth. Grandma was not in her right mind. The trauma of her long life on Mars had sent her mind spinning in the wrong direction. She had been one of the first settlers on this world of ours. Grandma was an historical personage, is what Da used to say. No matter that she was baying like a hound on that porch. No matter that her cries would come chasing us across the desolate plains.

Ma said it was a shame Grandma couldn't be given a knife like the rest of us, but Da just shook his head. He didn't want to be giving the old lady a knife. I could understand that. I understood more than they knew, of course. I was almost fifteen by Earth years, which was the calendar we were still using on Mars. I understood more than they wanted me to.

The sun scraped higher up the sky and soon the long, cool shadows were the best places to walk. The scorching trails of heat were already too tiring to move in and we had to conserve our strength for the picking of the corn. Da had drilled us all in the technique, though I knew it already, having snuck out to help him before.

The alien corn stood about three feet taller than me. It was green, with all these furling tongues and shoots. You had to seize and unwind them and pluck the corns out of the grooves in the narrow leaves. They were like springs that wanted to snap back and protect their precious growth. But we needed that corn. It was the reason we lived out here on the hot plains. Da had coaxed all of this green stuff out of the dry earth with such patience and care. It had taken him years to get it this rich.

But all of this would be ruined by nightfall. According to the signs, storms were going hit us and strip the land completely bare. Ma made us rest after the first hour of picking rows of corn. We gathered round her and each took a plaggy bottle of milk she had kept cooling in her picnic bag. The milk was bluish in the morning light and I watched my younger sister drinking greedily. My heart twinged a bit when I saw Hannah drinking. She was only three, but she was out here with the rest of us. Her hands were streaked by the dark-green sap, same as ours.

The burden beasts were panting nearby, and Ma slopped some precious water into their bowls. They bowed in deference, and sipped thirstily. On their backs were strapped the great wicker baskets containing our haul so far. It didn't look like much. If that was all we had harvested in the first hour, I wondered how much we'd end up with by the time the storms came blowing through.

I wondered if it would be enough.

Da was being hearty and confident. He jollied everyone along, exclaiming over what a great start we had made that morning. He was so proud of his girls, he told us. And of his son too, he said, clapping Al on the back as he drank up his milk. He almost spluttered it out. Al was younger than I was by a year, and more delicate, even if he was a boy.

My back was breaking, and my fingers were splitting and bleeding from teasing open the corn fronds. I shielded my eyes and looked back along the groves towards the Homestead. And I saw Toaster ambling his way up the green avenue towards where we worked.

The old machine was bringing us water. A great big vat of it, hoisted over his shoulder. He was just in time, too, because we were running out, as the sun hit its height. I watched him labour up the dusty track on those shaky, hydraulic legs. Toaster was so old even then and he was just about in pieces. Da had to keep patching him and looking for spare parts whenever he went into town. Sometimes I'd heard Da mutter to Ma that, really, the best thing to do would be to deactivate the old thing. Toaster was just a sunbed. What did we need an old sunbed for on the roasting surface of Mars?

Toaster came in the very first ship, with Grandma's people. It had been a luxury ship, stocked with all kinds of devices, the likes of which we'd never seen, and were unlikely to see again, Da said. Many were destroyed early in the settling period, but Toaster had lasted as long as Grandma. She wouldn't hear of his being deactivated, of course. Toaster reminded her of the days on Earth when ladies were pale and lived indoors, away from the sun's harmful rays. When they lay within the glass innards of machines like Toaster and burned themselves slowly orange.

In more recent years Toaster was determined to prove he was still useful. He stood on his hind legs and fetched and carried. He was slow though, and sometimes Da would get kind of exasperated waiting for him when he got the jitters. I sort of liked him though.

'Well, now, look at this!' Toaster gasped, as he struggled up to us, bowed down by the heavy water. 'Look at all this you've been doing!' He peered into the baskets at the corn we'd gathered. He was right, too. We'd put on a burst of speed as the morning advanced, and we'd done well.

Da opened up the vat and Toaster helped him fill up our bottles. 'Thanks,' Dad told the Servo, and Toaster looked gratified by this, his metal face wincing as Da clapped his shoulder.

While we were all drinking our chilled water, and Al coaxed my sister out from under the cornstalks where she'd been dozing in the shade, Ma took Toaster aside. 'Has the old lady settled down?'

Toaster lowered his voice tactfully. 'She was shouting for quite a long time, madam, I am afraid to say. She is convinced that you will be caught out in the dust storm. She fully believes that you will all die today out here, and that she will be left to starve, alone in the Homestead.'

Ma nodded. She was fretting, I could see. Ma hated anyone to be upset, even Grandma. 'I wonder if I should go back,' Ma said to Da. 'And check that she's OK.'

Da shook his head. 'I need all of you here. You too, Toaster. I reckon that we've got about four hours' work left.' Da stared into the boiling soup of the red skies. 'See that?' He nodded to the far horizons, where a peppery darkness was building up like a swarm on its way. 'That's what's heading here.' He sighed, gazing at the swaying green of the cornstalks. I looked round and saw how little we had actually tackled. Only a tiny portion of the precious crop would be saved and I could feel the terrible weight of Da's sadness. All that work of his would be ruined within minutes of the dust storm touching down.

And so we worked with renewed concentration and vigour. I was amazed at Toaster's speed. He tore into the cornrows, both hydraulic arms lashing out with mechanical precision. Dry chaff and waste flew in all directions as he worked.

It wasn't too much later when Da stopped us all. 'I was too generous in my estimation,' he said. 'I think we'd better go home now.'

It was barely three hours into the afternoon and a dry, nasty wind was rippling through the corn. It lashed at us like hot tongues saying bad things at our backs. Ma and Da and Al and Toaster worked busily packing up all the equipment, and covering up the panniers of fresh-cut corn.

Staring into the storm as it lowered on down through the heaving clouds, I imagined a whole desertful of sand up there, flying about. About to slice right through us. Everything living would be torn to shreds. Wild grit was flying through the air and landing in our hair, stinging our exposed skin. Ma tucked Hannah into her arms.

'How long have we got?' she shouted at Da. 'Do we have time to get home?'

Da looked like he knew he'd cut it fine. He'd kept us out till the very last minute. He frowned and shook his head. 'Of course we've got time. If we go now, and we don't stop.'

He kicked the beasts into action. They were lazy, slouchy lizards but with the weather coming up even they were keen to get going. I'd never seen them so swift.

So we hastened home with the storm behind us and as much of our crops as we could carry in our baskets.

Al came walking alongside me. 'Sometimes I could really hate Grandma,' he said, softly, so that no one else could hear. 'Not for all that she's crazy and she shouts at us and does weird stuff. I mean, I could hate her for coming here in the first place. She had a good life on Earth. They were rich, weren't they? And yet they had to come to Mars. Our lives could have been so different on Earth...'

Of course I'd heard Al going on like this before. He would start imagining what his life could have been like. On Earth, he would have been like a prince, maybe. He would have worn a cape of gold and gone walking in the rain. He would have had a yacht and gone sailing their oceans. He often came out with these dreams. That was just Al, though. He was my little brother. He was OK.

2

We only just made it.

The dust storm came roaring across the plain even earlier than we thought. We were loading the baskets into the store shed. First we knew, my brother Al gave a squawking shout of fear. We turned about and there they were: the worst storm clouds we'd ever seen. They rushed billowing out of the skies and they were in the fields of crops now. Destroying everything as they came.

Da spurred us on to unload the baskets and quickly secured the barn. I saw him look worriedly at the building. He was hoping it would stand up to the dust. If it didn't, then we'd been wasting our time. And what about the Homestead? Would that stand up to the storm? But it had to. There was nowhere else to go.

We got home in time. Just as the eerie howling of the wind and dust could be heard like a threat rolling up the valley towards us. Ma hugged Hannah to her chest as she flung open the door of our home and we all toppled into our small house, finding it dark and still inside. I had never been so relieved in all my life.

Da was tethering the lizards into their pen at the back

of the house. The creatures would have to take their chances in the storm.

Inside the Homestead, we found stuff ruined, flung down, torn into bits. Some of Ma's good rugs and wall coverings had been rent apart. Pots and dishes had been smashed on the tiled floor of the kitchen. There was a strange, nasty smell.

None of us had to wonder who had messed the place up while we were out. It was always Grandma who did bad stuff like this as soon as our backs were turned. Although we were used to her strange goings-on, the wreckage was worse today. Da said it was likely the old lady had been super disturbed by the scary noises of the rising storm. I saw Ma break down in tears in her kitchen when she thought no one was looking.

Al and me went round upstairs, finding more damage, looking for Grandma in her favourite hiding places. Toaster was busying about already, putting things to rights and cleaning up the mess she'd made. 'Oh dear, oh dear,' we heard him say in his singsong voice. 'Someone has had a busy day. Oh dear!'

Upstairs, through the thin roof covering, the sounds of the approaching dust storm were louder. Closer. More ominous. Al looked pale as he lit the lamps. He knew that the natural daylight coming through our windows would vanish, all of a sudden, very soon. None of us wanted to be sitting in the dark when the dust came.

'Grandma, are you in there?' Al asked, sounding such a scaredy-cat now, I wanted to push him aside and yell at her myself. I didn't feel like she was venerable or historical. I felt like she was a dumbass old woman who was making our lives hell. She was giving Ma way more work and heartache than she needed to have.

'You better get out of there, Grandma,' I said, pounding on her door. 'Come on. Open up. Da says it's best if we're all together, downstairs. He wants us all gathered together.'

'Go away,' came the old lady's voice. Now she sounded weak. But I knew she was just weaseling. She was scared we'd be mad about the mess she'd made. Now she was turning back into being the sad old lady who wouldn't do nothing wrong.

'Please, Grandma,' said Al, in his most winning voice. He knew that Grandma had a special soft spot reserved for him. He knew he was the best at getting her to behave. Apparently he was just like her brother at that same age. Her lost brother, the fantastic hero, Thomas. Sometimes when Grandma was crazy confused, not even knowing what year she was in, it was like she thought her Thomas was still with her. Al didn't mind.

The door opened and she stood there, in her nightgown smeared with ashes. She had eyes only for Al.

'Dust storm's coming, Grandma,' Al said, though it was kind of pointing out the obvious. By now the noise was pounding through the whole house. The windows had gone dim already. When I looked at the landing window there was a grainy fuzziness out there, like the haze on a broken monitor.

Grandma's expression went clear like she briefly stopped being mad. She said, 'Did you rescue the crops?'

Al nodded. 'Yes! Yes, we did it. Well, we got some of them. Enough, Da thinks.'

Grandma looked down at her hands. 'That's good,' she said. 'I wish…'

'Come and sit with us,' said Al. 'Ma's making some broth and some soda bread.'

As he led her away, Grandma said, 'I wish I could have helped you all.'

'Hush, now,' Al said, taking her towards the wooden stairs. I followed on behind, listening to the skittering and tapping noise on the tarp roof of the house. I was feeling bad, I guess, because I couldn't feel sorry for Grandma. I felt kind of cold inside about her. I just didn't care as much as Al did anymore and I thought that probably made me bad.

Downstairs Da had gathered everyone around the table where we ate our meals and prayed together each day. 'Lora,' he told me. 'Come and sit down with us. Look, we're all here. You sit with us now. Remember – nothing bad can happen to us. Not when we're all together.'

That time, at least, this was true. Nothing bad happened to us that night. None of our family was hurt or killed by the storms that raged till the next dawn light came.

I don't think any of us slept except Hannah and Grandma. We stayed together in our kitchen as the walls were battered. It was as if wild creatures were out there, trying to come inside to get us.

I think we sang every song we knew that night. When it seemed we had run out of singalong songs, Ma played her harp. It was a miniature harp, all gold, and she kept it wrapped in cloth underneath her and Da's bed. It always made me feel drowsy, and half-awake, the liquid strings sent me dreaming of the rivers and seas of Earth. I had heard the grown-ups talk of such things, and I had even seen pictures. And I dreamed about them on music nights.

The storms raged and howled in the darkness outside and we did our best to ignore them. Then, when we were almost too tired to move or think, Da started telling us the old stories again. He told tales about Earth and our family and who they had all been in that other life. And then he told the story of Grandma and Grandpa's generation, and how they had given up almost everything to create a new life for us.

We heard once more about the first landings and the first wave of settlers. The early disasters and the fights that broke out between folk when they tried to make homes for themselves. The constant struggle each day to bring subsistence out of the hopeless soil. They had it so much harder than we do, he said. We must be so grateful for the sacrifices of the previous generation. We were second and third generation settlers and we had an obligation to create a better life for those who came after us: that's how it all worked. Each generation made it easier for the next, and they did it all out of love.

I guess I slept for a while that night in my chair, with thoughts like those going round in my head. When I woke up I thought I'd gone deaf. The roaring and the howling had stopped.

It sounded like a great big emptiness. I cleared my throat, just to make sure I could still hear anything at all. Then the whole kitchen started coming to life. Ma clattered about, cleaning our crocks with sand. I could hear Da stomping, carrying Grandma upstairs to her bed. There was the mechanical whirring of Toaster's ancient joints as he began work again.

We had survived!

I felt like jumping up out of my chair, running outdoors and doing a lap of honour around our Homestead. Al grinned at me like he felt just the same way. Da came downstairs and he started to take down the wooden boards that covered the windows and doors. He got us kids to help him and we were so excited, we felt like we hadn't been outside for several weeks. Martian sunlight felt so good on your face when you'd been shut inside like that. It felt slow and old. It warmed you right down to your toes.

Da tackled the door. It was stuck. The sand had been swept into a dune against the front of the Homestead. We all put our backs into it. It was only when Toaster put his hydraulic strength behind the door that we got it open.

We stepped out into an alien landscape.

Really, in the new morning, it looked nothing like it had the day before. My heart was hammering with excitement and shock.

Someone had reached down from heaven, or wherever, and smoothed his great big palm over our world. The sand had blown over everything so deeply it had smothered the whole lot. We were worried about our crops being damaged, but they had completely disappeared. Even the shape of the horizon had shifted, at the far edges of our familiar prairie. It looked hillier now.

Da looked grimly disgusted. He knew the storm was a bad one. He knew that chances were it would wipe the slate clean. But we checked on our storage hut and – amazingly – the building was still standing safe, and the crops we collected the previous day were all fine.

'Praise the Lord,' Da muttered, under his breath. I thought I even saw him wipe his eyes with relief.

We did a circuit of the Homestead. Da said we had to be careful of the shifting sands; they could be treacherous.

At the back of the Homestead we found our burden

beasts. They were dead, of course. Their heads poked out of the new dune, and I stared at their closed eyes and their fringed lashes. I had names for our lizards. I called them Molly and George. Which was stupid and sentimental when they could die so easily.

Da sighed as he started digging the dead beasts out. 'We'll have to train up another pair,' he said. 'We'll be lucky to get two as good as these. Will you come to town with me, Lora? Al? There's all sorts we need. Plus we have to check on the townsfolk. See that everything's OK there.'

Both Al and I nodded, holding back our excitement. We loved to go to town.

'Come on. Back indoors,' said Da, staring at our dead animals. 'We'll tell Ma she's got her work cut out for her filleting and salting these beasts for storage. At least we know we won't starve, eh?' He tried to make light of it, and talked about us having a grand barbecue maybe, and inviting all our friends from town.

But I didn't want to think about eating Molly and George.

See? I was sentimental in those days. I tried to focus my thoughts on our trip to see the townsfolk.

And if I remember rightly, it was on this trip that we heard about the Disappearances. They had started up again.

3

The going was hard. Usually Molly and George would pull the hovercart all the way into town. With our beasts dead Da had to tinker with the complicated insides of the engine to make it hover again. The circuits of the instruction manual had long ago fizzled out. Like so many of the devices we'd inherited, we'd forgotten the original instructions and everything was a guessing game.

Da was a kind of super genius and he battled away with his whole box-load of greasy tools and what do you know? Pretty soon that old hovercart was lifting off the sand upon a cushion of jellified air. It quivered like heat haze on the prairie.

Al and I whooped, clambering aboard, and the cart wobbled underneath us. Da was busy kissing goodbye to Ma and Grandma and fussing over Hannah. He was always like that. He departed as if every trip was his last. He had seen too much calamity during his life on Mars. He had seen too many folk set off and never come back.

But Al and I were impatient that day. I wanted to feel the air streaming past us, all cool and sharp on my face. We both wanted to experience that lurching excitement in the pits of our stomachs as the hovercart accelerated to what would seem like impossible velocities.

As Da gunned the engines, Grandma stood alongside us in her old woollen dress and shawl and she had that crazy glint in her eye again.

'You be careful in that town, do you hear?' She narrowed her eyes at us. 'You watch after these kiddies.'

Da nodded, pretending he was paying heed to her madness. We could tell that he was as keen to be off as we were. He jumped up in the driver's seat, let out a yell, and wrenched the rusted wheel around. The hovercart shivered and bucked, and then we were off. Riding across the newly smoothed dunes that the storm had created.

We found town busy. People were out and about, using shovels to clear away sand drifts that had settled against the fronts of stores and houses. Folk were up ladders fixing windows and signs and tiles on rooftops. There was a cheery, businesslike atmosphere, as if the town was determined to carry on as usual. They wouldn't let something like a storm get in the way of their everyday lives.

Al and I watched all of this as Da steered the hovercart down Main Street. He called out to a few men he knew and they answered him with gruff replies, or waved as they concentrated on their tasks. Da parked in a sandy lot behind the abandoned Post Office and gave us a handful of coins each, plus a list. He had the bigger list, detailing the heavier goods he would pick up at the Storehouse. Our list consisted of the no-less-important smaller items we could get from Mrs Adams' store. Da always sent us there, so that we would have a vital task of our own to perform, he said. But Al and I knew it was also because Da couldn't stand gossipy Mrs Adams holding court in her fancy goods emporium. I was surprised though, because that day he said, 'Be sure to invite the Adamses to our barbecue. Don't you forget, Lora.'

We watched our Da lope off towards the Storehouse where he'd be meeting up with other farmers and men from town and they'd spend the remainder of the afternoon discussing the storm. They'd be jawing about the impact of the disaster and drinking the homebrew. Then they'd be congratulating each other on getting through the worst of another stormy season.

But more had been blowing through town than hot wind and sand.

There were rumours. Tales of something terrible. Everyone was talking about it, as Al and I found out in the cool interior of Mrs Adams' store. There were hushed voices and a kind of electric nervousness in the air. Al and I joined the huddled group of ladies and we eavesdropped.

I breathed in the hundred spicy scents of Adams' Exotic

Emporium. I examined beautifully arranged displays of dainty soaps and candles and dried flowers. Everything was scented with lemon verbena, cinnamon and white musk. I gazed at ribboned boxes of jellied fruits and sugar biscuits and all kinds of unguents in jars for prettifying and pampering yourself. All these things were lavishly displayed, even though none of the townsfolk could afford them.

We went to Mrs Adams' place to spend money on things such as flour and sugar, powdered milk and eggs. All them costly frou-frou things from the Earthly past were left to rot luxuriously on the shelves and in cabinets. Really, Ma would say, whoever had need of talcum powder from Paris?

Tittle-tattle would tell you they were all thieved goods anyhow. The Adamses were profiteers from other folks' misfortunes and everything in the Exotic Emporium had been filched from a shipwreck out in the desert.

It was true that once upon a time it was thought a good idea to transport luxury items from Earth to Mars. This was back when they were expecting the rich to come here in great numbers and to find this a world full of hope. That seems like a fairytale now – to think that they sent their expensive goods ahead of themselves, as if pampering was the most important thing those Earthlings could imagine.

As we stood among those clucking women, Al was

twisting and pulling faces. We were so crushed between the starched pinnies and the wooden baskets we couldn't even see Mrs Adams behind her glass counter. We knew, though, that she was weighing out goods on her silver scales and talking all animatedly.

We caught the odd phrase echoed by the ladies around us. We heard the word 'Disappearances' several times and this made our ears prick up. I heard 'just a baby' and 'one of her lovely twins' and then a kind of ghoulish excitement rippled through the shop. A shrill voice piped up: 'Like she foolishly left a window open … and during a storm! What did she expect to happen to her precious babies? Of course one of them went flying out the window…'

'Or it was snatched,' snapped another, croakier voice. 'Snatched from clear under her nose. Just like it used to happen before. They could always get at you and yours, no matter how secure you thought your Homestead was. Even when you were under lock and key and all your hatches were battened down they could still get at you!'

This particular raspy voice rose above the others and I recognised it almost at once. It belonged to Grandma's only friend, Ruby. Ruby was an engineer and a legend in Our Town. She was also Grandma's only surviving contemporary. She had more memory and knowledge than anyone still alive on Mars. She was revered and respected and it was surprising for us to even find her here, wasting her time gossiping with all these old dames. If Ruby was here then it must be important, she was no idle chatterer.

'Tell us, Ruby, tell us,' urged Mrs Adams.

'What's to tell?' said Ruby, smoothing down her tangled white hair. She glowered at everyone in turn. 'It's the Disappearances. Seems like they've started up once again.'

A horrible pause followed this pronouncement, as everyone struggled to take in what she meant. It was something we'd heard the older people saying. The Disappearances. The very word made the colour drain out of the ladies' faces.

Then Mrs Adams saw Al and me standing there with our wooden baskets and our list and our handfuls of coins. She decided we ought to be protected from all this gloomy adult talk, so she brightened her voice. 'Why, it's the Robinson children. Thank the Lord that you're safe, my dears. I take it you all came through the storm in one piece and that your family is well?'

I nodded firmly and the ladies sighed with relief. They knew that we faced the brunt of the storm on the prairie. Here in town they'd have been hunkered in their shelters underground. I admit that Al and I basked in their admiration as we went up to the counter with our empty baskets.

I gave Mrs Adams our list and watched her frowning at Ma's handwriting and then set about filling our order. I felt Al's hand reach out to take mine and I knew straight away how he felt about what we'd heard.

Da had heard similar things from the men. In the great wooden Storehouse, where they traded and loaded up their wagons with heavy sacks of grain and barrels of oil, the men gossiped just as much as the ladies did. They just swore and spat more, is all. He always said that we weren't the same as town folk. We lived on the Martian prairie and we were made of tougher stuff. Yes, we traded with them and we were still related to them, and all of us sure depended on one another for survival, but Da insisted that we were crucially different. They were used to their huddling together with their softer, sheltered living and their fancier things. They had time on their hands and idle tongues to match.

That day, though, it seemed that the gossip reached out and snared Da's attention too.

'Old Man Horace. He's gone,' Da told us tersely, as we loaded the hovercart with new provisions. Da didn't believe in sugar-coating the truth, even for kids. He thought it was best we knew the worst from the very start.

Old Man Horace had been the town vagrant. Going back way before I was born, he had been racketing about the town. He may have been a filthy tramp, but he belonged to us, and every single Homestead had taken him in at Christmas time or Martian Thanksgiving. I could remember the Christmas I was eight and he came out to stay in the Homestead with us; he'd carved wooden animals for Al and me.

Now, according to the men in the Storehouse today, after the storm came rampaging through town, and left the whole place smothered in dust and all topsy-turvy, there was not a single sign of Old Man Horace. No one could remember who had volunteered to give him shelter. It was assumed that the storm had simply borne him away like an old rag swept out of the road.

'They're taking it to be an omen,' Da told us, as we strapped the last of the sacks into the hovercart. 'Damn fools. They're talking like that dirty old guy was our mascot or something.'

Al looked as if he was longing to tell him about the baby that flew out of the window. But I jabbed my brother with my bony elbow. I didn't want him troubling Da right now. This was unsubstantiated tittle-tattle and Da surely wasn't in the mood for it. I distracted them both by asking about our replacements for Molly and George.

'They'll be ready in two weeks,' said Da. 'They're still too young to leave their mother. They're having chips implanted too. But before the month's out we'll be able to take them home with us.'

I wished I'd gone to the livestock pens with him, just so I could have seen the young burden beasts.

On the way home Da chatted brightly about the feast that we'd be having the following evening. He'd invited everyone he'd seen and now word would go round the whole town. Everyone was welcome at the Homestead barbecue. We could celebrate the fact we were all still alive and the summer storm was, hopefully, at an end.

And nothing more was said for the rest of the day about Disappearances.

4

Molly and George turned out to be delicious. Ma cooked them up right. Great hunks of meat marinated in sauces all the afternoon before our party. I helped hoist them out onto the makeshift cooking range outdoors, but most of the work was Ma's. She was brilliant at this stuff. Obviously it was easier when supplies were more plentiful, but Da always said that Ma excelled at any time – feast or famine. She could keep us going on the most meagre rations.

The aromas swirled and drifted all the way into town, enticing folk out of their boltholes, attracting many more than we knew we'd have to feed. Their carriages and hovercarts came pulling up in our yard and some of these faces we didn't even recognise. They were cousins and friends of townsfolk. All were welcome, Da announced.

Some folk brought kegs of foul-tasting homebrew. Noxious drink was passed around in plaggy beakers and as the sun went down, fizzing golden into the dunes, the party was getting rowdy. With the landscape so changed about, I wondered whether everyone would find their way home after darkness fell.

Grandma enlisted help from Al and Da to drag her

heavy old armchair into the yard and there she sat, looking like the queen of our world. She wore a silver frock that she must have unearthed from the very bottom of her trunk. It shone glamorously in the moonlight and she was very proud of herself. She watched the revels going on with a strange expression on her face. I guess it was the kind of face you'd wear if you'd seen everything and done everything the world had to offer and now you were watching all the young people doing it all again.

There was music. Old discs that had been handed down from the first settlers. Later, when everyone was tired of those ghostly, over-complicated songs from Earth, we made our own music. Da fetched out his guitar and someone beat time on the empty kegs. Mr Adams played a shrill penny whistle and there were jigs and reels. I hung back when the dancing started, keeping a watchful eye on the proceedings. The grown-ups were drunk and enjoying themselves, but there was no way I was making a fool of myself.

The only dancing I'd ever done was away from anyone watching, with Hannah, when she was a baby, moving softly round as I held her in my arms and tried to get her to sleep. In all of the raucous music that memory came back to me and it caught my breath sharply. I looked for Hannah and saw her in the dress she'd had for her birthday. Ma had cleaned and pressed it and Hannah looked a peach. She was clapping and trying to join in, though she was too small for most people to notice. I kept a careful eye out in case my sister strayed too close to those stamping feet.

One cracked voice cut across everyone else and started to sing an old song. It was a story song: about the voyages that the settlers had made from Earth to come here. It was a song no one had heard in a long time.

By now it was properly dark. The stars were out, but we all felt safe because we were together. The whole town was here. We listened in respectful silence as Grandma rocked back and forth in her armchair. Her voice was like old creaking water pipes or ungreased engine parts. It told a tale come from the distant past and it was our duty to harken to it. Paying our respects to the sacrifices of those who had gone before us.

Her song went on forever, it seemed like. It was truly horrible. Even worse than the last time she'd inflicted it upon us. In the end, Toaster stepped forward to pat her on the shoulder and whisper in her ear. Her dirge-like singing faded out and she submitted to his hydraulic embrace, allowing herself to be manhandled indoors to her bed. It was too late for old ladies to be squawking at the tops of their voices in the cooling desert air.

The music and the party were over, and everyone became conscious of being out of doors in the dark. All of a sudden it was time to leave. In all the milling about – that was when the gossip started. People were tired and jumpy and whispers were going around – insidious and shivery – spoiling the party mood. People were talking about the Disappearances. It was as if our light and warmth and noise couldn't keep the dark thoughts at bay forever. The shadows were creeping in to claim us.

Clearing stuff away, Ma caught those whispers and went straight up to Da. She was shaking with anger and fear. 'You never told me about this. You never said what you'd heard in town.'

He froze. He was aware others had stopped to listen. They had caught the tension in Ma's voice. 'It's only a rumour,' he told her. 'Old Man Horace just wandered off, probably. He was a drunk old man, weak in the head after years of being ill. It's sad, but one day they'll find his body in a dune out of town.'

'And the Simcox child?' Ma asked. Her voice was getting shrill and others were murmuring. The Simcox family were absent from our shindig that evening, most unlike them. It added credence to the rumour they had lost one of their babies. It had flown right out of its cot and through its nursery window into the eye of the descending storm.

'So you don't believe it?' Ma asked Da. 'You don't believe that it's happening again?'

He growled, 'We need more evidence. We can't all turn hysterical.' He took hold of her and tried to shush her down.

'Disappearances, Edward,' she hissed. 'You know the stories. You know what your mother said. Or have you forgotten?'

He smoothed down her hair. She wriggled out of his grasp. She beckoned to Hannah, who ran into her arms.

'We've forgotten nothing,' said Da.

'The weather isn't the worst thing,' said Ma. 'It isn't the harshest, most deadly thing on Mars. We've had it easy for years. We've had it soft. Compared with the settlers.' Then she broke into tears. This shocked both Al and me. We'd seen Ma cry before, but not in front of people from the town. She just crumpled up and fell down on her knees in the dirty cinders from the barbecue.

5

At the weekend Grandma took a bad fall. We heard a tremendous crash and all this cursing from her room and, next thing, Toaster came to us looking all concerned. Grandma's cybernetic leg had seized up – sand in the joints. It was all corroded up and getting to be no use. Da said the only thing to do was to take her into town when we went for the replacements for Molly and George. Doc Eaves could fix up cybernetic limbs pretty well.

Grandma didn't complain, even though she hated to go into town, on account of her looking so beat up and old. She hated to be seen by people these days. I reckoned she must have been hurting for real to agree so readily.

So we all went – apart from Ma and Hannah, who waved us off from the veranda. Grandma and Toaster were strapped onto the back of the hovercart like bits of old farm equipment and I guess we made quite a comical sight, buzzing along on the sand. Grandma kept yammering all the way across the plains. I could hear Toaster hushing her and placating her in reasonable tones.

Al and me sat up front with Da. We were both paying attention to how he drove the machine. We knew that our day would come when we'd have to know how to do everything Da could do, to support our own families in the future. One day we would have our own Homesteads somewhere on the prairie.

We were settlers – third generation – and it was our duty to grow up and spread out and occupy new land and have more children who'd carry on the sacred mission after us. Me, I couldn't imagine doing anything else with my life and, for as long as I could remember, I'd been learning and memorising all the skills and knowledge bound up in Ma and Da about surviving in our world. Al was the same. Well, I'd always assumed he was the same.

But something weird was going on with Al. He had started to question things. He wanted to know *why* our whole purpose was to thrive and proliferate and multiply and colonise Mars. He was thoughtful, Al. Thoughtful and deep and troubled. At first he only voiced his questions to me, his older sister, and I only half-understood what he was talking about. I mean, what else would he or anyone else do with their lives? What else was there to do but try to survive?

Ma once said, 'Mars doesn't want us here. This whole world wants us to go back where we came from. The planet is rejecting us and trying to kill us off.' She had been sick with a fever for some time after Hannah was born.

Funny thing was, the questions Ma asked then were just like the ones Al was asking lately. All that why why why.

It shook me up and made me uneasy. I preferred just to get on with things.

In town we took Grandma to her appointment with Doc Eaves and left Toaster to wait for her while we took ourselves off to visit our new reptiles. The new Molly and George gazed at us sadly, I thought. As if they knew they had a whole lifetime ahead of nothing but servitude until the day they died and we chopped them up for another neighbourly barbecue. What was wrong with me? I should be happy. We had new members of the Homestead.

Then we found out that we'd have to stay in town overnight. Grandma didn't just need work done, she needed a whole new cybernetic limb. She kicked up a ruckus and Da didn't look too pleased either, when we returned to the surgery and heard. The good news, said the Doctor, was that he had just the right model of leg in stock and it was almost the correct size. He could effect the replacement almost immediately. But it was going to be expensive. Da blanched when he heard the figure.

'Don't pay it,' cried Grandma, lying there on the Doctor's bench. 'Just take both my legs right off, why don't you? What does an old biddy like me want legs for anyway?'

But Da told her she was shaming him, carrying on so. He said, yes, she would be having the leg, thank you, and he quickly made an appointment for the fitting the very next day. Grandma was helped down from the examining bench by Toaster and now she was looking smug at the prospect of a whole new robotised limb.

That night we stayed at the home of old Ruby, Grandma's last surviving girlhood friend. Over the years we had stayed with her a number of times and her ramshackle place was familiar. She was a gruff old lady who'd lived through some rough times. She always boasted that she'd buried three husbands and nine babies and whenever she said that she always scared Al and me half to death.

Her house was pretty dirty and nasty inside. Ruby kept small lizard birds as pets and they left their slimy droppings just any old place. They skulked about in the rafters of every room and it was easy to imagine they were thinking up ways of doing their mess on us, or pecking out our eyes.

Ruby also had great piles of papers everywhere. Books and magazines in sliding heaps, dangerous as the shifting sands. All these things had been salvaged years ago from one of the crashed ships. Ruby's home was the town's unofficial library, though no one ever came by to read. Maybe because everything was stuck with lizard mess and old feathers.

Grandma and Ruby greeted each other noisily and straight away Grandma started bragging about the new leg her beautiful and marvellously generous son was going to buy for her.

Ruby talked as we ate the meal Toaster had made. She talked about a new spate of mysteries. It had now been confirmed that the Simcox baby was gone and the mother was inconsolable. Old Man Horace's body had not been found, plus there were two other Disappearances rumoured in the past week. So it seemed to become official. The Disappearances were back.

'Exactly like before,' said Grandma so gloomily that Al and me didn't dare ask what had happened. We sat at Ruby's table under a giant orange lamp, eating our supper capsules off of china bowls. The whole wooden table was covered with an exotic rug. Because Ruby believed in equality for all sentient beings Toaster sat up at the table with us. He looked very pleased to be there. Da said Toaster would be incorrigible after. He said the two old women were giving the sunbed ideas.

Bedtime, and Al and me were sent off to the attic where we always slept, going back years of visiting Ruby in town. Da hugged and kissed us goodnight at the bottom of the staircase. He told us to pay no heed to those crazy old ladies. It made them feel more alive when they dwelled on stories of terrible things in the past, but we kids weren't to feel frightened or upset by it.

I looked at Al and he looked at Da. Al's pale, wide-open eyes were luminous in the dark hall. But like I say, he was always more sensitive than me, plus he was younger. I told Da we were disturbed by none of it. Da chuckled and gave us each a five-credit note. We were absolutely stunned by this. As our reward for recent help and support, we were free to spend all this cash at Adams' Exotic Emporium on just anything that we liked.

Al and me went up to the attic. We were so tired we fell asleep almost at once. I was in my clothes, clutching my five-credit note in my fist.

I woke up in the early hours to the noise of Al and the lizard birds snoring. Something told me I had to get up at once and move to the window. I don't know why. I had to clamber up, peer out of that dusty old window and look down at the street below.

Ruby lived at the corner of First and Fourth. You could see the red rutted Main Street from this gable window. I'd always loved the view from here. In the daytime you could see all the townspeople passing by, but not now. The streets at night were deserted. The red sand looked pale under the Earth light.

I stayed there, looking down at the street, as if I knew something was about to occur.

And, sure enough, after a minute or two, it did.

They came out like dancers floating onto an empty stage. There was no music, just my brother and the lizard birds breathing heavily in their sleep.

Down there, outside, the dancers moved along dreamily, as if to music of their own. Music I'd never heard before.

They were the ghosts of Martians.

6

These weren't townsfolk out there, down on the streets. No one I had ever known looked anything like this. They were taller than the human beings I knew, and skinnier – way skinnier than anyone I had ever seen. Skinny like old bones you find sticking out of the sand. They had no facial features I could see – just eyes. Glowing purple eyes, flickering like candles in a window. They were mostly naked. Some wore red-and-white striped hats, others wore socks or gloves. One had a scarf streaming over its shoulder.

There were eight – no, nine – of them below on the street. They were coming off Main Street, round the corner of Ruby's house. Mostly they clung to the shadows, but one or two dared to stroll down the middle of the road as if they just didn't care if anyone saw them.

They moved stealthily on those long naked legs. They paused now and then and I realised that they were peering inside the shrouded windows. They gathered together, and the pale beams from their eyes seemed to shine into the buildings. As if they were looking for something in particular.

I called to Al. It took me a few moments to find my voice. He woke with a cry, like he didn't know where he was. I told him to get himself over here, and take a look out of this window. My brother stood there in his rumpled sleeping shirt and pants and gazed down into the street.

'What? What, Lora? What am I supposed to be looking at?'

He was right to look so mystified and perplexed. Because when I looked again, I couldn't see them any more, either. The ghostly dancers had completely crept away.

'Why do you say they were ghosts?' Grandma snapped at me. 'And why do you insist on saying they were Martians?'

I had waited until Da was out, off to see his friends at the Storehouse, before I brought up what I'd seen in the night. The old ladies clearly didn't believe a word of it, and they delighted in quizzing me, turning me round in circles.

'Martians and ghosts!' old Ruby guffawed. 'Damn girl doesn't know what she's talking about. She ain't seen nothing like what we've seen in our lifetime!'

Grandma cawed loudly in agreement. 'We've seen Martians. And we've seen ghosts. We've seen things like you wouldn't believe. Things you would never brag about seeing afterwards. You kids these days – you're all soft and mollycoddled.'

Both old dames were looking at me and Al defiantly

but I shouted right back, 'I saw them in the street outside! In the Earth light. They were looking in people's ground-floor windows. They were peeping and prying.'

'Hoodlums,' scoffed Grandma. 'Simple straightforward bandits and robbers. Why, they most probably come in from some other town. Some place we don't even know about.'

'They were Martians,' I said.

'All the Martians died,' snapped Grandma.

'They were their dead ghosts,' I said. I don't know how I felt so sure.

Al touched my arm gently. I shrugged him off. He said, 'Lora. You're scaring the two old ladies. You're getting them all worked up.'

'Toaster,' I called, and he came scooting in from the kitchen. 'Did you detect anyone – anything – lurking about outside last night?'

He mused on this, drying a cup with a tea towel. 'Outside last night? I was deactivated last night, I'm afraid, Miss Lora. I never detected a thing.'

I tutted. 'You're no use,' I said.

There was a complication with the grips for Grandma's new leg and Da asked Al and me whether we'd mind staying one more night at Ruby's place?

So we'd have another day of eating the weird concentrated foodstuffs the old ladies loved so much. Stuff like that reminded them both of their glory days when they were space travellers and early settlers and everything they ate came in dried-up capsule form.

Also, they loved to watch ancient videotape of the take-offs and landings of various spacecraft they'd been aboard. 'I'm in there! So are you!' 'We're both in that one!' And they'd dissolve in giggles at the absurdity of it: of surrendering your life to such fragile-looking devices. The video films were crackly and it was hard to make out what was going on. But Ruby and Grandma sat there clapping and then blubbing together as they re-watched hours of this footage.

Occasionally they saluted the flickering screen.

Al and me watched and waited for the most interesting parts. The pictures of places on Earth. I have to admit that we were both fascinated to see folk in old-fashioned dress waving to the camera and going about their everyday business on this alien world. The cities were huge and impossible. It was like they were made out of boxes and tubes of cardboard and spray-painted silver. Did anyone really live in places like that? I tried to imagine what the din must have been like. Why wasn't everyone driven completely mad living in crushed places like that?

But there are only so many hours you can sit looking at scratchy pictures with the old folk. Al and me decided to go out in the afternoon. Those five-credit notes were burning holes in our pockets. Grandma caught wind of what Da had given us and she was scandalised. 'You'll waste it! Kids with so much money to fritter away! No wonder your family hasn't got anything! It's like when you have a barbecue and go inviting the whole town! You lot will never amount to anything and then you'll all starve!'

She shrieked this at us, standing on Ruby's porch. Then she went back in to watch more of their movies behind the closed shutters.

Out in the street I examined the red dust of the road, trying to find marks left by the strange people I had witnessed in the night. Al sighed with impatience. 'If they were ghosts, like you say, they'd hardly leave footprints, would they? They'd be lighter than air.'

The road was a blurry mess of different tracks. Already that morning too many people had been down this way. I gave up and we headed to Adams' Exotic Emporium to blow our cash.

Mrs Adams' store was relatively quiet. She was presiding over her counter, watching us like a lizard bird as we entered. I always got the feeling that she distrusted us. She thought because we were country children we were dirtier, rougher and inclined to thieve. Though I resented that, I was of course a first-class thief. As I moved through the store, my hands had a life of their own. I lifted trinkets and gee-gaws – rubber bugs and gobstoppers – and slid them into my pockets. I had warned Al many times never to copy me. His lack of subtlety and skill would get us caught.

Right now she was levering open the lid of a rusted steel drum. Dust swirled in the air. Mrs Adams drew out a brown paper parcel. Al and I stepped nearer. By the markings on the drum it was plain to see that the consignment had been sent from Earth many, many moons ago, and it wasn't addressed to anyone still alive in this town. This was contraband, whatever it was.

Of course, it didn't help that our town didn't have much of a name. Being the earliest settlement of houses in this landmass, it had always simply been known as Our Town. Sometimes I thought that was a purposeful thing. Like we wanted to keep separate from everyone else. We didn't really know what was happening on the rest of Mars. And very few of us even cared.

Al and I watched over her shoulder as Mrs Adams donned white cotton gloves to unwrap the ream of brown paper. Inside was a case of pale wood. And inside this was a mass of blue tissue paper. Between each sheet was a set of glass slides, each no bigger nor thicker than a fingernail.

Mrs Adams looked almost glad to see us. She'd had a shipment, she said, in which I would be very interested. A long-looked-for consignment of reading matter had come into the shop at last. I had been waiting along with her and several others in the town who were also avid readers.

We had already read every scrap that Mrs Adams stocked in her lending library.

She flicked through them. Each bore a vivid smudge of colour. They were shimmering, beautiful objects. I was dizzy at the sheer profusion of slides, knowing that each contained a whole book. There must have been over two hundred inside that canister. I don't think I had ever seen so many in one place before.

I forked out a good portion of my five-credit note to Mrs Adams that day. She let me choose a bunch of those glorious slides and she said I could keep them for a whole month. Take them back to the Homestead and everything. She gave me a printed list of titles so that I could choose the most exciting ones. I used the colours of those slides to help me, imagining that dark purple meant Romance, steely blue meant space adventures and green – for some reason – meant grand historical epics.

Meanwhile Al went round the shop filling a basket with novelties and sweeties. Give him five credits to spend and the whole lot would disappear in a flash. He'd always toss it away on rubbish.

I was the eldest child in our family and so I would always be in charge. Ma and Da had drummed that into me. If – God forbid – anything ever happened to them, I was to look after my brother and sister. I understood, didn't I? Of course, of course I understood. Sometimes the thought gave me nightmares.

Not that anything bad was ever going to happen to our parents, they said. They had a great deal yet to offer, and life on Mars still had much in store for them.

For some reason I was going over this in my head that day, as Al crammed stuff into his basket: handfuls of marshmallows, toy telescopes and pointless card games. I flicked through the colourful slides and chose five. I imagined evenings when my chores were over, sitting in the dark of my room, all peaceful, with the screen glowing and words from old Earth marching past my eyes. Half my mind was taken up chasing alluring titles like *Vanity Fair* and *Wuthering Heights*, but the other half was roving over and over the thought that one day I would have to be in charge.

It was like we were all waiting, all the time, for disaster to befall us.

7

Grandma was furious with me.

It was Al's fault. He let slip that I'd dropped most of my season's allowance on books from Mrs Adams' lending library.

Ruby cried out against the greed of Mrs Adams and how she'd been exploiting the townsfolk for too long. 'Three credits! And for only a lend, too! Not even a keep!'

Grandma was more inclined to be cross about my stupidity. 'Your Da works so hard! And what do you do with your pocket money? Why, you throw it back in his face!'

I managed to find my voice and answer her back. 'We all work hard, Grandma. And besides, he said the money was mine to spend on what I liked.'

'See?' hollered Grandma, gnashing her plaggy teeth. 'No respect! This is where your soft living and luxury gets you!'

'Luxury?!' I shouted back. I was really mad now. 'What luxury do we have? You say it yourself, Grandma – when you were my age, you had Servo-Furnishings to do everything. Shopping and cleaning and tending the crops. You even had a robot to cut your toenails and do your hair!'

Al was staring at me in horrified awe. I'd never been as openly rebellious as this before. Something had touched a raw nerve, I guess. Them thinking I was wasting the family's money with my library books. I wasn't hurting anyone, was I?

'Why do you want to read made-up books, Lora?' Grandma asked, close to tears. 'Things like that can only make you unhappy. They make you hanker to be elsewhere, and to be someone else. We only have the here and now. And that's what we've got to concentrate on.'

Oh no. The crazy glint in her eye was back again. I'd pushed her into one of her dreadful moods. But it seemed that Ruby knew how to placate her. Toaster joined in, shuffling forward and rubbing Grandma's back.

Ruby's idea was that my remaining two credits would be spent at a certain fancy establishment called Lucille's. Grandma had talked about having fittings at Madame Lucille's for corsets and other ladieswear things I didn't understand as yet. Lucille's was where town ladies with more money than sense hung out, and they came back gussied up in paint and lipstick with ludicrous hairdos. Worst of all they came back in horrible dresses that winched them into unnatural shapes and prinked them out in flounces and frills, like they'd stepped out of some old history tape.

I could feel the blood chilling in my veins. Ruby announced her generous intention to supplement my remaining credits with five of her own, from her very own savings, and I was to think of it as this year's birthday present from her. Both she and Grandma were getting flushed, prodding me and examining my figure and demeanor like I was their very own dressy-up doll.

Next thing I knew, I was being dragged along and we were heading on out.

I wanted to struggle but I knew it was no use. I knew that I'd have to be a lady some day.

I was at their mercy. They driiiinged the bell and the door clicked open.

Madame Lucille was painted eggshell white and she was very tall and muscular. When she bent close I could see that her face paint was covering a thick moustache on her top lip. Her hair was done up in a turban and she wore a very tight, wraparound dress. It seemed plain to me that she was a man. She didn't even try to disguise her voice. But no one said a thing about it. They just called her Madame Lucille in this very polite way, even Grandma.

Madame Lucille made me stand on a chair and she went round examining me from all angles. I was pretty mortified, standing in my raggy underwear. When Madame Lucille leaned in close, it was like her moustache was bristling at me.

My nerves and the musky heat of the dressmaker's shop made my head spin. Her perfume and stinky breath made my stomach surge upwards into my throat. When she sent me into her cubicle with three heavy outfits to try on, I couldn't stop myself. I made a horrible squawking noise and threw up.

We all got thrown out of Lucille's. Grandma and Ruby were given no choice but to buy the horrible purple – and now sicky – dress. Madame Lucille called her brutish husband down from upstairs. He stood intimidatingly over us until all the cash was handed over.

We went home to Ruby's. I was in disgrace. I was holding the vomity dress in a large paper bag and it was reeking. I was told by Grandma that I would have to scrub it myself. I felt like saying the rotten food at Ruby's had turned my stomach. Those space capsules she kept serving up were decades out of date.

The whole day felt like a disaster.

Al was in his element. He got to laugh even more when Dad returned from hanging out with his Storehouse cronies. He smelled of booze and was swaying slightly. I'd hardly ever seen Da drunk, especially in the afternoon.

Grandma said, 'Go on, girl.'

I opened the bag to show him satin ruffles and lace and ribbons. The stench of sick came rising up to meet him and he looked puzzled. Da was too tired and drunk to ask any more. He went up to his room and didn't come down for supper.

I spent the evening rinsing and rubbing my hideous new frock in the zinc tub. I wrung out the dress, dunked it and hung it up to dry in Ruby's scullery. It looked wrinkled and lopsided and quite a lot like an old rag. It was nothing like how it had looked in Madame Lucille's shop. It seemed to me like a headless spectre, sagging there on the line. This was the lady I was supposed to grow up to be. She was lopsided and wrong, and trying her hardest to seem feminine and sophisticated.

We had supper and I avoided the chewiest, rankest-tasting cubes. The evening hurried by, with none of us really talking to each other. I was keen to hide away with my stories from the lending library. At last I'd have a chance to be alone and simply read.

I dozed over my electronic *Vanity Fair* and by one a.m. I was in a deep sleep. By then Toaster had shut himself down, leaving his leads plugged into the mains for charging to the max, as was his habit when at Ruby's. He knew that, following Grandma's operation tomorrow, we would be leaving for the Homestead just as soon as we could.

At ten minutes past one Ruby felt 'a great big wave of weariness, hot and dry like the sandstorm itself' sweep over her. She told her oldest friend on all of Mars that she was ready for her bed. Ruby reminded Grandma to unplug the television and to do the usual stuff. Checking windows and doors and lights.

The window had been open all evening, it being such a sultry and close night. Grandma knew the drill, so Ruby told her good night and headed off to bed.

There was no noise. No almighty scuffling sound. No shrieks or protests in those early hours. Not one of us was woken up. We all slept till first light came flooding through the blinds.

Ruby was first downstairs. She went hurrying down in her night things – startled because the television set was still buzzing.

And the windows were open, letting in cooler air and street noise. It was obvious they had been open all night.

At that moment Ruby felt her old heart was going to burst right out of her chest. She knew something terrible had occurred.

Grandma was gone.

Only her leg remained.

8

It was late in our Martian autumn when we were allowed to hold the funeral for Grandma's leg.

F.E. Baxter wasn't a very reliable town sheriff. No one felt any safer because he was in charge of law and order. Now he said we had to hang on to that left-behind leg for ten whole weeks before we could legitimately bury it and only then could we assume that Grandma was officially gone.

'It's ridiculous,' said Ma, with Hannah grizzling on her lap. 'What does he think? The old woman went off on a whim? Dragging herself along on one leg just for fun? And that some day soon she's gonna come hopping back to the Homestead and surprise us all?'

Da told her, 'Hush now.' Da was grim-lipped and subdued that autumn. Chill winds were coming in from the wasteland west of us. He never said much about Grandma's Disappearance but what he said was enough. It was a bad business. An unfitting end to the life of an Historical Personage.

Of course he tried to say as little as possible in front of us kids. Al and me were as upset as our parents, but we were also secretly thrilled. Grandma was gone forever. The old Martians had taken Grandma away. We whispered this to each other at night and then lay awake, wondering what it could all mean.

Ma went about cleaning and baking and making the house nice for Ruby. The old lady was bringing a letter of permission from the sheriff to hold a small ceremony commemorating the loss of Grandma. The white-haired old lady also brought with her a parcel tied up in brown paper. At first we wondered what she might be bringing us, and then we realised. Of course. The leg.

Toaster shuffled forward and took possession of his owner's last remnant. He took it away to the shady spot we had picked out, where he'd spent all of the previous Saturday digging a hole to bury her in. He was extra quiet. He'd been very attached to the old dame.

Ma saw to it that Ruby felt at home. She had fixed up Grandma's room, making it fresh and habitable. Ruby couldn't have been a more gracious guest, complimenting Ma on the comfort of her home and the excellence of her food – especially the feast Ma put on in her honour that night. We had all our favourite Sunday night foods: salted lizard steaks and hickory sauce and mashed taters. Ruby joined in as one of the family. She listened to stories and told her own and cracked jokes – and she never once got nasty-mouthed and crazy like Grandma often did. It was nicer having

Ruby than Grandma with us. Al and me were starting to think it was a decent swap.

However, this old lady in her khaki fatigues and her soft sugary hair wasn't ours to keep. As she told us, her place was in town and her own house off Main Street. Even the Disappearance of Grandma couldn't put her off living there alone.

'I told her,' she said, looking upset for the first time. 'I told her about closing the windows. Over fifty years I've lived in that house and shut the whole place up each and every night. I never thought to go on about it, in case it insulted her – of course she knew the windows had to be fastened tight. Not because I thought night creatures would snatch anybody away. No, it was on account of the vapours. I didn't want the poisonous vapours leaking into my home.'

I saw Da roll his eyes at this old-timer superstition. The first-generation Martian settlers thought that the planet was a living organism that resented the very presence of human beings. It exhaled poisonous gases every night after dark, so everyone had to seal their homes up tight or face certain death. The dark fumes would creep into their lungs and drive them demented.

Of course, farming folk like Da and third-generation people like me – we all scoffed at such stuff. Why, we practically lived in the open air. We knew all about terra-forming and how our new world had been made safe for us to live and breathe. We camped out under the stars and by Earth light. We never had one whiff of these so-called ghastly vapours.

Da shook his head. No, something far more solid and real was responsible for making off with his much-missed mother, he said.

Hannah was packed off to bed and Al was drooping by now. I stayed awake later than usual and heard the grown-ups discussing important things in lowered voices. They had a nightcap of brandy and Ruby told them that, yes, there had been further Disappearances in town. Two more that she knew of. And naturally people were getting scared. There had been no public pronouncements yet. The Sheriff and the town Elders hadn't said anything about the Disappearances at all. Even the weekly news-sheet hadn't reported anything. They'd not said a word about Grandma, which had angered Da. He'd gone to the office and took issue with them, but still there was no obituary.

I lay awake in my room until all the adults were in bed and the house Da had built for us eight years ago settled down creakily into its timbers. All I could hear were the hot winds cooling as they blew over the dunes. Then I heard Ma and Da murmuring to each other in bed, in the room next to mine.

He said to her, 'It'll soon be time to start again. Can you bear it?'

Her voice – when she answered him at last – was so sad

and desperately tired. 'I'll have to, won't I, Edward? We'll all have to start again.'

There was a long pause. 'I think we will, yes. We have to go somewhere else.'

I heard Ma crying softly.

Da said, 'We know this is happening, it's happened before. This is what we heard about, isn't it? The tales and rumours in those other towns. We knew that it could happen here. We knew it was possible ... even inevitable.'

'You're right,' Ma said. 'I know.'

'It's already too late for my mother,' he said.

9

One night – not too long after – Al shook me awake. I knew right away that something was up.

'I dunno what it is,' he said, looking worried. He was in his little-boy pyjamas, but his face in the starlight looked older than his thirteen years. You could see the softness was starting to leave his features. For the first time I saw that my brother was growing up. 'Something is happening.'

The house was reasonably quiet. Squeaking timbers and the clink and hiss of the cooking range as it cooled in the kitchen below us. It was a still night outside with no wind. The house smelled of that evening's dinner. Al was annoying me now, just standing there, ears pricked. I climbed out of my bed and he seized my arm.

Clunk. There was a definite clunking noise from downstairs. There it came again. Someone was moving around heavily. It'll be Ma or Da, I thought. Or Aunt Ruby, who seemed to be living with us now after all. One of the adults would be up in the night, unable to sleep. Plagued by cares and vexations, the way that adults seemed to get.

Clunk, clunk, it came again.

Then there was the precise noise of the front-door lock. Someone was easing it round. *Thunk*. It was open.

'OK,' I said. 'That's not right.'

No one was ever allowed to mess with the seal on the front door of the Homestead except Da. Especially not at night.

Yet someone was heading outside.

'Come on,' I told him. Downstairs we went. How eerie it was, seeing the front door open, casting moonbeams on the scrubbed kitchen table and floor.

We ventured outside, where the air was chill and the prairie looked even wilder than usual. All the warmth had leached out of the sand and the jagged pillars of rock standing at intervals on the wide open space. Shades of cinnamon and hot paprika had drained from the land. All was pale and frosty blue.

Soon we found disturbed sand. Muffled prints of someone dragging their feet like a sleepwalker. We followed the unswerving trail into the shallow hills, where sprigs of gorse were growing and a few murky shapes dashed hither and thither. Martian hares. Blue Jack Rabbits. Bad eating. We'd tried them once and never again.

'Uh, we shouldn't go too far,' said Al.

I agreed with him. Looking back, I saw that the ground had risen almost imperceptibly and we could see the whole Homestead in all its modest glory. Here was the main house, the outbuildings and the sheds where the new

Molly and George were sleeping. It looked so peaceful and vulnerable. The land about us was seething with mysterious and secretive noises which we – when I actually thought about it – knew very little about.

Still we ploughed on, carefully testing out the safety of the ground. The last thing we needed was one of us stepping onto shifting sands and getting caught up and lost forever. When the sand became the consistency of finely milled flour, that was the most dangerous sign.

We hauled ourselves over a craggy brow of rock and beyond there was a shallow bowl about a mile across. Once it had been the bed of a vast lake and usually it was a broad expanse of smooth, dry perfection. I'd been out and seen it before, though Da didn't like us to come out this way. Yet here we were, looking at this one-time lake, like a silver mirror under the stars.

Al pointed. I jumped when I saw what he meant. It was impossible to miss.

It was Toaster we were following. Of course, it had to be Toaster.

Those clumpy, square feet dragging along. The clunking noises we'd heard. I think Al and me had known from the start that we were pursuing the sunbed into the night, but neither of us had liked to give voice to the thought. There was a definite possibility that Toaster had gone rogue. He had broken every rule in the Servo-Furnishing book. He had endangered and abandoned his human family, striking out into the outdoors at night and even leaving the door open. This was very bad news and it could only end with his total deactivation.

I called out to him. I called his name again and again and he took no notice. I set off at a run. Al flew alongside me, his breaking voice filled with panic. 'If he's flipped out he could be dangerous, Lora! Be careful! Don't get too close!'

I was in no mood to be careful. I had known Toaster as long as I had been alive. He had been nursemaid to all of us, and nanny, butler and cook, babysitter and tutor and everything. Our family had drawn upon his great reservoirs of knowledge and energy and generosity for decades. We'd even played horsies, riding around on his back, when we were little. He was one of the only touchable links we had left with Earth, and this was the first time I saw that for the plain truth it was.

'Toaster!' I screamed and started to run onto that dead lake.

Still he didn't turn. As I got closer I saw that his tanning bulbs were on. They flashed spasmodically in his bodily cavities, ultraviolet in the night. I wonder if he even knew they were malfunctioning so badly. They would drain his energy away, along with all this exertion, and he was in danger of getting stranded out here.

I caught up with the errant sunbed and saw with a shock he was crying. It should have been impossible, but there were certain things that Grandma's Servo-Furnishings had been customised for, over the years. Her second husband had been some kind of whizzo robotics man. And so Toaster the sunbed could express his emotions just as freely – why, much more freely – than the human beings we knew.

His unlovely geometric face turned to look down at me and it was streaming wet.

'You shouldn't have come after me, Lora.'

'Are you running away?'

Al came pounding up right then, raggedly out of breath. Toaster said gently, 'You two should have wrapped up warmer. I blame myself for this.'

'What are you doing?' shouted Al. 'None of us should be out here.'

'We heard you letting yourself out of the Homestead and we came after you. You shouldn't be here.'

He shrugged and gave us a look like he didn't care about that stuff. He was intent on some mission of his own.

He felt around inside his chest cavity with his strange, telescopic fingers. He flexed them and produced what he wanted to show us. It lay in his metal palm and we stared at it uncomprehendingly. It rolled a little, like it had a life of its own. It was a blue sphere, about as big as a marble.

'I found this,' he explained. 'I found it in the red dirt. I picked it up and dusted it off and hid it away inside my chest. I found it the day after they took her away. It wasn't just her leg that got left behind.'

Al and me both felt like that little sphere was looking back at us.

Grandma's false eye.

'She must have struggled against whoever was kidnapping her that night,' said Toaster softly. 'In the fight as they dragged her outdoors, her eye must have burst right out of her head and landed in the street. No ordinary eye, this, of course. Engineered on Earth in the olden days at unimaginable expense. Blue crystal technology. That's why your Grandma could see things that no one else could. Because of this.'

'You hid this from us?' asked Al.

'I tucked it behind a broken bulb in my chest. I didn't know what to do. I tried not to think about it too much as I went about my duties. And yet, I told myself, my first owner had been Grandma, right from the start. I owe her the greater loyalty. So I walked around with a precious secret locked inside my chest and, I admit, it's worried me ever since. It's her final gift to old Toaster.'

Al and me looked at each other. The sunbed had inherited Grandma's crazy-assed thinking, too. We all three of us looked at the blue eye again and it was like Grandma had found a way to keep a watch on all of us.

'You humans had your ceremony to mark her passing,' said Toaster. 'But I wasn't even allowed to attend. I was indoors doing the Homestead chores when you were under that tree, round the grave I'd dug. You were sharing your memories of her, and all the while I was thinking: my memories go back furthest.'

None of us had even thought of asking Toaster to take part. There were quite a few mourners that day. Ma had said she needed Toaster to be in the kitchen, preparing refreshments.

'I'm sorry,' I told him.

Toaster shook his head. 'So. I choose to mark my owner's passing in this way. My own way.'

Al was grossed out by the sight of the eye. 'What are you going to do?'

Toaster closed his fist and drew it back, high above our heads. Then he used every ounce of his strength to fling the eye as hard as he could into the sky. It flew across the breadth of that barren lake.

The three of us watched, amazed, as the tiny point of blue light sketched a tall parabola and started to fall. It landed too far away for us to see.

10

The whole of the lake bed started to ripple and shudder. The three of us cried out in alarm, not quite sure what we were seeing. We turned and started running for the rocks, but Al kept looking back. He was shouting what was happening; about the jagged black cracks that were spreading out from the centre of the dead lake. They looked like cracks in a mirror, or the dangerous ice that people would skate across in the old stories.

Toaster was low on energy after his trek out here and the two of us were held back by helping him. 'It's an earthquake,' screamed the sunbed. 'I have precipitated a ghastly catastrophe! Leave me! You must abandon me to my deserved fate.'

Toaster could be dramatic like this. All we could do was put all of our strength into it and yank him along to safety, to the hilly crags, away from the shattering lake. The zig-zagging cracks were widening and the dense weight of sand spilling through.

When we reached the relative safety of the rocks, we stopped, panting and wheezing. Then we looked back at a bizarre sight. A crazy web-work of fractures filled the whole expanse.

Al said, 'What have we done?'

'It is your grandma,' said Toaster. 'It is her furious spirit, wreaking vengeance on the world.'

'Rubbish,' I snapped, wondering when Toaster had become so illogical and superstitious. 'It's the shifting sands. It's got nothing to do with Grandma and her eye.'

The two males – my brother and the sunbed – weren't convinced. We set off for home, wondering if the rippling impact of the strange disaster had woken anyone up, hoping they had slept through it so we could return to our beds unnoticed. We were caked in filthy, blood-coloured sand and I think we were in shock.

Secretly I believed, just like the others, that this had everything to do with Grandma's eye. It was as if, when Toaster flung it and it landed upon the sand, the eye triggered some kind of response from the landscape. Mars itself had claimed the remains of the ancient settler.

As we approached the Homestead Al seemed to be thinking along the same lines. 'We could have fallen down those cracks,' he whispered to me. 'And never be heard of again.'

'I know,' I said. 'But there's no use dwelling on that. We're home and safe now.'

But the thought stayed with my brother from that night on. That the ground could open up and swallow us at any moment never to be seen again. Or maybe hostile creatures would emerge from those cracks in the land and steal us away.

It spooked him, is the best way of putting it. I'd always complained about my being the older and most grown up of the pair of us. But Al was growing up overnight, into a wary, dubious person, who expected to meet with danger everywhere he went. In truth, I'd have preferred to have my childish brother back, who wasn't yet scared of the world.

And what did I feel? I felt excited. Even when all those crazy cracks were appearing and we were trying to outrun them. I felt so thrilled and alive. At last, I thought, something is happening. Here is the truth. Here is the proof. There's something living on Mars that's bigger than us. There's something alive and intelligent here. And it's watching us, and waiting.

Of course I never shared these feelings with anyone. They would have thought me insane. And maybe I was. Maybe the hot Martian dust had got into my head and corroded my wits.

So we survived the weird night of Grandma's eye and pretty soon it was Hallows Eve. This was an excuse for another small gathering at our Homestead. Ma prepared traditional loaves and sweets and she tried once again to teach me the traditional womanly roles for a festival such as this. I knew it was important, but I wasn't in the slightest bit interested. I'd always known I'd one day be running a whole place myself, like Da had. I wasn't going to be just some man's wife, staying indoors to bake stuff. I told her, 'Ma, it's kind of you – but if you want to teach someone, teach Hannah. Teach Al.'

Ma looked so hurt, each time I had to tell her like this.

Da and I spent time breaking in the new beasts, Molly and George. They were so much younger and hardier than the previous pair. I saw how we had been making do with feeble burden beasts for some time. These two were obedient and strong and they'd both been – for considerable extra cost – supplied with a command chip, which made practically everything much easier. Now they could understand when Da explained what they needed to do. They didn't need instructions dinning into their ears or whipping into their hides. The command chips were amazing, but I wondered if the beasts having the rudiments of our language might make it even harder, later on, when it came time to put them down and eat them. Da didn't seem to think so. As he put it, animals and humans and Servo-Furniture were united in the effort to ensure human survival on Mars. Everything was subordinated to that effort – most especially the lives of beasts, and the beasts would naturally understand that.

Al did, in fact, help Ma prepare the sweetbreads and sickly drinks for Hallows Night. We sat up till late as guests told tales that were pretty dumb and harmless, mainly.

Then Mrs Adams volunteered to tell a tale. She was done up in her finery, standing by the range and looking haggard in her ritzy purple dress. She was holding her glass of punch with one little finger sticking out all elegantly like she thought she must set an example of deportment. When she stood there and promised us a story to top them all, I was expecting something pretty corny.

'Alice, don't,' said her gentle-faced husband, Vernon, but Mrs Adams shushed him and looked annoyed. Then she started telling us a story that happened several weeks back, to do with the fancy goods that the Adamses imported – or rather, salvaged – from the wreckage of the giant ship in a valley to the east of us. And the Adamses getting spooked that day.

She began by reminding us that she and her husband rode out twice a year to the wreck of the *Melville* in the eastern hinterland. I noticed Da and a couple of the other adults exchange a glance at this. No one ever knew for certain which wreck the Adamses took their supplies from. Usually it was hushed up. It was known that the *Melville*, *Hawthorne*, *Fitzgerald* and *Stein* were within a few days' ride from our town. Twice a year the Adamses took their hovercart into the eastern hinterland and stole stuff from a ship named after a man who wrote a book about a giant fish. A ship that was a hundred years old and not going anywhere ever again.

'I hate those expeditions,' Mrs Adams said. 'Over the years we have made so many. It's become a familiar feeling. The dread when I even think about that smashed ship, all rotting away and only its tail fins jutting out of the sand. Each time we climb aboard we have to go deeper and deeper into the hold, searching for supplies. Each time I feel we are grave robbers.'

That was true enough, I thought. And what was worse, they were bringing back all their loot – the tinned essentials, the dry foodstuffs and the fancy doo-das – and forcing us to pay money for them.

'I hate it,' Mrs Adams said. 'For twenty years we've been raiding the *Melville* and the others lying out there in the wasteland. When we went there a couple of weeks ago, it was different. This is the tale I have to tell you.'

This was breaking our Hallows Eve rules. Didn't everybody have to tell a made-up tale? Something horrifying and gruesome that had come straight out of their head?

Her moon-faced husband crouched by our hearth, looking up at his wife, telling her that she needn't do this. She shrugged. 'They all need to know.' Then she launched right in. How she and her husband made their bi-annual pilgrimage on the first of the month into the hinterland. It was a journey that would seem impossibly far to the rest of us, she declared. She was really playing up her part, making herself and her husband sound like great adventurers.

They drove through days and nights, taking turns at the controls of their hovercart; soothing the fever that their little girl Annabel was coming down with; fixing their broken engine when they were halfway there; spending a night lying under the stars; shooting one of those tall, purple hares and roasting it over a fire.

'Our journey was so much more hazardous than usual, we were relieved to see the wreck of the *Melville* on the horizon. That oh-so familiar rusting hull looked almost welcoming…'

They clambered aboard through a breach in the side, taking ropes and torches and all their usual equipment. Their pretty daughter Annabel was back on her feet, though choking with sneezes that echoed in that cavernous interior.

'Poor child, I felt cruel,' said Mrs Adams. 'But we only went that way twice a year. Only Annabel is small and limber enough to fit through the twisting nooks and crannies deep within the *Melville*.'

So the Adamses sent their nine year old down into the hull of the fallen ship. At nine Annabel was an old hand at having a rope tied around her waist and being lowered into the waiting darkness. Oh, she was very used to shining her torch around in the inky spaces – looking out for boxes, crates, anything useful. Anything she could lay her little hands on.

Annabel was sitting by the front door, on a hard wooden chair, staring into space. She didn't seem aware of her mother holding court. She was in a pretty dress that was too small for her and she was unfazed by all our stares.

Mrs Adams went on. 'This time, I knew there was something different about the *Melville*. I guess we knew that supplies aboard the ship couldn't last forever. The past few years we've had to probe further into the hold. We've had to carry more and more rope with us, lowering Annabel deeper into the darkness. We've scoured room after room, breaking open doors that have been sealed for decades. Never mind the danger.

'But there is also treasure. Things we all need. Things we have become used to by now, eh? Remember the lobster bisque? The sherbet bonbons? The steak and kidney puddings? The freeze-dried shrimp?'

She had us licking our lips. Thinking about the exciting days when the Adamses threw open their shop doors following one of their expeditions.

'This time the *Melville* seemed vaster, more echoing and chillier within. Its hull rang with clangs and bangs as we let ourselves in. It seemed like we were disturbing somebody's peace, just by being there.'

'Don't, dear,' said Vernon Adams, but he was shushed by everyone in the room.

Mrs Adams went on. 'I thought it was ghosts in the ship. Come out at last to ward us off. But it wasn't. They were people. Real people. We could hear them distantly, deep in the bowels of the *Melville*. They were blasting down doors and tramping about. Moving aside great big hunks of bulwarks and ramparts. Drilling and burning through sheer metal walls.'

My Da asked, 'Who were they, Alice?'

She shook her head. 'We don't know. They had serious equipment. Stuff we'd never heard. We listened to the disturbed echoes and thought about it. They could have come from anywhere on Mars. Places we don't know nothing about. There was an urgency and an ugliness to the sounds we heard, as if they were wanting to rip the *Melville* open to see what it hid. We take from the *Melville* twice a year, but I hope that we respect her. We even say a little prayer to the *Melville*'s soul, each time, before we leave her behind.'

If it had been Da, he'd have done everything he could to find out who the strangers were. He looked excited by the descriptions of the sounds of their heavy-duty machinery – the blasting and the drilling. He looked hungry to know more about people who could use such technology, in order to tear open a cruiser like the *Melville*.

'Annabel was sick,' her mother said. 'We thought we could keep away from the invaders. We thought we might creep in and out without them even knowing we were there. So we tied up Annabel and lowered her through the high ceiling of a new storeroom we'd found. She was crying and vomiting and suffering mightily, but the brave girl never lost heart – even through all that hullaballoo. Down and down she went and straight away started putting the things she found into the bags we lowered after her. We kept hauling up bags of clanking tins and sending Annabel down for more.

'Poor Annabel was feeling even worse by now and I was scared we had pushed her fragile health too far. Her ears were ringing with all the noise and she was dizzy. Her hands were covered in rope burns, the poor child. I had to keep telling her about the almighty feast we could have when we got home. Now all we had to do was finish loading up the hovercart and steal away. Before any of the noisy ones realised that we were there.'

Mrs Adams paused. I knew she was enjoying everyone looking at her. She was drinking all that attention in.

'We worked and we packed our hovercart with all these essential goods and then – miraculously – we got away unscathed and flew home.'

She threw up her hands to receive our applause, which was thunderous. Only Da looked perturbed and annoyed by her words and I knew why. The Adamses had only thought about themselves – their own business and their safety. To him, they had a duty to investigate further. Me, I shared his feelings.

The evening went on and more tales were told. Silly ones and old ones – about people who ate human flesh and drank blood and those who turned into four-legged beasts with fangs and wings. And skeletons that came out of the sand, back to life, and pumpkin heads that haunted the cornrows and prairies.

Later I was out back, feeding the new Molly and George. The animals hunkered down, snuffling and grateful as I patted them and whispered. But after a few minutes I realised I wasn't alone at the back of the Homestead. A small figure was sitting there, staring at the sky.

'Those germs still ain't gone away,' I remarked, sitting beside her.

'Nope,' she said.

I looked sideways at her. 'You're braver than I thought.'

'Yeah?'

'I never knew, till your Ma said. I never knew how they put you on a rope and all.'

She sighed. 'Yeah. Just about as soon as I could hold a torch and lift boxes. Just as soon as I stopped screaming when they put me down in the dark.'

'That's horrible,' I told her.

'Ma sure was the star of the show tonight,' Annabel said.

'I guess she was,' I said.

'One thing she got wrong,' Annabel said. 'The people who were drilling and lasering and cutting open the insides of the *Melville*. I saw them. When I was down in the hull.'

'You did?'

'I tried to tell my mother. I tried to tell my father. They didn't want to know. But I am telling you, Lora.'

My heart was thumping, because I knew something bad was coming.

'They weren't human beings.'

11

Colder days came in. There were ice crystals in the air some mornings. Al and I would go to stand on the tallest dunes and open our mouths, sticking out our tongues, even though Ma always said it wasn't safe. One evening Da came back from the fields coated in frosting like we'd spray on the tree at Christmas.

Molly and George were stamping and groaning, complaining about the cold. Their smelly breath came out in long trails of vapour. When I had Da on his own, I decided to broach the subject that had been bothering me for some time. I told him what Annabel Adams had told me, standing in that very spot, late on Hallows Eve.

Da was pulling blankets over the beasts and he looked at me, surprised, when I finished my account. 'You believe what this girl told you?'

'She was pretty serious about it. She sure seemed like someone who'd seen something awful down there in the *Melville*.'

Da scoffed at me. 'Lore, you're telling me that you'd believe a single word that spoiled and pampered Adams child would ever say?'

I hung my head, ashamed of his mockery. Didn't sound to me like Annabel was all that spoiled and pampered. Yeah, she had fancy clothes and they let her wear garish face paint and scent, but Annabel was still like their slave, doing scavenging work for them.

'She never heard nor saw anything down there,' Da insisted, glaring at me. I wasn't to go blabbing this stuff indoors. I wasn't to go unsettling Ma, because Ma was coming to the end of her tether. As if she too had been lowered into the dark on a long, fraying rope. But the darkness consisted of her own fears. Some of the wild talk in the air those past few months had just about made her sick. None of us wanted to see Ma get sick again, did we?

'All I'm saying is what Annabel said to me,' I told him, feeling defeated by Da's hard expression. 'And I was figuring that, if there were – well, non-human beings scavenging aboard the *Melville* ... well, maybe that's who it is, coming into the town at night and making people Disappear ... stealing them away and all that.'

I knew at once that I'd made a mistake. Molly and George mumbled and stirred in their pen as if they could feel the furious tension rising off Da. His face was black with anger as he advanced on me. 'Lora, I've warned you now. You're putting half-truths together and coming up with dangerous lies.'

I resolved not to say anything else, but I knew what I

knew and what I'd seen. I thought I could trust Da to listen to me; to take me seriously and not to treat me like a little kid. Thank God I never told him about the night Toaster threw Grandma's eye into the dead lake and the ground opened up to swallow it.

'OK, let's go back in,' he said, his smile warming up. 'You're missing Aunt Ruby's tales from the olden days. Come on, cheer up, Lore.'

He called me 'Lore' when he was feeling fond of me.

'I've heard enough about the olden days.' I sounded rude, I knew I did, but I just couldn't help myself. Why did all the adults hide away from stuff?

'Lore,' he said, warningly.

'In the olden days they would have believed me,' I said. 'Back then they knew the Martians were out there. They didn't deny it.'

His eyes widened. 'Martians? Lora … is that what you're worrying about?'

I wouldn't meet his gaze. 'I'm not saying I am. Just that … I might be.'

He sighed. 'They are long gone. You don't have to worry about them coming back in the night and snatching people away and eating them.'

I couldn't believe he was laughing at me. I burst out, 'What about Grandma? So where did she go?'

I met his eyes and he was on the point of tears. Oh no. I never wanted to upset him like that. I wanted to take back each of my stupid, careless words. Forget about the Martian Ghosts and Grandma.

'Lore, your grandma was very old. She was hardly her old self any more, was she? Remember how she'd rave and bust stuff up?'

'Yeah, I do.'

'When she was most like herself, she realised that she was making life harder for us. She was being a burden and she was too proud for that. She loved us all too much. And so that's why – I believe – she took herself off in the middle of the night. I believe that she went out into the wilderness to die quietly.'

Da had his hands on my shoulders as he told me this. He was acting like he was disclosing some great adult truth to me. Something he felt I'd grown up enough to hear.

I nodded, and tried to seem as if I was absorbing everything he was saying. Acting like Grandma was some amazing and noble woman who had sacrificed herself for the good of the rest of us. Inside, though, I was seething. I wanted to yell at him: so, how come she left behind her faulty leg? And what about all the other Disappeared townsfolk? The babies and tramps and husbands and healthy young people? Did they all crawl off into the wilderness to die?

I could feel the objections piling up in my head. My brain was throbbing with angry logic. For the first time I felt like my Da – my Da who I worshipped – had made himself into a fool. And all for the sake of an easier life.

He led me back indoors, out of the cold and the whistling dune winds. In the kitchen everyone was singing *Adeste Fideles*. That was an old song written especially for that time of year, in a language that none of us could understand.

12

At the end of the year the Disappearances increased. The town's leaders simply couldn't ignore them any more. As Da said, they had all turned a blind eye for far too long. Doctor Eaves Disappeared and that was really serious. He left behind a surgery stuffed with books and potions and mechanical parts, but they were of no use to us now. There was no one in Our Town with any knowledge of how to use them.

Only when the wife of Sheriff F.E. Baxter went missing did they call a town meeting. Everyone knew that Sheriff Baxter didn't give two hoots about his wife in her gaudy dresses, always looking elsewhere for male company. But now the Sheriff had to be seen to care, after she'd been carried off into the night. Also, he had given chase, onto Main Street, alerted by his wife's unholy screaming. Others were woken and looked out of their windows. That night several townsfolk had caught glimpses of the Martian Ghosts, just as I had months previously. Skinny, dried-up things with lamp-like eyes. Mostly nude, but some were wearing stripy garments that flapped behind them as they danced along the lane through pools of shadow.

As we ate a frugal supper of winter greens and corn bread Da was telling the tales he had heard that day at the Storehouse. About the skinny, giggling men and how they had been seen by Sheriff Baxter and others, carrying away the Sheriff's screaming wife, Eliza. How she had gurgled and howled. The men in the Storehouse had laughed uneasily as the tale was related. But their laughter was fooling no one. Everyone was frightened.

'You saw the kidnappers, didn't you?' Da said to me. 'You tried to tell me you'd seen them, when we stayed at Aunt Ruby's. I didn't listen to you.'

I nodded and stared down at my plate, flushing. He wouldn't listen to me. He'd told me to keep it quiet, in case I scared the others. I could feel all their eyes on me – Ma, Ruby and even Hannah – shocked that I'd been carrying such an important secret. Al and Toaster were looking at me too, and I don't think I'd ever felt more important.

I nodded again. 'I saw them. They creep into town and they take folk away, one at a time. Sometimes screaming, sometimes silent-like.'

Ma's face was white. The dinner she had so carefully prepared was going stone cold on the plates in front of us. She was rigid, with her hands like claws on her knife and spoon. 'What do they do with us? When they take us away?'

'I don't know,' I admitted. I'd wondered about it a lot and I knew it couldn't be anything good.

'Oh, poor Margaret,' said Ruby softly. At first I didn't know who she meant, but then I remembered that Margaret was Grandma's actual name that no one had called her for many years. To Ruby she had always been the same girl. 'She was always so scared the Martians would get her,' Ruby revealed, sighing. 'She said she could glimpse into the future, now and then. And there were lovely things to come, but terrible things, too. And she used to tell me that the Martians would come back and it would be the death of her. I'd tell her to hush her mouth. No one wants to hear awful stuff like that. The Martians were long dead to begin with, I'd say. Even if all of the Martians weren't exactly dead, then they had retreated so far underground so as to be no real danger to us…'

All my family were staring at Ruby. The quiet old woman in the patched and stained safari suit had never made such a long speech in all the time I had known her. The words came tumbling out and we could hardly keep up. She was bringing out secrets from the long past.

'M-Martians underground?' said Ma, looking very troubled.

'That was one theory,' Ruby shrugged. 'Just one theory among many. During the first settlement we found cities that had been abandoned. Not ancient cities or cities that had been nuked or burned to the ground or smashed by sandstorms. No, just cities where everyone had seemingly stopped what they were doing, got up, and walked out.

There was food on the tables, some folk said, just like our food here. They left things half-done and simply Disappeared themselves.'

A chill ran through every one of us.

'You knew more about them than you've ever told us,' said Da. 'I've never heard this stuff before.'

'It was a long time ago,' said Ruby. 'We've spent all these years making this part of the planet our very own. Pretending no one else was ever here. We didn't want to rake up the past by worrying about who might or might not be still around…'

Da's eyes flashed with anger. 'You must have been crazy! How could you pretend there was no danger?'

Ruby jumped to her feet, shouting back at him. 'Because as far as we knew, there was no danger. Every few years or so, one or two people might have Disappeared. Just a paltry few. But the settlement was working out, against the odds. Babies were being born and the colony was expanding. People felt that a handful of Disappearances was a small price to pay, for us getting a whole new planet to live on. And they were usually the sick or the old who were taken, anyway. They were seen as the sacrifices that had to be made.'

'My God,' said Da, looking horrified.

'You can't blame me – or Margaret,' Ruby said. 'We were just kids then. We were Lora's age. What could we have said or done that would have made any difference?'

We all looked at her, until she slumped back down into her seat.

After that supper and Ruby's revelations, things weren't quite the same between Da and our adopted aunt. He no longer trusted her. He made a few remarks along the lines of, was there anything else that we should know? Any other sixty-year-old secrets about our world that she knew but hadn't cared to tell?

Evenings at that time would see Da unrolling maps and charts he had found among Grandma's belongings. The maps were brightly coloured in cheerful shades of orange and red. Some showed how early landings had found the planet in its native state, and others were projecting ahead into the then-future, showing the marvellous cities of glass and steel that mankind intended to establish there.

'It was all meant to be so much grander,' I heard Da mutter. He studied those maps long and hard. Grandma had always talked about the wealth of materials she had hidden away about the first settlements. But now she was dead, Da was left looking at these naïve versions of a future that had never come.

Toaster joined him, peering over his shoulder. I saw Da turn on him. 'Did you know what Ruby knows? About the Martians?'

Toaster shook his head. 'No, but my memory circuits are not what they were. I would hate to say anything against Grandma, because she was a very good mistress to me. But, over the years, she did tamper with my memory something rotten. Portions of my mind have been burned out – rather crudely, I must admit. So I am not an entirely reliable witness to the first forty years of my existence. I regret to report it.'

'Hm,' said Da, looking askance at the sunbed.

Next thing was, Sheriff Baxter and the town Elders called a town meeting. They were actually going to discuss the Disappearances in an open debate.

Da told us, 'We're all going to be there. The whole Robinson family. And that includes you, Ruby. This is important.'

13

All the town was in attendance. Our family – including a slightly unwilling Ruby – took up a long wooden bench quite near the back of the meeting room. Da was grim-faced and quiet, as was Ma. All the other adults present were gabbling away, as if they had been holding back these words for ages and now had received permission to let them all out.

We faced the stage, where every Christmas we acted out the Jesus story and every Martian Thanksgiving we performed the Tale of Landfall. That stage had been cleared of everything but a long table and sitting at it were the town Elders. It was all the oldest faces in town in one long row, like cabbages growing in a patch.

For the first time it occurred to me that although Grandma had been ancient, and so was Ruby, neither woman had ever to my knowledge been asked to become one of the town Elders.

Sheriff Baxter was trying to call the meeting to order. He looked tired and red-eyed. His voice cracked as he shouted over everyone's noise. When at last they quietened down he outlined what he called some key points about recent developments in town.

Hannah grew restless, muttering and clambering on Ma's lap, and to tell the truth I felt much the same. The Sheriff was dressing everything up in unnecessary wordiness as he talked about the important thing being our continued confidence in leadership and personal comfort and safety. Only once did he use the actual word 'Disappearances' and pretty quick into his speech I realised – along with everyone else – that he was dancing around the edges of the subject. Minutes passed and he went on talking in vague terms and soon folk were murmuring to each other. Why, his own wife had been borne away into the dark night. You think he'd show a little more gumption and resolve, wouldn't you now?

The Sheriff suddenly looked very young and too weak for the job he was supposed to be doing. As Da said, Baxter had never been called upon to deal with anything as serious as this before. Land disputes, drunken brawls, petty thefts – that was all he was used to. At last my Da got to his feet and interrupted him. 'Er, excuse me, Sheriff Baxter,' he said, holding up both hands so as to stop the blathering on. All eyes in that meeting room were on my Da. 'It's fine to talk about defending our town and night watches and so forth,' said Da – and he looked round at every worried face in that room. His voice boomed into every corner and held firm and strong. 'But I think we ought to be talking about what's really going on here. And by that I mean finding out who or what is causing these Disappearances. Who or what is taking away our folk – like my mother and your wife and all the others. No disrespect intended.'

The whole gathering burst into spontaneous applause. Da ducked his head and smiled into his beard, embarrassed. The Sheriff on the stage looked mortified. 'Mr – ah – Robinson. We don't have access to the kind of knowledge that you're talking about. We…'

There came mutinous murmurs from the crowd. 'Yes, yes we do!' someone catcalled. Another voice cried out, 'They have been witnessed! They have been seen in the night, going about their ghastly business!' 'Phantoms!' gasped another and a strange thrill went through me. I should have been scared and more grown-up acting. But I was thoroughly excited.

'It's the Martians – they're coming back!' This was a louder voice, closer to us and we all turned. Vernon Adams stood up, sweating and feverish. He clutched the back of the bench in front of him, his eyes staring crazily round at all of us.

Either side of him, Mrs Adams and his poor daughter Annabel were in their chintziest frocks, with their hair set in ringlets, as if they thought tonight's emergency meeting was gonna be some fancy social shindig. Mrs Adams was pulling at her husband's arm, tugging at his waistcoat. 'Come off it, Vernon. Please, my dear…'

But that small, pink-faced man stood firm. He had a bellyful of stuff to say. 'We've been burying our heads in the red desert sands. We all know that there's an indigenous population here. At least, our older folk do. It's only sixty-odd years since they came here from Earth. And yet somehow – in the scrabbling for existence and survival and keeping ourselves going – we've limited our horizons and put the wider and deeper world out of our minds.'

A ripple of fear ran through the room like a desert snake in wet grass.

'We heard them first,' Mr Adams said. 'When we were last aboard the *Melville*. One of our salvage operations. Annabel – my beautiful daughter here – she was deeper within the ship. And she saw them, didn't you, darling?'

All eyes moved to the pretty, powdered face of Annabel. 'Yes, father,' she said, in her singsong voice. 'They weren't human at all. They were tall and skinny and they were laughing.'

Da voiced everyone's question, 'Laughing?'

Annabel nodded. 'They went, "*Heeee heeeee heeee.*"'

She put on a warbling voice to do that laughing as she'd heard it, and it startled everyone present. It was like the laughing Martians were there in the room with us. Annabel carried on doing it, like she was losing her grip, '*Heeee heeeeee heeeeeee,*' until her father grasped her shoulder and squeezed hard. Then she got that distant look on her face again and Mrs Adams produced a lacy handkerchief and began crying into it.

'We didn't listen to our wonderful, darling Annabel at

first,' said Mr Adams. 'But really we knew. These Martians are out there. Watching us. And laughing.

'And then … last Monday night, they actually came to our shop!

'Now, we lock our doors and windows just as tightly as anyone else. But I'm here to tell you that it doesn't matter. They ripped that electronic scal away like it was silver paper round chocolate. The stark truth is, if they want to get inside – then they will.

'We sleep directly above our emporium and there was no mistaking the slapping noise of bare feet on boards. The scrabbling of skinny fingers on the shelves and in the drawers and the barrels. Dirty Martian hands touching our wholesome goods. Fingers rifling and patting, stroking and scratching.

'We sat up straight in bed, Mrs Adams and I, and we held hands, listening to this abominable racket. Annabel came from her room to sit with us. We three listened to the noise from downstairs … and the giggling. "*Heeeee heeeee heeeeeee.*"

'I thought, if we kept still and didn't draw attention, then they would forget we were there. After a while – we heard a closer sound. A footstep on the staircase. Then another, and another. We heard their fingers scratching at each of the doors in the hallway. And … at last the bedroom door. We sat up in bed, clutching one another. The door came squealing open.

'One of them slowly poked his head round the door and into the room. He looked at us and we stared back. He looked like he was smiling at us. Purple, swirling eyes, like blood running down a plughole.

'He was moving on horrid, twiggy limbs that actually creaked out loud. He said, "Now we've got you. *Heeeee heeeee heeeeee*."

'There was something so deathly about that creature's voice when he spoke our language. He sucked all hope out of the air we were breathing.'

The meeting room was absolutely quiet.

Da broke that silence, asking, 'How are you here to tell the tale?'

Mr Adams said, 'The creature said my family and I would be spared that night if I came here to tell you all what the … the Martians wish you to know.'

Sheriff Baxter spoke up then. 'I – I insist that you tell us what this message is, Vernon Adams.'

The shopkeeper said, 'The creature told us he and his fellows have shrugged off their slumbers and are about to reclaim their world. The Martians are, in fact, coming back.'

Anger erupted to replace the fear. People got up on their feet and shouted stuff out. Mr Adams looked white and sweaty and I knew we hadn't heard the full message yet.

The tableful of Elders weren't shouting out. They sat there, very still and shrivelled.

Suddenly Annabel Adams was up on her feet. 'He said they were going to eat us! Now they've got a taste for human flesh! That's what the Martian wanted us to say!'

14

Some of the men said they wanted to go on the offensive, and take the fight to the Martians themselves. They started to stockpile weapons, dragging ancient blasters and dusty automatics out of their basements and polishing them up. My Da tried to make them see sense. 'How will you find them? You don't even know how many there are! How do you know you even stand a chance?'

That was one of the most frightening things about the Martian Ghosts. They were subtle and slippery and numberless. They came and went by darkness, sticking mostly to the shadows.

That long winter was a tough time. The Disappearances continued during the months of snow. Peculiar footprints were left over town and traced all over the Prairie. Our enemies were starting to care less about being secretive.

There were blizzards and we bolted and sealed ourselves into our homesteads. Ma and Da gave us homemade toys and gifts and we tried to recapture the magic of the great Christmases we had known when we were much younger, but it was hard. Knowing what was out there, wishing us ill.

We tried to celebrate for the sake of Hannah. She was only four and these were the times she would eventually look back upon. Would she want to remember us all being scared and miserable?

When the winter weeks drew to their dreadful close and people emerged again into the sunlight, it seemed that fewer of us were out and about in town. Rumour had it that certain families were so scared about the Martians that they had sealed themselves up in their underground shelters. They would stay down there until they felt the menace had blown over.

'The fools,' Da said, knowing that nothing but desert dust was going to be blowing over any time soon.

Then came the gossip that certain families hiding in bunkers had taken lethal poisons and ended their lives before the Martian Ghosts came and dragged them away. Sheriff Baxter did a roll call in the February and seventy people failed to answer their names.

Da was perturbed by this.

'We have to stick together,' he said. 'That's what humans need to do. We belong together.'

He went to the Elders and told them how we all needed to leave right away and find somewhere new to settle, and we had best do it collectively, en masse, altogether. Da spoke passionately and Sheriff Baxter tried to relay his ideas to the line of withered old men.

Late that night, I looked out of the attic window of

Ruby's house and I saw a single Ghost, dancing slowly down the road. It looked smaller and more graceful than the others. My heart went crazy, banging with terror, but my brain was telling me not to be fearful. This Martian Ghost looked like a child. I stared and stared as it came down the street and somehow it must have sensed me, because next thing it looked straight up at my window.

I tried to duck behind the dusty curtains but it was too late.

Then – the strangest thing. The Martian smiled at me.

This was how I came to meet Sook.

She wasn't a child. I don't know what she was – how old or anything. I just know that she was very different from the others, and that she wanted to talk with me. She beckoned me down into the dark street, waving those skinny arms.

Hardly knowing what I was doing, I left my bedroom and went downstairs, really carefully not to wake any of the others. I agonised my way through the house, wincing at the cold of the boards on my bare feet, wondering if those lit-up eyes were making me do things my waking self never would.

I stepped out into the chilly night.

I was in the street, about to come face to face with one of our deadly enemies.

Already I felt like I had always known Sook. I was never very good at making friends. Al always made that kind of thing seem so easy, but I never got the knack. But this time

– at that very moment – I knew I was looking into the ravaged, alien face of a true friend.

She was purple in the Earth light. Her skin was corrugated and patterned so it looked a bit like when you cut into a red cabbage. Intricate and rough. She blinked at me, as if she was considering me and weighing up.

When she spoke I heard the words inside my head. They were very gentle and I didn't think it odd that she spoke in English. 'Come with me.'

It was the most foolhardy thing I'd ever done, and the most dangerous too. If I ever came back from this, Da would kill me. I recall thinking this and wanting to giggle as Sook took my hand in hers. It was dry and felt like gnarled tree bark.

She tugged on my arm and she started dancing off down the sandy road, which was still frozen solid. She was dancing and running at the same time, moving faster and faster, so that her thin, flapping feet were hardly touching the ground.

Miraculously, I was being drawn along after her. I was feeling lighter and faster than I ever had in my life. It was like we were both transforming into another substance. No longer pinky-brown or purple human or Martian flesh. We were waltzing and whirling through the frozen streets of town. I heard my Martian companion laughing – a light, breathy noise – and suddenly we were shooting far beyond the boundaries of Our Town.

We went out in the wilderness, heading west over crags and rocky outcroppings, lopsided hills and dried-out seas. I looked for the lake bed Toaster had cracked apart with Grandma's eye, but it flashed by in a blur. Then we were tangled up in streams of frosty clouds, all sparkling pink, wrapping themselves about us. It hit me for the first time, properly, that we were flying.

We flew and I didn't know how long it lasted or how far Sook had taken me away from home. Hundreds of miles, it felt like. I was looking down at maps and charts far more detailed and lurid than those hand-drawn efforts I'd examined with Da.

I saw that this was a whole world we were living on. A vaster, much more complex place than I had ever considered.

We flew over a plain of bulging monoliths and icy hummocks, where everything was trimmed in black, encrusted vegetation. I blinked and looked again, but already we had moved on. We flew over lakes and mountains and mysterious forests and I thought about how much Al would have loved this. But it was me Sook had called out to.

By dawn she returned me to the dirty little road outside Ruby's house. She set me down and then danced off again, turning to points of light and disappearing herself.

I was left standing alone. Sook had danced me right around the world, the whole shining circumference, and dumped me back here without us speaking more than ten words to each other. I knew her name was Sook. She knew mine was Lora. I knew I had never been so excited in all my life. I stood there alone for some time, shaking.

I let myself back indoors and sealed up the front door before the rest of the family could discover what I had been up to.

15

I'd never had friends of my own age. At the Homestead I worked with Da, and I had Hannah and Al and that was quite enough. Occasionally when we went to town I'd see other kids my age, but I never really had friends. Not to confide in or share with.

Maybe it's weird Sook became my friend, what with her being a different species and all. To me she was just Sook. Our forays into the night never seemed like part of the life I led by day.

This nighttime creature was the most fabulous being I'd ever met. She was half-dream, half-real.

On our third or fourth trip into the night, she talked to me a little more. Until that moment, when her chiming, golden voice bloomed inside my head, it hadn't struck me as surprising that she hadn't said much as yet.

'Have you told your parents? Do they know you come out to see me?'

'No,' I said aloud, and she turned those big purple eyes on me.

'You needn't tell them about me,' she said. 'They hate us, don't they?'

'They're scared,' I said, trying hard to speak the words inside my head. The hardest part was making them come out in a line, because my skull was swarming with thoughts that were all jumbled up.

We weren't flying tonight. We were just walking into the wilderness and the parched scrubland. It was further than I'd ever been on foot. I was fascinated by the strange columns of stone and the weird trees.

'They are right to be scared of us.' She sighed heavily. 'You know, don't you? You understand what we do?'

I told her that I knew about the Disappearances. I said about Grandma and how we had found her leg and her eye.

'How I wish my people wouldn't do it,' she said. 'I've tried to explain to them. I've tried to tell them that you are just people like we are.'

'Of course we are!' I burst out.

'And you have your own feelings, too. You look after each other and care and you even ... love each other.'

'And what do they say?'

Her shoulders slumped. 'I'm the youngest in our whole tribe. Of course they won't listen to me. They scoff when I say humans have feelings.'

'But we're human!' I cried out. 'We ... we *invented* feelings!'

Sook looked at me, frowning. 'No, you didn't. How could you?'

I didn't know what to say to her. Then it came out in a rush, 'But we invented everything! We've got, like, civilisation and rockets that brought us here. We've got Dickens and Michelangelo and … and…'

Sook smiled. 'I hardly know what you're talking about. But I like that you care enough to get cross, Lora.'

We walked through blue sand. The sky was creamy, starting to glow at the edges where the dawn light was coming.

'Has there ever been a friendship like this before?'

'Oh yes,' Sook said. 'All this time that humans have been on Mars. There must have been friendships before, don't you think?'

'I don't know,' I thought, inside my head. 'We don't really know anything about you.'

'You will,' promised Sook. Then she noticed the time and took hold of my hand, running down the steep dune we had just climbed. We were taking off again, into the sun.

It was the most beautiful thing I'd ever experienced. Flying through the dawn light. Sook kept tight hold of my wrist in her dry, wrinkled hand.

We touched down a few hundred yards from my home. No lights were burning yet. The prairie was one dark, sullen mass. The beasts were snoring. Sook smiled and left. I would slip into bed and pretend I'd been sleeping. All day I would be yawning again. Maybe I could sleep for an hour now and that would be enough.

I was almost at the door when something jumped out at me. I nearly peed. It was Al. He grabbed hold of my wrist, just where Sook had held me, except he wasn't so gentle.

'I saw you,' he said. 'I know what you were doing. I saw that … thing.'

I shook him off roughly. 'You don't know anything.'

'It was a Martian.' His face looked spiteful.

'Ssssh!' I drew him into the shadows of the porch. 'You can't tell anyone, Al.'

'What are you doing?' he squealed. 'They took Grandma! They're taking everyone!'

'I'm learning about them. I'm friends with her. I don't know how yet. But I know it's really important.'

Al was staring at me something dreadful. 'How are you ever going to tell Ma and Da about this?'

'I'm not in danger,' I told him, but he didn't look like he even cared about that.

He went, 'You're a betrayer, Lora. That's what you are.'

I couldn't make him see sense, whatever I said. All that day and for a week or so, Al kept out of my way. He kept playing with the lizard bird he had brought to our Homestead from Ruby's house. He was training it to understand him and do tricks.

I was helping Da with the burden beasts, cleaning up their feet and scales and stuff one day, when he said, 'You and Al had a falling out?'

'He's a boy,' I shrugged. 'They get funny sometimes. He's at a funny age.'

This made Da laugh out loud. It was always a good feeling, making Da laugh. Then he looked at me. 'Still, there is something different about you lately, Lore. I'm gonna be relying on you a lot in the next few weeks. When it comes time to be moving on I'll be needing you to help and be strong.'

'I know that.' I stood up, to look taller and more sure about what was expected of me.

But, what if we went hundreds or even thousands of miles away? Would Sook still know where to find me?

Maybe when we went I wouldn't be able to tell Sook about it. Maybe that would mean an end to our friendship.

It was like a clock had started ticking in my head and my heart.

16

I went out to work with Da in the fields. There was stuff to salvage before we abandoned the prairie. Da and I patrolled the perimeter and it hit me that the land had never really been ours. It had just been on loan to us for a little while.

Da said, 'We got some good use out of this dry old soil. It kept us alive for these good years.'

It was like we were doing it honour by going round the edges and taking down Da's electric fences. We were setting the land free, to turn back into wilderness again.

We worked quickly, plodding alongside Molly and George, collecting up any grain or shoots we found: precious scraps of life we could hope to transplant elsewhere. Some days when we went further afield we took the hovercart. It was old and kronky and the innards had corroded from the sand whistling through it.

That day we parked at the furthest perimeter. There we were, surveying the reaches of the cornrows, which had become visible again now that winter winds had stripped away the dunes. Da decided he wanted to take some pictures. He never said much, just used Al's camera phone to take some snaps of empty ground.

When we walked back to the hovercart in the late afternoon, it was plain to see it was listing. The skirt had busted and there was no way it was gonna hover again without serious repairs.

Da sighed and muttered something about it giving up the ghost when we were so far from home. Next thing he was crawling underneath the hovercart and starting to tinker with the insides. He was getting me to pass his bag of tools. I was proud because I knew all the names for those implements, and what they did.

This was no easy fix. The hovercart had gone very wrong. Da was under barely ten minutes before the anti-grav packed in completely.

The front end of the vehicle smashed down on his legs just as he was repositioning himself.

I stood there, frozen. Holding a tool. A tool I knew the name and purpose of. I stared at Da. He was rigid. Screaming till he was all screamed out. His voice was bubbling somehow. It sounded like blood in his throat.

I staggered over to him. What could I do? Could I get him out?

His face was coated in dark, sticky blood. He was in a fever sweat, panting like he was scorching hot. He spat words out past the bubbles of blood. He took a few seconds to fix his focus. Wild white eyes stared at me. Then he started to tell me what to do.

His jaw juddered. He was trying to keep calm for my sake.

'T-Toaster,' he said. It took every bit of his strength to get these words out. 'Toaster can g-get me out of here. F-fetch him n-now, Lore.'

I couldn't think of anything else to say but, 'Yes, Da.' Then I turned and I didn't hesitate for a second. I ran faster than a mad Jack Rabbit over the dunes. I let my heels fly and my lungs burn as I pelted downhill.

I could save him, I knew I could. It was unthinkable that he was going to die today. I had to run faster across the prairie than I ever had before.

All the while I was shouting inside my head, 'Sook! Come and help! You've got to help me, Sook!'

But there was no reply. The heat was still beating down. Sook would never come until it was dark.

Da was lying back there with no water. With his legs mangled and crushed and blood in his mouth, drowning him.

'Sook! Will you come and help us?'

I don't know how long it took me to get home. It felt like it was several days, with the sun scorching through my winter dress all the way. Sweat streaming down my arms and legs. It was a shock to find the Homestead so peaceful, with everyone carrying on their afternoon tasks. Ruby was with Hannah at the well scrubbing out linens, and Ma was in the kitchen with Al. I could hear them clattering around, and their high, contented voices.

I went straight to Toaster, who was out back, feeding

grain to the chickens. He saw at once that something was dreadfully wrong.

'We will go at once,' he said, dropping the bucket of feed. The hens went crazy over the spilled grain as we rounded the outbuildings. That's when Ma caught us.

'Lora, what's going on?' she began, and then she must have seen something awful in my face, for she went very still all at once. She said, 'It's your Da, isn't it? What's happened? Where is he?' She had hold of both my arms and was squeezing them tight.

Toaster laid a cold mechanical hand on her. He made her stop shaking me. My teeth were rattling in my head. He said in a very steady voice, 'I must go to him at once. Lora will come with me.'

Ma let go immediately. It was like Toaster had been the boss of our family all along and we were programmed to do his bidding.

Ma stood quite still, hugging herself, her rough woollen dress billowing in the breeze. She stood outside the Homestead watching us go.

Toaster and I ran through the sand, past the low dunes. It was all uphill. Toaster ran smoothly. My lungs were heaving and I could taste my own blood, as if the harsh sand in the air was cutting me up inside.

I shouted out directions and tried to explain. Toaster locked onto his target. I followed in his wake and we ran and ran. I could hear broken glass valves and fizzing circuitry crashing about inside his chest cavity. We didn't slow for a second.

At last we came to the rise in the cornrow where the hovercart could be seen quite plainly. Just as I had left it, wonky and lopsided on the rocks. Its silver skin glistening in the diminishing sunlight.

Toaster pulled ahead, surging towards his objective. He was at the top of the hill several moments before I was.

I came crashing to a halt beside our robot. I stared uncomprehendingly at the disturbed sand and the vehicle lying there and the gap by its skirt where my da had been. I stared and stared at the drying streaks of blood but it was no use. There was no avoiding the plain truth of it.

Da had Disappeared.

17

Hannah didn't fully understand what was going on, of course. None of us could really grasp the full meaning. Life – our lives – without Da in them didn't make any sense at all.

Ma hit me. Hard across the face. I think everyone else present was more shocked than I was. I fell over and they helped me back onto my feet.

Men from the town were there, in our Homestead. Stomping about in their desert shoes, loading up their weapons. They organised a short, futile search. When Ma hit me they dragged her away to calm down.

Those stinging slaps gave me something to focus on. I felt I deserved them. I had let Da down. I should never have left him alone out there on the prairie. He was pinned to the rocks, helpless as a beetle on its back. He was under the hideous weight of that metal machine. Even if I hadn't directly caused his death, I was still a jinx. A Jonah, like they used to have on old spaceships, like in the old tales of discovery and disaster in the void.

The very worst had happened. We had lost Da.

Aunt Ruby took Ma away and put her to bed and made

her swallow the strongest pills she had. Old pills from supplies Ma had tucked away in her cabinet. Things they gave to folk freaking out during deep space voyages. Ma went into a comatose state to ride through the days of grief. She floated above while the truth slowly sank in for the rest of us.

Al and me, we looked after Hannah, who remained her bright and cheery self. This seemed kind of wrong, but as Ruby said, she wasn't to understand.

The town's men gave up their search for the body.

Night time, morning, afternoon, evening, night time again. The same again, and the same again. The days wheeled round and no Da came banging open our front door, stomping the sand off his boots. He didn't whip off his hat and laugh at our stricken faces. 'You thought I was missing? You thought I was dead? How could you think I'd ever leave you?'

He never came in and kissed Ma and the baby and ruffled Al's hair and mine. He just never turned up. It was like he had forgotten us in an instant, and turned his back.

Those first few nights were so weird. I put the electronic seal on the outer doors of our Homestead. By doing that I was admitting that he was out there forever and never coming back.

Ma slumbered and muttered and, as the strongest pills wore off, occasionally woke up screaming.

Several days after Da Disappeared, I snuck out into the night. I checked that Al wasn't following me, then I set off. I climbed the scrubland and crossed the crazed surface of the dead lake, and I thought about Toaster. I thought about his throwing Grandma's eye and creating all these fractures. I climbed the crags on the far side and I called out to Sook.

'You never came when I called last time. When I was more scared than I've ever been in all my life…'

Just thinking about it made my heart start pounding again.

'Didn't you hear, Sook? Didn't you care?'

'I cared,' she said. 'I heard you.'

She landed softly on the sand behind me. Her voice was clear and bell-like in my mind. I whirled about, frantic, glaring at her. She looked less like wood bark, more like soft flesh. Her eyes were glowing silver. She wore robes that looked like scaled wings, like a moth's wings. Had she changed somehow? Did the Martian Ghosts evolve like that?

'You let me down,' I snapped.

'I know.'

'You could have helped me. He was stuck there. I just needed some help…'

'I couldn't have helped,' she said softly, hanging her head. 'They wouldn't have let me.'

'Who?' I demanded. Part of me didn't want to understand, or to hear what she was going to say next.

Sook said, 'I can't hold my people back, Lora.'

'You what?'

'I have pleaded with them and reasoned with them,' said Sook. 'For your sake and the sake of your family and everyone else you care about.'

I gasped. 'You've told them about us?'

'I've told them that they should help you. That there is a great chance here. An opportunity to make peace and understanding between two great species. To give them their dues, they did listen. For a short while.'

'W-what are you saying, Sook?'

She looked me dead in the eye. 'They aren't interested in being your friends.'

'But why?' I said, sounding so childish I was ashamed. 'Why not?'

She looked worried about how she was going to break this next bit to me. 'We have been starving for so long, Lora. It's hard to get nourishment out of this world of ours. Poor vegetables and horrid algae. Bony little rodents. Making meals out of jewelled insects that come in plagues once a year and we treat the coming of those swarms like you do Christmas. It's a pitiful existence. No wonder you think of us as insubstantial Ghosts. It's a hard life on Mars. Harder for the Martians than it is for you humans. How do you suppose that makes us feel?'

'I – I don't know.' All I could think though, was – You ate Grandma. You ate Da. Your kind might be eating his body at this very moment. All that knowledge. All that experience and skill. All that kindness and love. And you're eating him. Grinding him up into smaller and smaller pieces and mincing him to paste between your teeth.

Sook sighed inside my head. 'You people are just so fat and juicy and chewy. That's all my people can see. Even when someone like me stands up and says, "Look! The humans are thinking, sentient creatures. They have music, mathematics, ethics and art. Just as we have. They have arrived at a civilised status. They have all the sophistication we have developed, in some ways they are even more advanced. They can travel to other worlds and make their marks on other planets." But none of these things impress my people. Not compared with the animal stink of you. The salty, milky, fatty, fleshy juice of you. They get distracted from their thoughts of civilisation and art by the saliva welling up in their parched mouths. By the acid rumbling deep inside their bellies, eager to digest. They can't think of anything but stealing you away, one at a time, depleting your townships and homesteads and slowly and gradually feasting upon you all...'

Now Sook looked and sounded different. Her voice was fuller and rounder and sweeter. I could hear other voices behind hers. It was like she had become a whole choir of voices inside her body. Her silver eyes glimmered. Her moth cloak was fanning out as the desert breeze caught up with us.

'Sook ... what should I do? I need to decide. Ma can't. Neither can Ruby. I think I'm the one in our family who has to do the deciding now.'

Then Sook's voice went high and panicked, rising up out of all the others that her body contained. 'You must take them all away, Lora. As many as you can get to follow you. Get them out of the town. Leave this place at once!'

A horrible change came over her face.

Startled, I fell back. I turned away and started to run. Ploughing through the pale sand.

'Run, Lora!' Sook shrieked after me.

18

'We're moving,' I told the whole family. 'It's time for us to go.'

Ma, Al, Ruby and Hannah looked at me as if I'd gone crazy. They were eating the oatmeal Ma had prepared, just as she had thousands of mornings before. The old clock was ticking on the mantle over the fire and the range was blazing hot on the chilliest morning of the season. Ours was a house that was grieving, but it was still full of life.

'We take what we can carry,' I said. 'We should go as soon as we can.'

Ruby suddenly looked like exactly what she was. An old, tired woman. As old as Grandma had been. 'Why the suddenness, Lora? What have you heard?'

Toaster came in from outside. He could tell straight away that something was up. 'What is it?' he said. His metal body was braced against more bad news.

Al told him, 'Lora says we have to go. Abandon our Homestead and everything.'

'Ah,' said Toaster. Like me, he had heard Da making his plans aloud as he worked in the fields. 'Yes, this is inevitable.'

'I knew it,' Ma muttered. 'But we can't now. How can we go now? How can we do anything without him?'

I said, 'I'll be in charge, Ma. I know what to do.'

They looked at me – half disbelief, half relief in their faces. Then Hannah did something odd. Maybe because everyone's eyes were on me and I was the focus of all the attention in the room. She climbed down from her chair and came to me. I picked her up and she hugged me round my neck. She was warm as oatmeal.

We would limit ourselves to one small bag each, and Ma would pack an extra bag of essential cooking implements. In the kitchen she went into a fit of panic over food supplies. What could we take? What could sustain us? I didn't know either. A plaggy tank of distilled water could go on the hovercart. A small sack of oatmeal, a side of salted meat. Not very much. We'd have to find food on the road. Somehow.

Already I was thinking about the townsfolk and who would come with us. How many? Maybe we could all pool resources, like they did in the old days; the early days on Mars before the town even existed.

In the kitchen Ma grabbed my arm. 'Your da would never want us to give up. To sit here waiting till we all got Disappeared.'

'That's right,' I said, and I marvelled at her strength of will. I'd watched her control her panic and horror at the truth of what had become of Da. She'd gone robotic and cold like Toaster, to make sure we survived. She left her harp in the kitchen. With so much other stuff there wouldn't be room for it. We were all leaving most of our lives behind.

Al said, 'Lora, we must make space for Ma's harp. We can't leave that. Her music, Lora…'

He was right. For once he was right. I gave the nod to the harp.

Then I found him supposedly packing his clothes into a bag. He'd left most of his clean stuff out, and was coaxing his lizard bird into his bag with a few rinds of bacon.

'You can't take that,' I told him flatly.

'I'm going to,' he said, looking squarely at me. Perhaps because of the harshness of his tone, the lizard did as it was told. It crept into the bag and crouched there, clutching the rinds and chewing them delicately.

'I mean it, Al,' I told my brother.

'You think you can tell everyone what to do,' he snapped. 'I'm taking Samuel Clemens, whatever you say. You're not the boss of everything, Lora.'

I left him to it, shaking my head.

It took us only three days to dismantle our life in the Homestead. Toaster fixed up the hovercart till it was running as well as it ever had. We loaded it up till it was full to bursting. I wished that we had a different vehicle we could use instead. It was our only means of escape and we just had to use it, even if Da had been crushed and trapped underneath it.

There was still blood on its skirts that I hadn't been able to scrub away. I hoped the others would think it was a patch of rust or red sand corrosion.

I fired up those engines. I was at the wheel, Ruby and Toaster either side of me, Ma and Hannah in the back. Al was riding atop George, and both beasts walked behind the hovercart lugging the bulk of our supplies. We made a pitiful convoy, I thought. But a brave one.

I don't know about the others – I was too busy driving, squinching my eyes against the dust in Da's old goggles – but I never looked back at the old Homestead. Not once. Everything that it had meant to us and everything that we had been when we lived there – it was all gone. Now we were fugitives. We were like bugs, scrabbling about on the desert floor.

No, we were settlers, all over again. That was a better way of seeing it. With everything we still called our own heaped onto our cart, we were looking for somewhere, far from here, where we could put down roots again. Da – and Grandma – would be proud of us, I thought.

In town we were met by astonished stares. We were supposed to be hardy and resilient. We were Prairie Folk. We didn't scare easily. We faced up to arduous times with fortitude. But they saw that day, when we rolled into town, a family on the run. We were mostly women folk, plus one jumpy boy and a kronky old robot. We had given in and we were running away.

'But where will you go?' Vernon Adams, at the counter of his emporium, looked neat as ever in his black uniform and white apron. His wife and daughter were standing beside him, and a whole storeful of shoppers stared at us.

I'd thought about this long and hard. So had Da. He had kept this one up his sleeve. Da's brilliant idea about where we should run to, when the day eventually came. I brought it out with some pride.

'We're following the source of the signals,' I said. 'All the meteorological reports we get on the radio. When the wind's in the right direction and the radiation calms and sun spots fizzle down. Someone's been broadcasting these messages for years, telling us about the weather. Someone with a powerful lot of technology, Da always said. A City, maybe. A human City. And that's what we're heading towards. That's where we're going, Mr Adams. Will you come too?'

19

Sheriff Baxter thought it was shameful that we wanted to run off and abandon town. He got up in front of the new public meeting and acted all scandalised at the suggestion. He even implied we had been sent off our heads because of Da's Disappearance.

'This is Our Town, our home,' said the Sheriff. 'How many years have we spent building it up? Why would we suddenly give up hope and turn it over to our enemies?'

A great many agreed with him that night. Rumbles and grumbles loud enough to raise the rafters on the meeting hall. The line of Elders looked smug at all the noise.

'They're content just to sit still and do nothing,' I hissed along our row to Al and Toaster. 'They think they're doing something good by doing nothing at all.'

Ma's hand crept into mine, and I was surprised. I suppose it was her telling me to shush, as well as a gesture of quiet support. We sat on those hard benches listening to all that complacent noise and I thought: Well, why should they even listen to a young girl like me? Why would they listen to some women, a young boy and a broken robot? Why should they accept our word about anything?

We spent that night at Ruby's house. Everything seemed like an anti-climax. After gearing ourselves up, here we were, under a familiar roof again. Sitting amongst Ruby's memorabilia and tat. We spent an uneasy night in the beds we always slept in when we were in town.

The next day Ruby lost it. She yanked out trunks and rotting boxes, all filled with old discs and mildewy books. She told us in a defensive voice that this was all history. It needed to be preserved. We couldn't just leave it here.

I agreed with her. I knew that it was all history. But she had to look again at the size of the hovercart. We couldn't take any of this stuff with us.

'But you've seen these films, Lora. Films of Earth! Films of life in the olden days and life during the settling!' She sobbed and I had to harden my heart. Now I had to be really in charge.

'One day maybe one of us will come back,' I said. 'Or somebody else will. You know, if you hide all your precious stuff away, in the cellar, say, then maybe it'll keep safe.'

The old woman started babbling. 'It's heritage. It's the legacy.'

But by now this just sounded like words to me. I got Al to help her shift the old junk into the basement. I knew we had to focus on practical stuff. I went through Ruby's kitchen for the concentrated capsules she had salvaged from her days as a space traveller. She had very few of the disgusting things left. Just one final parcel. She had opened this last box to delight Grandma when she visited. A shame. They'd have been useful on our trek, since they took up so little space.

How were we going to survive? I had seen for myself the vastness of the deserts. I had gained a glimpse of how huge our planet really was, during those stolen night flights with Sook. It seemed impossible that we could get very far on our hovercart, with our two lumbering burden beasts. I was glad no one else had seen things on the scale I had. They might think this whole setting off was futile. But I just knew we had to try. I couldn't let the Martian Ghosts take any more of us away. I couldn't bear to think of them Disappearing my family.

20

Though they couldn't be described as a matter of life and death, I made sure I brought all of those books – the ones about the men in the tall hats and tight britches and the ladies in their corsets and gowns with their cups of Chinese tea. Books about wills and big houses and misty moors and journeys taken on horseback or railway. I stole them from under Mrs Adams' nose, knowing that I would need them. I took my own books too, despite what I'd said to Aunt Ruby, and how I'd made her leave her things behind. But my books took up no space at all. Less than a handful of fingernails. And I never told anyone.

The day after the meeting, when we walked about town, still trying to convince folk to leave, lots of them were averting their eyes from us. I knew that they wanted to behave like there was nothing wrong. But it felt like everyone thought we had disgraced ourselves. Made fools of ourselves.

Al even said, 'Maybe we've got it all wrong. If we stayed here in Our Town … we'd be stronger in numbers. Maybe we can fight the Martians off…'

Even as he said this, I could hear the doubts colouring his voice. He was squinching his eyes up, trying to convince himself.

We went to the Storehouse to buy fuel and sundry other bits that the damaged hovercart would need for a long haul. These men were Da's pals and peers. They were respectful to us for his sake. They gave us good prices on the things we'd brought from the Homestead to trade. Stuff we wouldn't need anymore.

The men hung their heads in shame because they weren't heeding our warnings. I wondered if they'd have listened to Da more. One of them – a gruff old geezer called Spider – broke their uneasy quiet. 'He was a good fella, your Da. We all respected him.'

'I know,' I said, sounding curt.

'But still, he didn't know everything,' Spider went on. 'You think he did. But he weren't always in the right.'

I glared at Spider for that. How many times had he helped this lot, with a thousand things they couldn't do, or got wrong? How many times had he fished them out of trouble? 'Da knew more than you lot,' I snapped. 'More than anyone in this town.'

They never said anything to that. I paid up and left that small collection of worn-out goods we'd been bartering with. Al and I carried the plaggy cases of supplies out to the parking area at the back. This was the place Da had brought us so many times when we were kids. This small lot was where he had always parked, leaving us to explore town while he went to see his cronies. What if he could have heard what they said today?

Al and I didn't feel like the same kids anymore.

Ma, Hannah and Ruby were sitting in the hovercart as we loaded up the fuel and the last few supplies we could cram aboard.

I sat in the driver's seat and gunned the engine. It coughed and wheezed like it was choking on the red dust of the prairie.

And that was how and when we left.

Our first few days on the road were peaceful. Deceptively peaceful, Al said.

The terrain levelled out and smoothed and the going was easy. Like the land itself wanted us to think it was gonna be plain sailing. And then, when we were far from home, it was gonna turn on us. Al always was a worrywart, though. I told him to get back to training his lizard bird to do something useful. He was full of talk about how bright that dumb-looking beast was.

Ma sat on top of the hovercart wearing her best bonnet, clutching her carpet bag of her most personal and precious items. Those first few hundreds of miles she barely said a word or cracked a new expression. Staring straight ahead, she seemed frozen there. The rest of us shared scared glances with one another. She kept her face fixed straight on the horizon like a monument that we were transporting somewhere better.

'She's just recovering, that's all,' Aunt Ruby told us, in a wise tone. 'Losing your Da like that. It's a shock to her system.'

Ma sat Hannah upon her knee and Hannah looked scared the whole time. She didn't get what was happening at all.

We camped under yellow starlight, and then, when it rolled into phase above us, the blue light of old Earth. The first few nights were colder than I expected, but luckily we had brought enough blankets and rugs. We lay on the exposed ground and I listened to my family members dropping off, one by one, into sleep. Hoping we'd be safe here. Surely this was safer than being at home and waiting for the Martian Ghosts to come for us, one at a time?

I lay awake plagued by awful thoughts. What if I'd taken responsibility, only to place us in even more danger?

This was me, staring up at the great big skyful of ink, too fretful to read a word to help me to sleep. I basked in the wild Earth light and eventually I slept for a few hours.

First thing in the morning I was awake, tuning in the hovercart radio and listening out for those meteorological broadcasts. Was it my imagination, or were they clearer than ever out here? I took this as a good sign even though, unlike Da, I couldn't make head nor tail of them. The messages consisted of a list of numbers – presumably temperatures, wind speeds … stuff like that. And strange-sounding names. Lodger, Digger, Moribund, Spaniard, Eventide, Kestrel and Turk. I listened because they were evidently important, but I didn't have a clue what they meant.

The increasing clarity I took to mean that we were travelling in the right direction. The reception was good, even if it made no sense. I memorised the words as best I could and made a mantra of them. Digger, Eventide, Turk and Softspot.

As we travelled through those early days, Aunt Ruby sat in the passenger seat beside me. I fired off questions at her and she told me all that she could remember about all those years ago. Back when our town was first settled and how all the humans separated out across this hemisphere. They made townships all over the place. All these places that we – two generations later – had never even heard of.

'It's such a long time ago. You must excuse an old woman's haziness and the gaps in her recollecting. We all fell out of touch with each other, after just a couple of years. Everywhere was so far apart, and radio and TV signals, they got blotted out by the rays, you know. And the towers fell down, and the dishes. And we were so busy just concentrating on keeping ourselves alive. There were storms and insect plagues and the blighted crops. They seem so commonplace now. You've grown up knowing how to deal with these things. But back then we had to learn everything new. There didn't seem enough energy or time left for keeping in touch with those other places. And they had their own concerns, too. It seemed like a luxury or an indulgence to discuss them over the crackling airwaves. Why, when everybody had problems, why spend all your time yattering about them? Especially with folk so far away? Folk that you're already starting to forget about?'

I shook my head, listening to Ruby, keeping my hands on the wheel, keeping us straight and level on the desert floor. Would I have thought and felt the same thing, had I been alive back then? Would I have made the same decisions? I felt sure that I would have seen the sense in staying in touch with my fellow human beings. I know that I wouldn't have let it all drift apart.

Ruby went on. 'The Elders always told us we had no time to waste, thinking about the cares and woes of other folk. Not distant relations, doing their own thing elsewhere. What were those others to us? Competitors, if anything, in the ecosystem. So when the dishes and masts fell down and the transmissions went hazy and faded to nothing, we didn't fret none. We didn't mind that our town suddenly felt alone on the face of this planet. The darkness dropped around us and it was a strange and new feeling. Alone on this world of Mars.

'Why, I remember the night it happened. The last strand of connection snapped. It was New Year's Eve and the signal faded in the middle of the chimes from some famous clock. We had to pick up the counting ourselves and we all cheered and before the noise faded the last contact was gone. And you know what? Being alone there, in just our little town … why, it even had a kind of cosy feeling. As far as we were concerned, we were the only folk.'

I was used to everyone acting kind of ignorant like this. The Adamses were regarded as great travellers because a couple of times each year they went to loot more stuff out of ships like the *Melville*.

Only my family had come out of the wilderness, hadn't we? Eight years we had been in our Homestead on the prairie. We weren't part of the townsfolk, Da had always made sure we were aware of that. But where were we before? Another house on another prairie. I'd been too young to even know where it was.

Da had brought us from somewhere else. We weren't the same as the folk in Our Town. That was something I'd known all along

Five days into our journey, we got the biggest surprise.

Aunt Ruby stood up, looking backwards in the cart, wielding a brass telescope she claimed was an Earth antique. As she adjusted it she gave a squawk of triumph.

People from Our Town were coming after us. They were a blur of dust at first, then they were gathering pace. They had come to join us.

'Yooooo-hoooo…!'

Not many of them, but who it was surprised me. The Adamses had abandoned their Emporium, loading everything they could on their own hovercart. As had Madame Lucille the dressmaker and her quiet, hulking husband. Hardly anyone had seen Madame Lucille out of doors for years and now here she was, in full glare of the sun and several days away from home.

When they caught us up, they said they had realised it was a big mistake, staying in town. They would have been fools to listen to the Elders and the Sheriff.

I was heartened and amazed and so was all my family. It had always seemed to me that the Adamses' emporium was kind of like the heart of the town. Yet here they were, in a hovercart twice the size and much more splendid than ours, packed to capacity with everything they could think of.

My heart was only just calming down. When we'd first seen them on the red horizon I didn't know who was chasing after us.

'You convinced them, Lora!' Aunt Ruby crowed, grabbing me about the shoulders. 'They saw sense in what we were saying!'

It was like Da used to say: we stood a much better chance in greater numbers.

'But it isn't exactly the whole town,' I said. 'Just five people…'

But it was enough. It was a sort of vindication. They made us feel less alone on the face of the planet.

I tried to explain to Ma about it, but she just looked at me blankly. She shook her head, as if to clear it of sand or noise, and eventually I saw understanding coming into her eyes. She surprised me. 'That's good, Lora. You've done what your Da would have done. You've made people see sense, and follow you.'

Even if they weren't exactly the nicest people in town...

We pitched camp early that night, building an extra big fire and cracking open supplies for a welcoming feast. Welcoming folk we thought we'd never see again. Mr and Mrs Adams and a shy-seeming Annabel, plus the glamorous Madame Lucille and Ray, her burly husband. Everyone hugged each other and made a whole load of noise. Even Ma came out of her shell that evening. Al said that she ought to play us some harp after supper. Music and the old rituals were important, he said, for making us feel at home, wherever we roamed.

Vernon Adams told us how his family hadn't been at all happy with the Elders and the way we had been treated and virtually dismissed by everyone. 'We were sorry to watch you setting off on your own like that. The next day we felt so ashamed. The women in our Emporium were laughing and joking about you all, and how you'd soon be back with your tails between your legs. Well, we knew you were right. We Adamses know better than anyone what's coming to that town. We knew we should have left with you.'

Mrs Adams was nodding vigorously. 'We're so glad we didn't leave it too late. And that we have found you...' As she snuffled weepily by the campfire, her face was kinder and softer than I'd ever seen it. All of a sudden I felt guilty that I'd stolen her library books.

Madame Lucille told us how she and her husband had decided to follow us, too. She added, 'Ray and I – we never fitted into that town anyway. They only just tolerated us. I barely went out, did I? We lived most of our lives behind shutters. We figured we would be losing nothing by lighting off after you. Maybe going somewhere better. Somewhere with no danger.'

In the silence that followed this hopeful pronouncement, I thought back to my single, embarrassing visit to their dressmaker's shop. I shivered with shame when I recalled how I'd thrown up on one of the gowns and had to take it home in a bag. I hoped they'd forgotten all about that day. It was just last autumn, though it felt a lifetime ago already. It was around the time of Grandma's Disappearance. Though so much had happened since then, I could still feel that crinkly, fancy material against my skin.

We all sat there around the fire, eleven of us, now. We were lost in the wilderness, but we were making much more noise this night than we had been capable of the night before.

21

Because we were so used to being sealed indoors as we slept, it took some time to get used to the noises at night. I suppose I was better equipped at dealing with them, thanks to my night flights with Sook. But still, it was disconcerting, to lie there in the midst of a million rustlings and fidgetings, whoops and cries. These sounds came from close by and from miles away across flat prairies, echoing about the hills. We refugees slept huddled round the fire together and our hovercarts formed a barrier around us, sheltering us from whatever life was out there.

I tried to sleep. I tried not to think that all these people were my responsibility. They were looking to me for leadership. Even the grown-up men. Ray had never left town before, and Vernon Adams was much too sweet and gentle to announce he was taking over.

Late one evening the shopkeeper came and sat by me. He said, 'When I look at you, Lora, it's like your Da is still with us. I can see his wisdom in your face.' Mr Adams was almost weeping as we sat there by the fire. The strain of recent days and weeks had been too much.

'I know you'll do great things, Lora. I know you'll get us through all of this.'

In a suspicious part of my mind I wondered whether those men – Mr Adams and Ray – were just relieved to become mere followers. They didn't want to take charge and have everyone looking to them for answers. I was amazed at the way they trusted their lives to a girl like me.

I was fifteen now. My first birthday without Da. I had a muted birthday celebration one night, quite early during our journey. Al and Ma conspired to make a cake out of handfuls of ingredients they'd stowed away. It was a flat honey and flour cake they made in a shallow pan on the fire. It was delicious but, even as we crowded round to share it, I thought it was probably wasteful.

Mrs Adams produced a fancy bottle of pink liqueur from the depths of her shoulder bag and they sang to me under the bright Earth light.

I looked at the beaming, well-meaning faces around me and I thought about just a year ago – and still being a kid. On my last birthday I'd wanted toys and childish stuff. Back then I'd thought it was exciting to go into town for a visit. It was a momentous trip, travelling in to see a picture or to visit Adams' Emporium. A year ago, when I was just turning fourteen, Da was still around and so was Grandma and they were standing there as I cut into my cake.

Everything had changed.

We ate our honey cake and each had a sip of the cloying citrus spirits Mrs Adams poured. Then later I wandered into the desert alone as the others were settling to sleep under the stars.

There were no grown-ups who could tell me when or where I was allowed to wander. Not any more. Under the pretext of scoping out the land, checking our position by the stars and spying out signs of wild animals, I wandered away to find some quiet. These nocturnal checks had soon became second nature after two, three, four weeks on our journey. Also, I took the transistor radio Da used to carry with him, when he wanted to pick up the meteorological reports. I turned it on and tuned it into the dry, implacable voice again, telling me about the weather on Mars. Or at least, regaling me with the lists of numbers and strange names.

'Desperado, Turnstile, Leastways … Mousetrap, Seizure, Cuttlefish…'

Was it my imagination, or was the weatherman's voice even clearer tonight? It was still gibberish. I understood nothing of what I heard, but I felt we were closer. Much closer. That night of my fifteenth birthday I wandered to a spot far beyond our camp. A spot sheltered by blood red rocks and there, when I was sure no one could hear me or see me, I called out to Sook.

I knew she would be out there. I'd had a feeling for some days that she had been tracking us. I knew she wouldn't let me down. In the midst of all those nocturnal noises I'd heard the brushing whirr of her wings, I was sure.

Also, she knew it was my birthday. Though Martians didn't have the same concept of birthdays in their culture, she knew that the day was a special one.

She arrived out of the clouds and dropped lightly onto the sand. Her wings were gorgeous things, more elaborately formed since the last time I saw her, covered in golden scales. When her feet reached the sand, her wings folded tidily into a cloak about her slim body. She was more beautiful and graceful than ever, I thought. I felt so cloddish and dirty before her. So heavy and stuck to the ground.

We hugged and it seemed like months since we had been together. She pulled me into that heavy, scaled cloak of hers. It had a strange, heady smell – like pollen, I guess. I was shivering at her touch. Suddenly I felt able to give in to all the feelings I'd been carefully holding back.

'Why be upset?' Sook laughed. 'You're doing so well. You've been amazing.'

'Do you think so?' I looked into her eyes. By now I was used to them, those kaleidoscopes. I could even read her expression, I thought. She was amused.

But all at once I stiffened. I sensed there was something different about Sook. Something had changed her.

'You've come a massive distance, you know,' she said, and the words bloomed inside my head. It was a long-absent sensation. 'That's why it took so long for me to find you. You've done better than anyone would ever expect.'

'We just keep moving,' I said. 'Following the signals. Moving on. Surviving.'

'It's extraordinary,' Sook said. 'I wish you'd let me tell my people all about you. Your determination. Your fortitude. I know they would be interested and impressed. They might start to see human beings as something better than a mere source of nutrition.'

I shook my head fiercely. I didn't want Sook telling them anything about us. I wanted to be off their radar.

'Have you been through Our Town?'

She smiled. Again this was a calmer, changed Sook. I felt she was slower in her expressions and choosing her words more carefully, like she was holding back secrets. There were long, considered pauses before she replied to anything I said.

'I've been through your old town, yes,' she said. 'But really, those people are of no concern to you now, you know. You left them all behind. They were given the choice. You were most generous. Only a few were brave enough to follow. They are the important ones. The others … not so much.'

Sook wouldn't say anymore about Our Town and I was keen to suggest something now. I had a prickling in my feet and a tingling in my palms. I had an urge to demand a birthday present from her.

'A flight?' she laughed. 'A night flight? Like we used to?'

Already it seemed like too long ago.

I told myself it wasn't just for fun, this was practical as well. I would get to see the land all around us. I would get to see where we were going.

'I'm afraid not, Lora,' Sook said. 'We might be observed.'

'Who by?'

She looked troubled. 'These are foreign territories to me. You have travelled far. There are people here watching all the time. They aren't my people. I don't even know their language. If they saw us flying together…'

'Oh, OK,' I said, knowing she was right. I was so disappointed though. I'd imagined floating and zooming about on those new dark, golden wings of hers. They were strong and supple and now that I looked closer, indigo and chocolate brown as well as gold.

I could have felt braver, if I could have flown again with Sook.

But there were other eyes watching us both. I understood that.

Soon enough it was time for Sook to leave, she said, and we parted. I watched her soar away and again I wondered about the changes in her. She had aged. Perhaps she saw the same thing in me. I was fifteen now, after all. And I was a leader.

I walked back to our camp, exhausted.

Ma was awake and waiting for me, some distance from the slumbering mass of everyone else. She was rigid with fury as she grabbed my upper arms. Always stronger than she looked, Ma. I felt that strength now, like electricity jolting through me. She seized hold and shook me until my feet left the ground.

'Where have you been?'

I'd never seen her looking like this before. I'd seen her worried, upset and crazy, but never as angry as this. It was like there were sparks shooting out of her.

'You can't go wandering off at night.'

'It's OK, Ma,' I told her, trying to regain my calm. 'I was quite safe.'

But it turned out that she wasn't worried for me.

'What about the rest of us? What becomes of us if you go away and Disappear? You've made us depend upon you. We can't afford to lose you now.'

Then she broke down and hugged me to her.

I felt a great coldness come up inside me. I needed to harden my heart against Ma. I couldn't help it. She just saw me as the person in charge now. Not even a daughter anymore.

The following days were difficult. We weren't really talking to each other. But Ma had enough to do, seeing to Hannah. My sister had come down with a dry desert cough and she turned feverish for forty-eight scary hours. Old Ruby thought she was coming down with the same thing, and declared she couldn't move an inch further while her lungs and feet were paining her so badly.

The three of them sat atop the hovercart at the rear of our raggy-tailed convoy and dragged along so slowly. I was leading at the front, with Toaster beside me. Toaster trained his electronic eyes ahead, all around us, like an old sea captain exploring the wet deserts of Earth. He was scoping out the land for us as the dusty coughs of our womenfolk rang out pitifully.

Mr Adams walked with us some days and he was glad of the company. His own wife and daughter were feeling raspy and poorly too, and they had decided they weren't talking to him. They had now come to the conclusion that joining our gaggle of sickly refugees had been an almighty mistake. They were poor, homeless and destitute and it was all his silly fault.

The Adams women sat atop their hovercart in their best bonnets as their vehicle went puttering along on its skirts. They looked stupidly snooty. Mrs Alice Adams and Annabel stuck their noses in the air and they wore every ruffle and bow that they still possessed. The blasting heat and scorching winds blew them about, but still these two silly females sat there on show, as if they were on their way to a garden party and we were just their servants.

Madame Lucille walked alongside us up front for a while. She made humorous remarks about the way some people carried on. I couldn't help thinking that Madame Lucille looked a bit of a ridiculous sight herself, with several weeks' worth of chin stubble growing through her cakey layers of make-up. At times I felt like I was travelling with the circus, or a troupe of human freaks, and we were looking for a place to set up our show. I longed to run off – leave them to their own devices and see how far they'd get. But I knew of course that I couldn't. I'd catch a glimpse of little Hannah or hear her poor hacking cough (too big and loud for that tiny body of hers) and remember how much I loved her. I'd remember how much I loved the rest of them – even Ma when she was being so chilly and brusque. Or Al, who seemed to be in a stupendous, ongoing sulk with me.

'I'm the boy,' he'd reminded me, one night as we sat in our camp, eating a fiercely spicy goulash Mrs Adams had prepared. She had sprinkled her priciest spices into the cauldron over the fire, and let us know just how richly she was treating us.

'So what?'

'Why should you be in charge? You should at least let me help you more.'

But I knew Al didn't really want any kind of responsibility. He was just letting off steam at me. He was allowing his resentment to spill over, like milk boiling out of the pan onto a hot stovetop. One night he let out Samuel Clemens, the lizard bird he had smuggled out of town under his coat. Oh, everyone knew he had it. Everyone knew he'd brought it from Ruby's attic. He thought he was being so clever, stealing tidbits of food and snaffling scraps away for that evil-looking critter. In recent days he'd been trapping desert rodents for the ugly thing to tear to shreds. If any of us hadn't known about Samuel Clemens before, we certainly did once he started gurgling and gobbling up the desert rats.

Al got cocky. He let the lizard bird fly free one night. He was showing off to snotty Annabel and little Hannah. I could hear them whooping with delight, some distance away from the camp. At first I was alarmed that Hannah was up and about with her fever only just gone. I went to investigate and, sure enough, there was Al, making Samuel Clemens turn cartwheels in midair while the little girls clapped and cheered him on.

The creature puffed out pretty jets of flame. He blew rings of bright pink smoke. Even I was impressed by the display. I was about to say so. I was also going to tell Al what I thought of him leading the girls so far away from the safety of the camp. These two things were on the tip of my tongue when something terrible happened.

It happened – not in a flash, because the thing that dropped out of the sky was so dark. A flash is a brilliant thing. This was a vast piece of darkness. It fell out of the evening sky. It fell onto the lizard bird and swallowed him up in one go.

Samuel Clemens had time to let out a startled cry, and then was gone.

Al fell backwards onto the sand and I darted forward

to grab Hannah. I was just in time to see the strange assailant rear up again.

It had a massive, undulating form that was hard to get a complete sense of. It was like a colossal silhouette of a monster, cut out of black card. Out of the skies had fallen a paper doll of a behemoth, here to prey upon us, soundlessly and savagely. A Shadow Beast.

I clasped Hannah to me as she screamed. Al was flat on the ground, yelping with shock. Only Annabel was still standing. It was like rigor mortis had set in as she stood there. She gazed up into the dark form of the unknown beast as it reared up again.

I could see it was about to pounce. I could see all at once how it would be. This wretched girl, who hardly had a nice word for anyone and who was never really a friend of mine. This hoity-toity madam who'd been forced by her parents to steal luxury items from wrecked spaceships; who'd been lowered on a rope from the very earliest age into the terrifying deeps. This girl was about to be eaten whole by a creature we had never encountered before.

Annabel simply stared into the hideous face of death as it rose up in two dimensions before her. She didn't look scared, or even all that bothered. As if she didn't like her own life enough to be that upset in her final moments.

The behemoth roared *silently*. And, without even knowing what I was doing, I put Hannah down safely and bolted forward. I pushed Annabel in the small of her back, hard, with both hands. Then I stood before the creature and I screamed at it.

I hollered with all my might and waved my arms about like a crazy lady. I made more noise than I ever had in my life.

And the monster recoiled.

I shouted at the others. 'Help me! Come on! Make as much noise as you can!'

By then the others – the adults – had realised that something awful was going on and they were heading over, making noises of their own.

'We need more noise!' I yelled. 'He can't stand it!'

Even Annabel – lying in the dirt in her finery – gave a few bleating cries. When our screams and shouts reached a crescendo, the Shadow Beast rolled up like a paper blind. It twisted in the air in a weird kind of way. It was hard to pin down with your eyes. And then it was gone. It shot off into the darkest reaches of the sky.

We all cheered like mad. Making such a noise had never felt so good. I hugged Hannah and Al to me until they squeaked. But even though we had beaten the monster back, this wasn't really great news. We had a new deadly predator. Something else to fear as we inched across this arid terrain.

'And Samuel Clemens is gone forever,' muttered Al, looking woebegone. 'He was my pet. I taught him everything…'

I tried to commiserate, I really did. I told him that the smoke rings had been very pretty.

After that it was decided – by me – that our troupe of refugees had to make as much noise as possible, at all times. If these Shadow Beasts hated noise, then we would ward them off day and night as best we could, by singing and laughing and talking as loudly as possible. By turning on all the mechanical and electronic devices we had in our possession. I turned on the transistor and the hovercart radio so we had those cryptic broadcasts in loud stereo.

'Wherewithal, Coconut, Salt-Tang, Rubicund…'

We hit metal parts with improvised drumsticks whenever we could. We made our loud, percussive way across the desert, raising decibels with dust clouds as we went. Ma sat atop our hovercart, strumming thoughtfully on her harp, which gleamed in the midday sun. Her sounds unified our cacophony into a strange kind of tune. For some reason, she wasn't talking to me at all now. Everything I did – including saving Annabel's life and coming up with the idea of noise to ward off silent monsters – just seemed that to make her resent me all the more. I was floating further and further away from being someone she could love.

But I really couldn't afford to get caught up in silly things like feelings. I had to keep my eyes fixed on the road ahead and whatever tribulations we would have to face next.

Just a few days after the horror of the Shadow Beast, Toaster came and told me some striking news.

Even the usually implacable sunbed seemed excited to announce that there was a town up ahead.

22

For a few awful moments I thought I had made a huge mistake.

As we stood there in the middle of the road, I felt sure that I had managed to lead us around in a big circle and we were back where we had started. Surely this was Our Town? We were clearly back again on our own Main Street.

But a few long, silent, ominous moments passed by. We stared round at the buildings and we started to see the differences. Yes, the wooden boards that made up the buildings were the same, and the whole look of things was similar. All were copied from pictures of buildings on Earth. So far, so familiar. But there were differences. Here was the inn. At home it was The Dragon. Here it was McCaffreys. And the big store was McAndrews, and not Adams' Exotic Emporium. Also – and this was the biggest difference, so obvious that it should have leapt out first of all – this place was utterly dead.

The windows were dark and cracked. Every surface was coated in crimson grime from desert winds. An eerie breeze riffled down Main Street, making shutters and loose doors creak on their hinges. These were the loudest noises in the whole place. There wasn't a single living soul anywhere to be seen. I was against it, but the others were determined to explore. They split up and went all over that town, shoving their way into stores and private houses, hunting for life and preserved foodstuffs. To me it seemed disrespectful somehow.

'Ah, now, Lora,' Ruby said to me. 'You can't go bossing adults about all the time. People are allowed to do what they want, whatever you think...' She chuckled at me.

So they were doing just what they wanted. Barging into these abandoned houses and coming out with armfuls of loot. Tins, jars, bottles and capsules. They looked almost elated by their findings. I felt disturbed, though. I couldn't help imagining strangers ransacking our own town.

Al voiced one of my troublesome thoughts. 'But where did they all go? Are they all dead?'

No bodies were found. None of our party came back to announce they had found skeletons sitting up at tables or lying in bed.

'Maybe the whole town just got up and walked,' said Ma, digging through a small case of fancy toiletries Al had brought her. 'Just the same as we did. Maybe they felt the danger and the need to flee, just like us.' There was a strange expression on her face, as she sniffed the jars of unguents and sprays. I recognised the signs of her rising panic and dismay. I knew she was liable to cause a scene if we didn't get ourselves sat somewhere calmly, in safety. The noonday heat was making her mad.

I watched the others – the Adamses, Madame Lucille and Ray – coming back to our vehicles loaded down with gear. They were consuming stuff already, winching open tins of lobster and chicken. Al spilled a whole can of olives in the dust. Aunt Ruby came over proudly to show me three tins she had found – mandarin segments in sugar water. She joined the others in digging out the contents of these rusted tins with fingers and pen knives and feeding their faces right there on the spot. Even Mrs Adams was eating like that. It was every man for himself, with no sharing.

Madame Lucille was in one of her fancy get-ups. She was watching me watching the others. She gulped down sardines in tomato sauce, and blobs of bloody, fishy stuff were stuck in her thick beard.

'You think we're all disgusting,' the dressmaker said.

'W-what?'

'Grabbing and being selfish and greedy and gobbling all this stuff down at once,' she said. 'That's what you think we're like, don't you? You think we should be fairer and nicer and share everything out properly.'

'Well,' I said. 'I suppose I…'

But Madame Lucille interrupted, 'You're just a little girl. What do you know about real life or real people? You think everyone should listen to you because they all respected your

Da and you knew what his plans were. But your plans don't sound so great to me. You don't really have the right to tell us how to carry on. No one's gonna listen to you forever.'

She stopped then and all that could be heard was the noise of my family and the others chewing and swallowing.

'Listen, Lora,' said the dressmaker. 'Can you hear it? That's the sound that human beings make. Greedy, rapacious human beings. Consuming stuff. That's what they do. That's human nature. And there's no use pretending – little girl – that it can be any nicer or nobler than that.' Madame Lucille leered at me and crammed the last fistful of ancient sardines into her mouth.

People were dropping cans on the ground when they emptied them. Plaggy wrappers and packets, too. Who would care about litter, here in this dead town?

Dead Town. That's what I started calling the place, right that minute.

I turned away from the bearded dressmaker and went to my family. I wanted to concentrate on them and push out of my thoughts what Madame Lucille had said. I was seriously wishing that the other townsfolk hadn't come along with us. I hated seeing the Adamses carrying looted boxes back and forth, working so expertly on renewing their supplies.

I found Ma feeding Hannah pink pressed meat. Hannah's eyes were gleaming. 'It's good,' she grinned at me. 'Have some!'

Truth was, I wasn't even sure that I liked any of the people who'd tagged along with us. Maybe excepting Vernon Adams, who could be quite decent. But hadn't he always made it his business to profit from supplies found in tombs?

After Hannah ate her fill of the fake-looking meat she dozed off and I picked her up. It was time to find some shelter out of the sun. Toaster helped with Ma (who was starting to flip out, clutching her new toiletries case, staring wildly about) and we went to find somewhere to rest.

'They've all Disappeared, haven't they?' I asked Toaster. 'The people here didn't wander off or leave to find somewhere new. They were all taken away and Disappeared.'

The sunbed nodded curtly, as if he had been thinking that exact same thing.

'I don't like it here,' Ma grumbled.

The problem was that she had run out of the tablets that she took every day. As soon as we found somewhere indoors to sit, I checked her purse and found the bottle was empty. I couldn't make sense of the label. All I knew was that they came from Adams' Emporium. They were purple and she got them in jars of one hundred at a time. She had been getting them for as long as I had been alive. Foolishly, I'd always imagined they were some kind of lady's thing for keeping your breath nice and sweet.

'They're for my nerves,' Ma confided, looking panicky. 'They keep my nerves in check. They are nerve medicine.'

We were sitting just inside an opened doorway. A dark hallway led into the main body of someone's home. We perched there, Ma staring fixedly at the storefront across the street. McAndrews. It looked very like the Adams' place.

'I thought I could do without them, Lora,' she said, thickly, as if she was dying of thirst.

Across the street our friends were ransacking the McAndrew's Emporium. The doors hung open and there was a flurry of activity within. I left Hannah sitting with Ma and went to see.

Shelves and drawers had been emptied. Boxes, packets and jars had been opened and there were spillages all over the wooden floors. Mrs Adams was behind the till, just as she would be in her own shop, glaring at ledgers with an expert eye.

It seemed that not all of this damage was caused by our party. There had been other refugees who'd been through this way. Some of the damage was old. There were dried, sticky stains on the counters and a nasty smell from rotted supplies.

Al was filling his pockets with confectionary. 'How long do you suppose it is, since the original people cleared out?' Gobstoppers and lollipops were dropping out of his clothes.

I shrugged at him. It was impossible to know how long Dead Town had been as dead as this. There were no calendars up. Mrs Adams was hogging the ledgers and papers, so maybe she'd uncover some details. The wooden clock was smashed and frozen at just after midday.

I went into the store cupboards and found the pharmacy supplies. There were little drawers and ranks of colourful jars. Mercifully, they were mostly untouched.

'The purple ones,' Al said, peering over my shoulder. I sighed and pointed out at least four types that looked similar to Ma's favourites. 'What do you think all these are for?' he asked, whispering. 'I didn't know folk could have so much wrong with them…'

'Ailments and diseases,' I said. Both my brother and I had always been really healthy. No childhood illnesses to speak of. Much the same for Hannah. We were advertisements for prairie living. Ruby and Grandma had both lived to ripe old ages, too. (I reckon they must both have been over sixty, at least!) In many ways life on Mars was really good for human beings.

In other ways, not so much.

Al took up a large, clean, empty jar. He picked up dozens of all four kinds of purple pills and dumped them in the jar.

'They'll do,' he said. Then he looked at me. Suddenly he seemed much younger. 'Did they all Disappear, Lora? Everyone in town?'

'I'm not sure,' I said.

'They did, I think,' he said, very sure of himself. 'They were taken away one at a time by the Martians and then they were eaten,' he added.

I thought about those bits of sardines and tomato stuck in Madame Lucille's beard.

We were interrupted by an electronic shout from Toaster, outside the shop. There was a big disturbance in the road. A survivor had been found in Dead Town. An older woman, she was dishevelled and frightened. She had come crawling out of one of the cellars when she heard all our noise. Now she was blinking in the unaccustomed daylight, staring all about like she recognised nothing.

She was as pale as the lobster meat in those old cans. It was obvious she was really scared of us. Toaster shielded her away from the others with his body. I didn't understand. Did they want to harm her?

Madame Lucille spoke up. 'We only wanted to know who she was, and what happened here. But she went all peculiar on us.'

They must have panicked her with a barrage of questions. This wild-haired woman must have been hiding away for some time. She was wearing something like farmer's overalls and they were filthy.

In the end it took several hours to calm her down. I sent everyone away to carry on with the exploring and scavenging. I fetched out some food for the woman –

some concentrated cubes from the McAndrews shop. She stuffed them ravenously into her mouth.

I saw that under the tangled hair and ingrained muck she probably wasn't as old as all that. Maybe about Ma's age. As she ate and made lip-smacking, gnashing noises, it struck me that I didn't even know if she'd speak our language. But she did. Her words came in halting, broken sentences.

'Am I – the only one?' she asked me. By then we were sitting on a bench on the veranda outside the store. The shop was quiet now, having been stripped of anything edible. My fellow refugees were all foraging elsewhere, along with my family. Only Toaster remained behind, in case the survivor turned nasty.

'You're the only human being we have seen since leaving our own town,' I told her, speaking loudly and clearly.

Her face crumpled. It started to look like one of the hand-drawn maps Grandma had kept hidden away. 'They came here again and again. They returned a hundred times, night after night. They used to sneak-sneak about. *Heeee heee heeeee.* And only one or two people would vanish. But then they got … *heeee heeee* … then they got bolder and soon … *heeheehee* … soon…'

The woman burst into tears. Horrid, jagged tears. Toaster and I stared at each other over her head. After a while she said, 'They are devils. Coming up from underground. Like in the Good Book … *heeee heee heee …*

they are come to punish us. We were a lawless town. We had liquor and gambling and dancing and fornicating. We didn't think there was anyone who could tell us what to do. *Heeeheeeheee* … and then the devils came and started taking us away. One at a time and then … then rounding us up in great numbers. By the tens and twenties and thirties … they cracked whips and they tied everyone together. *Heeheeee heee* and they giggled as they did it. They all were going *heee heeeee heeeeeee*…'

She was rocking where she sat now. Suddenly it was obvious that her ordeal had driven her completely insane.

Toaster asked her, 'If they were coming to take everyone away, then how did you escape, madam?'

His courteous phrase rang hollow when I looked at her wretched, desolate face. She spat at him, 'Well, I'm clever, aren't I? I let them take everyone. Every single soul. I let them take them all, one by one ahead of me. All the little children. The plump little children. And my neighbours. *Heeee heeee*. And my family. My husband. My kids. I'm a good survivor, I am. I am quite ruthless, really. I have learned I have to be. Would you think I was ruthless to look at me?'

I swallowed. 'You gave them your kids?'

She sneered. 'Horrible kids anyway. I gave them life and I gave them everything they had. Me and their dad – the sacrifices we made for them! *Hee heeee heeee*! And how ungrateful they were. Yes, of course I gave them away when the devils asked for them. *Heee heeee!* They needed punishing. They were bad kids. I couldn't cope with them. The devils – the Martian devils – they were going to teach them a lesson. *Heee heee heee.*' She was overcome by her weird laughter for a while. 'Oh ... *heee heee*... the Martians were glad because I had all the registers in my desk. *Heee heeee heee*... Oh, they were glad to get their hands on those.'

'Registers?' asked Toaster.

'The name and address of every kid in this town,' she said. '*Heeee heeee heee!* It made the Martians' job so much easier when they were foraging for food! Of course they enjoy eating children the most! *Heee heee!* And I could help them easily, couldn't I? *Hee heee hee!* What with me being the school's headmistress? *Hee heeee heeeee!*'

23

I had to get away from the terrible woman. I needed some air. I left the supposed headmistress with Toaster and went to the dusty, abandoned saloon bar across the street, where a temporary camp had been set up. It was shadowy in the large, wooden room, and it was comfortable, even if it did still smell of smoke and booze. Bedding had been rolled out and there was orchestral music playing thinly out of somebody's speakers. It was cosy in there, with pink candles glowing in glass tankards and the aroma of good food. Vernon Adams had got the gas supply to the kitchen working and he was frying kidneys and strips of bacon. It smelled really good.

In one quiet corner of the saloon, Ma was sitting with Hannah. I gave her the jumbo-sized bottle of pills that Al and I had filled. I prayed that they were the right kind, some of them, at least.

Then Ma blurted out something that I'd been thinking the whole time we'd been in Dead Town. 'This is what will become of Our Town, isn't it?'

I nodded. 'Yeah. We got out in time.'

'The Martian Ghosts were here first, picking it clean.

That means they must be moving east. We might avoid them…'

I was surprised to hear her thinking rationally like this. I wasn't sure she was right, but it was good to hear her being lucid.

She went on, 'But if that's so, does it mean that all we'll ever see is one empty town after another? Each place we come to is going to be dead, isn't it?'

Her voice rose as she considered this hopeless picture. But she couldn't be right. I didn't think the Martians actually worked like that. I didn't think they progressed across the face of the planet systematically, like a swarm or a storm. I think they mostly just pleased themselves…

I hated the idea that, as we moved west, everything we were heading into was already dead.

I encouraged Ma to take her pills and to wash them down with the delicious, foaming hot chocolate that Mrs Adams was heating up.

Then Aunt Ruby tried to get everyone involved in a singsong. Soon voices were raised, mumbling and crooning along with 'Show Me the Way to Go Home'. The singing became rowdier when some dusty bottles of rum were found, stowed away under the bar.

Evening was dropping down over the wooden rooftops and I wondered if they shouldn't be trying to be a little more quiet and inconspicuous…

Just in case.

Toaster brought the survivor woman – the only human in Dead Town – into the saloon. Now she looked calmer and less wild. She had cleaned herself up some in a bathroom. She was wearing someone else's clothes and she was standing straight. You could see how she'd once been a school headmistress, just like she said. Her back was so straight and she'd put her hair up in a knot. I could picture her standing at the front of the school in Dead Town, addressing all the boys and girls in assembly. Telling them how they ought to behave and how they ought to grow up.

Except she'd have a school hall with an assembly of no kids at all, because she'd given them away to the Martians. If she had a school hall full of children to talk to, then they'd be dead, ghost children with grey faces and no eyes. With holes bitten in them by the hungry Martians. And she'd still be standing there at the front, telling them all how nice folk behave.

I shook my head, clearing it of these terrible imaginings. I was way too tired. I wondered if Toaster had taken the headmistress to the McAndrew's Emporium and found her a sedative. She was so different from how she'd been earlier.

Toaster brought her over.

'My name is Cassandra,' she said. 'I'm sorry about my earlier behaviour. It's been so long since I've seen another living being. I do hope you understand.'

Ma and Mrs Adams and the others all broke off from singing and nodded politely. As if, yes, they all quite understood. They all knew how easy it was for a grown-up adult to turn the way she had. They all knew the dangers of being left alone in Dead Town.

Cassandra sat down beside Ma and Hannah, gratefully accepting the mug of chocolate she was offered. She seemed charmed by my little sister. I swallowed down the impulse to burst out, 'Get her away from my sister!'

I kept all of that in. She had just been babbling earlier. Of course the Martians never came into town, asking to see school registers and suchlike. It was just nonsense from the troubled fever dreams she'd been having. Who really knew the truth of what had happened here in Dead Town?

The music went on, with Ruby leading everyone through every single song we knew. The old woman's face was shining with excited sweat. As she capered about, dancing on the wooden bar in her stained and patched safari suit, I realised I'd never seen her so pleased and happy. For some of the songs she only remembered a few lines, but we sang them round and round again, even when they made no sense to us. Aunt Ruby kicked up her legs and acted the clown, making us laugh harder and harder.

We all bedded down at last, when it was pitch dark outside and we were exhausted.

Much later I woke in the blackness. Everyone was sleeping contentedly. I had woken up because there had been a noise.

A rustling, fumbling noise.

I was instantly on the alert. I crawled out of my sleeping bag and stared around me, frozen like a hunter in a crouching position.

There it was again. Rustle, rustle, clink, clink.

It was someone rootling through a bag, and through pockets. A thief in the night.

Almost at once I found her.

Across the other side of the room, beside the barricaded saloon door, Cassandra was hunkered down. She was rifling through Mrs Adams' knapsack, who was sleeping in the arms of her family, just a couple of yards away. Mrs Adams was doing her horrible snoring, that we'd all become so used to in recent weeks, and there was no way the thief's subtle noises would get through to her.

Cassandra had amassed quite a stash of trinkets and nibbles, I saw, as she had worked her way around the room. When she realised she'd been rumbled by me, she looked up sharply. Our eyes met. Her lined face twisted up at the sight of me. The headmistress snarled.

'You shouldn't be doing that,' I told her, trying to keep my voice level. 'We have been kind to you. Everyone has been very welcoming to you, Cassandra.'

She straightened up. 'How dare you talk to me with

such familiarity, girl? Have you never been taught to address your Elders correctly?'

'I guess I haven't,' I said. 'And I'm glad we never had a school ma'am like you to teach us.'

Her eyes flashed with fire. She whispered something I couldn't hear.

'What was that?'

She spoke up. 'I said, it's dog eat dog eat dog eat dog eat dog…' She was looking wilder by the second. It was like she was turning into a Martian Ghost before my very eyes. '*Heeee heee heeeeee.*'

Then, in an instant, she whipped around and ran out of the saloon bar on a pair of high heels, with her tweedy cape flaring out behind her. She burst through the double doors and hurtled out onto the street. Without even thinking about it I gave chase.

What on earth was I thinking of? I had no idea how dangerous this woman could be. All I knew was that I was furious. We had tried to look after her and, against my better judgement, we had trusted her. This was how she repaid us.

I tore off into the dark of Dead Town after the headmistress. I was surprised to find that the Earth light was bright on the bare streets, once my eyes were accustomed. So it was easy to keep the fleeing woman in my sights. She was a stick-thin figure in borrowed clothes, running awkwardly in those shoes. Her hair had fallen raggedly out of its bun and was streaming silver behind her.

I called to her, 'Cassandra!'

She flew to the very edge of town, where the worn-down buildings were seedier and grimmer. I got the feeling that they'd been like this, even before everyone in town Disappeared. This place was dead before the rest of Dead Town. The scrubby bush and rocky terrain started again at the end of one particular street. This was where the headmistress stopped running, right where the desert resumed. She tottered to a standstill and turned to look back at me.

'You think you're so clever, girl,' she snarled. 'You think you can survive all of this . . . but you can't! You've all been trying so hard, but you needn't bother! This world is going to be the death of us all!'

I realised her eyes had changed colour. It wasn't just starlight catching them and making them flash. Her eyes were actually silver now.

Something alien had got into her. She really was turning Martian.

But I didn't have much time to think about that. Next thing, several slender forms came out of the desert to surround her. They were rushing soundlessly, and appeared in a second. I yelped out loud, I couldn't help it. It looked as if they were crowding around Cassandra to embrace her.

But then I saw that they were smothering her.

'*Heee heeee heeeee...*'

The light breeze from the desert brought their giggling to me. They were skinny-limbed Martians, with burnt and blistered skins. They worked together as a team, squeezing and tethering their prize. And then they carried the headmistress away.

'No!' I shouted, thinking too late that I shouldn't draw their attention.

They looked at me.

I swore.

There was nothing I could do for Cassandra. She had invited this. She had called out to them. She clearly wanted to be with her Martian Ghosts, and go the same way as the rest of Dead Town. But I didn't. I left her to their embraces and I turned back and ran. I didn't dare look behind me and I didn't run back to the saloon. I didn't want to lead the Martians to my family and friends.

I took a weaving route through the empty streets, past shells of abandoned houses. I was soon breathless and the thin night air was hurting my lungs and making my legs shake. For a while I could hear the slapping of Martian feet and the thrilled '*Hee heeee heeee*' of their laughter. I could imagine their graceful movements, but I didn't look back and eventually they faded away.

I decided it was time to abandon this morbid town. We had uncovered everything useful or edible that it had to offer. I gabbled out my story about Cassandra's fate and the encroaching Martian Ghosts. No one wanted to stay a moment longer.

Dawn came up brilliantly as we hitched up our burden beasts and started the engines of our hovercarts. Ma took a couple of her purple pills and smiled at us. 'Where next, kids? You're the ones in charge!'

I had to admit that I wasn't sure at all. All we knew was the general direction we had to head in: the source of the weather warnings. Always keeping west, where the strange words came from. But beyond that, I didn't really know much at all.

Maybe that was a good thing. Maybe that was just as well.

24

I remember Ma saying, on the first day out from Dead Town, that she felt the whole of her world had been turned upside down. Why, just a few months ago, it had been the adults in charge. Grown men like Da were in command of our destiny, knowing all the answers and making all the decisions. And now it was just little bits of kids telling everyone what to do. A little girl, at that.

I stared back at her when she said this, catching a bitterness in her voice and I saw she was looking at me like I was a stranger again. She was as high as a kite on her tablets, of course. All she had to do all day, through these long days of travelling, was sit atop the hovercart, cuddle Hannah, and keep swallowing the pills.

Over the next few days and weeks we travelled hundreds of miles, all without much incident. Our initial supplies dried up and we had to rely on what we had looted from Dead Town. I found myself being thankful that we had stopped in that place after all. Their dried foodstuffs, their capsules and even their water were of a better quality than we were used to.

Mrs Adams took over cooking duties each evening, after

Ma decided that she didn't want to do any more of that stuff. This surprised her children and the people who knew her best. We all knew how she loved to cook and feed folk.

With Mrs Adams keen to show off her culinary skills we were living the high-life for the next few days. We consumed rehydrated sticky ribs and hoisin duck; tinned champagne that fizzed so fiercely it made us sneeze; star fruit in syrup served with powdered custard. This was bounty like we had never known and our suppers together became celebratory affairs.

But we knew our lavish evenings couldn't last forever.

There was one curious night when, buoyed up on that sharp, cold champagne, Madame Lucille opened up a trunk she had packed away in a corner of her hovercart. She pulled out yard after yard of gorgeous, shimmering material in a multitude of colours. Salmon and topaz and midnight blue. The bolts of cloth were followed by flourishes of silk and lace, feathers and fake jewels.

'You brought dressy-up stuff?' squawked Aunt Ruby. She was scandalised. 'We ran away with the few vital bits we needed to survive – and you brought your dressy-up trunk?' I knew Ruby was thinking about her precious tapes and historical records.

Madame Lucille simply grinned at the old lady and shook out a long, white sequined dress with a slash that went right up to the thigh. She thrust it into Ruby's arms and told her to go and put it on at once.

Ruby's eyes went out on stalks. 'Me?'

I couldn't remember seeing Ruby in a dress in all my life.

She was flattered. She dashed off with her prize and came back, not long after, looking really bizarre. But she felt – you could tell – ever so glamorous and fine. Aunt Ruby swept round and round our encampment that night acting like she was one of the flickering dames out of a picture show.

It turned out Madam Lucille had brought enough gaudy and marvellous outfits for everyone in our party of refugees. Quite by chance she had calculated the exact right number. That night she got her gruff, burly husband to put some old-time music on their wagon's speakers and she somehow whipped up a party out of nowhere.

It was a very fancy affair. We all got dressed up in items of fabulous apparel and we drank the whole supply of canned champagne.

Even the men dressed up. Madame Lucille insisted. By the end of it all, Madame Lucille with her dirty growth of beard and her over-painted eyes looked the most masculine of us all.

Oh, that was a great night in our journey. Al took pictures of us all glamming up and showing off. The next day, all the costumes – a little stickier with booze and grimed with desert sand – went back into Madame Lucille's dressy-up box. And we set off again, somewhat thick-headed, onto the next stage of our journey.

The day after we entered the canyons. I remember glimpsing this landscape once, when Sook flew me around the skies. It had seemed so far away. All these crazy zig-zagging patterns. Fathoms-deep trenches reaching into Mars. And now we were going to be trekking into them. We were stepping into deep purple shadows and entering a kind of labyrinth. The walls rose ever-higher above us as we went.

I wasn't sure it was such a good idea, travelling into the canyons, but there was nowhere else and at least the ravines offered us shelter and shade. And water, too, with innumerable rivulets coming down the rocky walls. As we advanced we soon lost track of our route through the maze. We came upon fountains and once even a deep jade pool. The lapping sound of cool waters was delicious to our sand-encrusted ears.

We stopped and carefully tasted the water. Would it make us sick? Toaster took a sample protesting that, as a humble Servo-Furnishing, his computer brain wasn't really built for chemical analysis. Nevertheless, after a few moments' consideration, he announced that he believed the water in the pool was non-toxic. That evening we drank deep and took off our dusty things and bathed and swam in the lucid waters.

We built a small camp beside the driest bank and settled for the night. Ma played her harp but, for once, the music wasn't as perfect and soothing as usual. She hit sharp discordant notes and grew cross with herself, cursing her clumsy hands. Her fingers had stiffened, she complained. This made her cry out in frustration. 'The old songs have left me!' she sobbed. The old songs had disappeared from her memory and her hands. 'It's because we have wandered too far,' she said, in a haunted voice. 'We have strayed too far from our own kind, and from civilisation.'

That night I dreamed about the Martian Ghosts and Sook. At night I felt as if they came among us. They would peer in my face and I'd see their round, purple eyes staring at me. They'd open their lipless mouths, showing needle teeth. They'd let their hot breath scorch my skin. Following our visit to Dead Town I could now hear their horrible giggling in my head: '*Heeee heeee heeeee...*'

In my dreams Sook came back to me, unfolding even bolder, more elaborate wings, stronger and more powerful. They could fly us both all around the world. In my dreams she would tell me the vile truth: that she had never been my friend at all. The whole thing had been a trap. She had been sent to my people to learn about us; to find out about our wishes, our hopes and our weaknesses. To find out anything useful about us. Sook had just been playing me along, anticipating the day that she would be able to eat me. She had earmarked me for her own personal consumption.

I would wake from these dreams panting with fear, my

body running with icy sweat. Did I really believe it, deep down? Did I believe in my hidden mind that she had betrayed me all along?

In some ways it hardly mattered. I had heard nothing from her in weeks. She had obviously lost track of us since we had come so far. I would hate to discover that my dreaming mind had guessed right — that she had been an envoy of the hungry Martians. That she had never been my friend at all.

I decided that these were gloomy thoughts to be having by the oasis. I looked around. Everyone was sleeping. I clicked on a small lamp and fired up my electric book and I spent my sleepless hours immersed in one of my old novels. I was reading my way through the Brontes. Sand had gotten into the workings of the machine and scrambled the pages up, so that all the Brontes had become one big, confusing story. I remember sitting up that night, trying to make sense of it all, and being impressed by the heroine of the amalgamated saga. How lonely and resourceful she had to be, and how far away from home she felt.

That was our quiet night by the oasis, where it was cool and calming. Other days and nights were less comfortable. We endured them. But one of us in particular grew angry and frustrated. Ray, the husband of Madame Lucille, became more and more impatient with being lost in the maze. One day he hunched his shoulders and summoned all his strength. To our astonishment he started to clamber up the rock wall. He was sick of hiding in shadows, he shouted. He would climb to the top and see how the land lay.

I knew it was far too dangerous. We stood watching. Madame Lucille shouted up at him, shaking with fear. 'The idiot,' she kept whispering. 'What's he trying to prove?'

Ray was about three-quarters of the way when there was a rattle of loose stone and a horrible, quick scraping sound. A handhold let him down. He slipped.

Madam Lucille screeched and darted forward. But what could she do? What could any of us do?

Ray didn't stand a chance, falling from that height. It was all very horrible, but graceful, the way he fell. And it happened right in front of us. He landed with a sickening crunch.

Madame Lucille was inconsolable.

That night she sat beside his body on the floor of the ravine. She covered it up in yards of very fine, silver fabric. She had her sewing kit out and her best needles and she stitched him a shroud. She knew she would have to leave him there on the rocks. There was nothing to dig into, to bury him properly.

'He looked after me, Lora, all those years,' she told me. 'He was a good man. We have lived in some very unfriendly places. Unforgiving places, if you see what I mean. Why, even in Our Town, where we felt we were settled at last, even that wasn't all that friendly. Oh, they tolerated us, I guess – but I had to keep myself indoors most of the time. I had not to show my face amongst everyday folk.'

Crouching by Madame Lucille, I thought about it. I'd always assumed she kept herself indoors because she was sick or too grand to go out. Or maybe her skin was too pale for the sun.

'He always stuck up for me,' she said, stitching away. 'He made my life livable.'

She sat up with him all that night, hunched over, spinning a web of silver lace about his crumpled body.

The next day we set off without him.

We turned one of those sharp corners in the canyons and saw that the way ahead became suddenly very much more narrow.

Dread clutched my throat. It felt like the red rock walls were closing in around us.

The way ahead wasn't wide enough for our three hovercarts. Nor would our burden beasts be able to squeeze themselves through. This was as far as they could go.

And so we had a big decision to make.

25

Of course we had to go on. Going backwards wasn't an option. We gathered everything we could carry in our arms and abandoned the hovercarts where they stood.

If I expected trouble from anyone over this, I guess I expected it from Mrs Adams. Having been pampered all her life, she wasn't used to walking anywhere. But she understood what had to be done. She, her husband and Annabel set about making bundles of supplies and tying them up in luxury sheets. They would carry everything they could on their backs.

It was my Ma who kicked off when we turned Molly and George free. It was hard for me, too. I was attached to these animals. I'd picked them out with Da when they were just infants. But when she watched those ugly brutes turning around in the canyon, Ma freaked out.

I slapped the beasts' hides, and urged them to leave us, to go find a new life for themselves, free in the desert. Molly and George looked totally mystified. Like they had no idea what to do with freedom.

Aunt Ruby suggested that we kill them at once for meat. Surely we could carry enough to see us through several days?

But the very thought of turning on our loyal companions and giving them such a reward was too much for me. Molly and George's eyes were wide with doleful surprise. The idea of slaughtering them was too terrible. We'd only be able to carry a few handfuls of flesh, leaving the rest here for the desert scavengers. It seemed ungrateful and cruel.

Ma watched me shoo our beasts back the way we had come, and she set up such a noisy protest she disturbed Hannah, who was clinging to her neck. I thought I knew how Ma felt. By saying goodbye to the beasts and by leaving our old hovercart to rust in the labyrinth, we were saying a final goodbye to the last vestiges of Da.

Al brought out her pill jar, giving her a double dose. He hoped it would quell her incoherent sobbing. She fell quiet and Hannah hugged her tight, singing a nonsense song to cheer her. We watched Molly and George plod off the other way, glancing back now and then to check there hadn't been some mistake.

Ma finally turned to walk with the rest of us. She shambled along, like she had given up all hope. Aunt Ruby walked alongside her, trying to look strong and dependable, muttering about lizard meat.

With the hovercarts we were leaving behind our electric navigational instruments, maps and the best radio. They had become erratic anyhow. We would just have to rely on the stars and our own instincts. We still had the small transistor radio, though reception was poor.

'Hecate, Balustrade, Liverwort, Fingerless…'

We were stumbling in the vague, twisting direction of what we hoped might be civilisation. But we didn't know what lay ahead. We didn't know anything at all, really.

Down in the canyons I started to feel doubtful. Perhaps it was the limited sun. The light came probing its long fingers into the labyrinth, as if seeking us out, but most of our days were spent brushing through curtains of blue shadow.

But there we were – Ma and Hannah, Al and Ruby, Mr and Mrs Adams and Annabel, Madame Lucille, Toaster and me. All of us clutching as much as we could carry. I knew better than anyone that in a matter of days we would be completely out of supplies.

Al helpfully pointed this out.

'We'll be out of the canyons by then,' I told him.

'Will we, though?' He stared up at the ever-loftier walls, until his neck gave an unwholesome cricking noise. 'This is an endless maze, Lora. You've been calling it that yourself. We could be wandering around down here forever.'

'Not forever,' I whispered. Of course, we'd be starved to death way before then.

I could see the rising panic in my brother. It fluttered away at his insides, just as it did with Ma. He had always been more like Ma. I was always like Da. Stoic, Aunt Ruby said. I was stoic and strong. Well, I don't know about that. Somebody had to be in charge without throwing hissy fits and panicking, didn't they?

About this time Toaster began to have trouble with his joints. He wheezed and clanked through these days in the canyons. His glass innards were making a horrible, grinding noise. He'd only just managed to scrape through the narrowest part of the ravine and we were all relieved we didn't have to leave him with the burden beasts.

He took me aside and lowered his voice, saying, 'You will have to consider leaving me behind. When I cannot look after myself and become useless.'

'No, never!' I gasped. I couldn't even imagine a life without Toaster. He had been in our family longer than any of its individual members.

'Lora, if I malfunction and cannot move anymore, what are you going to do? Push me along on castors?'

'If we have to, yes.'

I watched his stiff face pull into a smile. It gave a grinding noise as it did so. He was pleased by my reaction, I think. But like all Servo-Furnishings he was completely practical. 'I insist that, if the time comes, you leave me behind and you don't look back.'

'We'll decide that if and when we have to,' I said. I was thinking how our party was getting smaller and smaller. Was that how it was going to be? Until we got whittled down to nothing?

Toaster started talking about being the very last Servo-

Furnishing on Mars. He had no actual evidence for this – how could he have? None of us knew how many settlements there were on this vast world. What he really meant was that, out of all the grand luxury ships that had arrived here, so hopefully and bravely, sixty or more years ago, he was the final mechanical servant left. His faulty sensors could detect no other. From a roster of hundreds of drinks cabinets, trouser presses, armchairs, ovens and grandfather clocks, only Toaster the sunbed was still alive. Once they had all been splendidly alert and willing to help the human race in whatever it had needed. Slowly they had all crumbled into dust with just Toaster still somehow managing to amble gallantly along.

There was no way I'd abandon him. I'd walk away from Aunt Ruby easier than I would him.

That night our encampment was very subdued. We had no beasts or vehicles to protect us and the walls were closer. I found myself expecting Ma to start playing her harp, sending those delightful, liquid notes up the ravine walls, buoyant and sweet, taking our minds off our worries, as she had done so often in the past. Except, I realised, she had left the harp stowed away inside the hovercart, several miles behind us.

That night we went hungry, with only a few concentrated cubes left. We munched them silently, hating but making the most of their rubbery taste and texture. A plaggy bottle of distilled water was passed around between us.

Madame Lucille tried to lead us in a round of storytelling, but no one's heart was really in it. We listened as she told some dramatic tale about how she and her husband met. We were polite because she was still coming to terms with having lost him. Mrs Adams told a story about her mother, who was a first-generation settler and a very fine lady, a painter of portraits and landscapes. Mars' very first lady artist, she'd had a retinue of twelve Servo-Furnishings, each one of them a lamp of different height and dazzling colour. They all followed her about, illuminating her way as she slowly went blind.

No one else volunteered a tale that night. We turned in to sleep, dowsing out our own lamps early to save their charge.

26

We had enough water, so long as the rivulets came running down the walls of the ravine. We tried to eat some of the lichenous plants growing out of the rocks, but they just made us sick. I knew from the resentful, sidelong glances I was getting from the others that they thought everything was my fault. If I'd been in their shoes, I'd have been blaming me, too.

Why couldn't we have stayed back in Dead Town? Ma even asked me this one night. 'Sure it wasn't very safe,' she grumbled. 'But there were supplies. We could have at least lived for a while with food in our bellies…'

I thought back to the Martian Ghosts tearing after me through the silent streets. It wasn't worth arguing with her. I knew that we had done the right thing in moving on. We had to keep going. There was no choice about this.

The next day, as a total surprise, things took a turn for the better. The rock walls started receding. The chasm we were walking through was widening out. It didn't sound much, stated like that, but it felt like we could breathe more freely again.

Now we started thinking about the hovercarts and the

beasts we had been forced to leave behind, and how much we longed for them. But it was no use looking back.

The ground was sandy and soft and all at once there was more sunlight getting into the labyrinth. The light felt gentle rather than harsh on our faces. Our eyes streamed with tears, unused to the soft glimmer of sun.

'Is it my imagination?' Aunt Ruby asked. 'Or are we walking uphill now?'

With his usual slow thoughtfulness, Mr Adams confirmed it. Yes, the ravine walls were growing shallower, and the path was leading us uphill. I let hope start to grow in me: perhaps this was the end of being lost in this maze.

But then those hopes were crushed.

First we heard the noises. Horrible gurgling noises that welled up from deep inside the gullies. We walked on, puzzling them over. Thinking they were some natural thing. Maybe we would soon find another pool of spring water. Then the gurgling got louder and more insistent. They started sounding like words we couldn't make out. Like creatures conversing with one another.

Our party huddled together and moved along more rapidly. All that day and into the evening the vile sounds dogged our heels.

And then we saw them.

All at once. Creatures of a type we had never seen before. They emerged from the dark ravines, swaying, sticky tentacles first. Then globular, purple and blue bodies followed, glistening in the light. They moved towards us, closing in.

We kept very quiet and still, struck dumb by their hideousness. We shrunk away from the touch of their slimy, unnatural flesh. They were covered in jelly-like blisters that looked painful and ready to pop. As they came closer I could see that some of these blisters were actually eyes, swivelling about and studying us with keen, wordless intelligence.

A different kind of Martian, I thought. They had discovered us at our weakest, when our resistance was at its most dismal. There was nothing we could do to prevent them taking us prisoner.

Only Toaster put up a decent fight, once he was quite sure that these jelly creatures meant harm to those he was programmed to protect. He lashed out at them with laser bolts and electric shocks. They went crackling through the chasm like blue lightning.

But it was no good. We all yelled out as the jelly creatures swarmed around him and quickly sealed him inside a mound of horrible muck.

At that point I knew it was hopeless. No matter how far we'd come, or what we'd achieved, it was all over now these creatures had us in their clutches.

They herded us just like we'd herded our burden beasts. They waved tentacles and ragged claws in our faces and we had no choice but to go where they chivvied us. I looked at my family and friends and they all had the same shocked, wild-eyed expressions on their faces. None of us could believe what was happening, and how quickly. It had been sixty seconds since our first glimpse of the new Martians. And now we were helpless prisoners.

'Look,' gasped Al. One of the jelly creatures had reared up, stretching until it was twice its height, and made a guttural chanting noise that sounded like a kind of magical spell. All at once a wide section of the rock wall slid open, revealing blackness beyond.

Aunt Ruby swore. Her crabbed hand grasped my arm. 'W – where are they taking us, Lora?'

How could she expect me to have all the answers?

The creatures corralled us, nudging us along with their sticky bodies. They uttered threatening sounds and made it clear we had to go with them into the darkness beyond that fake wall. Grinding mechanical noises came from deep within the darkness. It was hot, too; it felt like we were being ushered into hell. Down we went: the Adamses, Madame Lucille, Ruby, Al, Hannah, Ma and me. Toaster was still trapped inside all that jelly, which had somehow taken on a life of its own, and was dragging him along behind us.

There was a nasty, sickly sweet smell. It reminded me of a jar of honeyed pears at the back of Ma's store cupboard one year. There'd been a crack in the glass and the stuff inside had turned nasty. It gave off this same scent of sugary decay.

The fake rock wall rolled back into place behind us. It wasn't completely dark in there. The walls glowed blue and pink. The colours were actually quite beautiful, but the creatures with us were hideous. More of them showed up, eager to watch our every move with their sticky, globular eyes.

We humans huddled together. Al tried to say reassuring things. 'If they wanted to kill us, they would have done it already.'

I wasn't so sure about that.

Annabel Adams voiced my thoughts neatly for me. 'They want to study us. They're taking a good look at us. Then they'll probably want to eat us, like those other Martians did.'

Ruby was staring at them thoughtfully as they pushed us about. 'They do seem to be fascinated by us. I think maybe they've never seen anything like us before, just as we've never seen anything like them…'

'So many Martians,' whispered Madame Lucille. 'All different kinds. We never knew we were sharing the planet with so many…'

Mr Adams said, 'Maybe we could have shown more interest in where we were living. Maybe we should have found out more.'

Everyone was talking as our captors led us deeper into their strange complex. As if we thought our voices would make us feel better and keep us from harm. I looked round to see Al holding Hannah's hand and Ma holding her other hand. My little sister didn't seem at all scared. She was looking at the gleaming, glowing walls with great interest.

Still those blistery eyes swivelled round and stared at us. Every single noise and move we made was being noted. I wanted to scream with frustration. How could we have let ourselves be taken captive? I felt Madame Lucille's hand on my shoulder, giving me a consoling pat. Her bearded chin was set grimly as she told me, 'We'll get out of this, Lora. You'll see.'

Deeper and deeper we were taken, until it felt so hot we thought we must be somewhere near the centre of the world. The ceilings receded ever higher above us and the walls started to look more elaborate. To our amazement there were carvings here, and jagged windows in the rock, revealing more creatures going about their business. Nothing made any sense, but it seemed these creatures had some sort of civilisation. And that gave me a kind of hope. Maybe they could be reasoned with, or at least talked to, I thought.

They put us in a room together and left us alone. There were no windows, just more of that polished blue and purple rock, threaded with glowing veins. We spent the time scooping handfuls of the jelly stuff off Toaster while he lay there. It took a while for him to come back to his senses, and when he did it was clear the sunbed was angry and frightened.

We all were.

Whatever these creatures were, we were completely in their power. No one said it but I was sure we were all convinced we'd be eaten pretty soon.

After a few hours stuck in our private thoughts, the rough stone door slid to one side with a grinding roar and one of the creatures appeared. He studied us all briefly, and then took hold of Mr Adams. Mrs Adams gave an over-dramatic cry as her husband was dragged away from her. Her husband shushed her quickly. I saw how quietly brave he was being.

'What will they do to him?' Mrs Adams shouted.

He was OK. They brought him back after about an hour.

Mr Adams, shamefaced, said our captors had simply assumed he was our leader because he was the oldest adult male.

We all listened as he told us about being taken into a large room, almost like a church from a book, all dug out of coloured rock. The jelly creatures placed him before a large pile of twiggy wood and stuff and he realised it was a nest. There, in the middle of it, sat what looked like a lizard bird. The kind we were used to seeing back at home, that Al had tried to tame. It was bigger, though. Gleaming and golden.

It snapped its beak and called to him in harsh, scathing tones.

'Yes, it could talk,' said Mr Adams. 'And it turns out to be the ruler of these … creatures. What about that, huh? We've gone and wandered into the valley where the lizard birds rule. There was a whole flock of them in the rafters of that churchy place and I could hear them snoring and stirring. I looked up and saw thousands of them.'

His daughter giggled at that. She always laughed at the wrong things. I looked at Al. He was always fascinated by anything to do with the lizard birds.

Aunt Ruby spoke up, 'What do they want with us?'

Vernon Adams shook his head. 'They are intrigued to know our story and why we are on the move.'

'Did you explain to them?' Madame Lucille asked. 'Did you have to explain all our business to a lizard?'

Mr Adams looked troubled. 'I don't think the lizard birds are as dumb as we always assumed. I think the ones we knew at home were always watching and keeping tabs on us.'

Ma gave a desolate cry. 'My God, is everything on this planet hostile? Has everything always been watching and waiting to feed on us?'

'I don't think they want to eat us,' Mr Adams said.

'Well thank heaven for that,' said his wife, fanning herself with her hat. 'Tell us what you learned, Vernon. Come on, out with it!'

'I think they have another use for us,' he said, pausing and rubbing his face. 'The way the lizard was talking, it was like she was considering ... a strange idea she'd suddenly had. She got excited as she warmed to her idea. She said something about 'The City Inside' and how she must talk to the people there. I didn't quite understand, she went back into lizard language and wasn't at all clear...'

Aunt Ruby harrumphed. 'Forgive me for saying so, Vernon Adams, but you're not being all that clear yourself.'

He smiled ruefully. 'I guess you're right there, Ruby. But it was a very strange and dislocating experience. And then ... then I was distracted by something that was there in that churchy room, something that I hadn't noticed. At first, when the lizard bird was talking to me, I just figured it was an ornament of some kind. But when the lizard went jabbering away and I couldn't follow, I happened to look again, and realised what I was seeing...'

'For goodness' sake,' snapped Mrs Adams. 'What was it?'

He smiled at all of us. 'It was a globe. Taller than a man in height and diameter. It was glowing red and purple and looked utterly beautiful. Lit up with patches of darkness moving like clouds over the surface, and there were spiny ridges of mountains and deep tracks of canals and dark blotches of terraformed forests. It was like a miniature world in itself. I realised that it was a glowing globe – of Mars.'

There was silence as we all absorbed this. None of us had ever seen such a thing before and our minds were boggling.

'A globe!' Aunt Ruby cried. 'A globe of Mars!' She was just about crying. 'The first settlers always said that when our ships crashed all the memory banks leaked onto the Martian sands and all that knowledge was lost. But they said that the best part of the planet had been chosen for us by the Earth Government, and we didn't really need to know any more about Mars. We never had to worry our heads about what the rest of the new world was like…'

All this stuff about the past came pouring out of Ruby again when she was excited. Could it be true? Could all the knowledge have dribbled out of the spaceships like that? Or were the first settlers content just to believe whatever they were told?

Mr Adams was grinning. We looked at him like we could see that glowing red globe in his eyes. 'I have seen the whole of Mars, and it is vast, let me tell you. There are so many places we could go.'

No one had the heart to point out that we couldn't go anywhere. We were still locked in a rock cell with weird jelly creatures guarding us.

Madame Lucille had been thinking. She turned quickly to Al. 'Have you still got your camera phone? Is it working?'

A protective look flashed across my brother's face. His

phone was an ancient antique Da once brought back from the Storehouse for Al's birthday. His tenth, I think. Of course there was no one he could phone with it, and no satellites to connect him to anything, but Al had always liked the buttons that made noises. And the thumbnail pictures he could snap with it had always seemed like magic to us.

All the time we'd been on our journey Al had been taking pictures of us and where we'd been. He was making a record for posterity, he said. Madame Lucille remembered his camera because one day he had her striking glamorous poses while he snapped away.

He realised why she was asking. 'I could take pictures of the globe…'

'If we can get you out of here and into that room,' said Madame Lucille.

'My phone's losing its charge,' said Al. 'I was hooking it into the hovercart's solar cells each night, but since we left the vehicles behind…'

'How much do you have left?' asked Mr Adams.

'Half power.'

'Then we'll make it last.'

Ma was impatient. 'This is all very well if we can ever get out of this place … we might have an idea about which direction to go in.' She looked unimpressed by Mr Adams' plan. 'How do we get out of here?'

But Mr Adams looked fretful, as if he had let

something vital slip his mind. Now Ma had jogged his memory and he looked dismayed. 'Oh, that's what happened next. The lizard bird made up her mind. She started talking to me in English again and she said they aren't going to eat us…'

'Oh, well!' said Mrs Adams. 'That's something, at least!'

'They want to give us away,' Mr Adams went on. 'We are a gift. We're going to be paid in tribute to the people of the City Inside.'

'What?' his wife barked out. 'Vernon, how could you leave this part to the end? The most vital part?!'

'Who are the people of the City Inside?' I asked.

Vernon Adams shook his head. 'She wouldn't say anything more. But it was clear that she and her people are very scared of this City Inside and its inhabitants. As she said the words, all the lizards above woke up, flapping their wings and squawking. Even the jelly creatures made some hideous noises out of fright.'

Mrs Adams howled. 'We've been kidnapped by creatures who are going to hand us over to their enemies, who they're terrified of…'

'That's about the gist of it, yes,' said her husband.

She glared at him. 'You've been completely and utterly useless, Vernon. They must have seen you and decided that we're all weak and pathetic. Why didn't you stand up to them? Why didn't you tell them that they can't just push and shove Earth people around?'

Mr Adams started to protest, and to talk about the globe again, and how marvellous it would be if Al could take some snaps and then we would have all of Mars to explore and escape into…

'Enough of your pie in the sky!' shrieked Mrs Adams. 'Enough, do you hear? We don't have all of Mars to explore, do we? Because we're prisoners!' She smashed her hat to the ground. 'I wish they had taken Lora instead. She would have stood up to those vermin! She would have told them – you can't just use us as gifts to appease your enemies!'

It sure was a surprise to hear Mrs Adams speaking up for me. She'd always been pretty dismissive of me in the past. But I didn't think she was being fair on her husband. How would any of us react, seeing what he'd seen that day? Mrs Adams was just being scared and nasty-mouthed.

We all had to calm down. We had to be quiet and think about this.

Al and I worked on Toaster, who gradually returned to life once he was free of all that jelly muck. We filled him in on what Vernon Adams had learned. All about the glowing globe and the lizard birds.

'I don't like the sound of any of this,' Toaster frowned, creakily. 'Except for the globe and the idea of taking pictures of it. That's a very good thing. Perhaps I can boost the power cells in your phone so they last a little while longer … let me see…'

Al beamed at this. Sometimes all he needed was a little encouragement.

'But this other business is bad,' Toaster concluded. 'This talk of our becoming tributes. I've never even heard of this place they call the City Inside…'

Though the light never changed deep inside the complex, we figured it was time we all slept. We had no more rations with us, and no one brought us food. We lay down in a huddle and all our minds were whirling with everything that had been happening. We needed to rest if we were going to face whatever the next day would bring.

27

We were woken early. I don't think any of us got much rest, but the jelly creatures ushered us out of our cell. Hannah grumbled a bit, but Ma shushed her. As we were led through the narrow passageways of rock, deeper into the complex, I had a wordless exchange with Al. Did he have his mobile ready? He nodded. He was ready.

The others were quiet, taking small, frightened steps towards this churchy room. Mr Adams led the way. He felt slightly braver because he had been there before, and he knew what to expect.

It sure was impressive. I looked up to see the thousands of lizard birds roosting in the rafters. They looked like stalactites made out of leathery reptile hide, and the folded wings moved, very gently, in time with the creatures' breathing.

And there was the nest, just as Vernon Adams had described it, with the biggest lizard bird you ever saw. She sat there so proudly, golden and bright. Her eyes blazed the same scarlet as the globe that spun on an invisible axis beside her. I heard a few gasps from my fellow humans as they stared at that globe. It was like a livid ball of flame, lighting up the whole room.

I just knew that morning that everything was about to change for us. We were standing there together for perhaps the last time. The refugees from Our Town. We had come so far to be there. We had been blown along on the desert winds and survived one thing after the next. We still didn't know what was going to become of us, but none of us had imagined anything like this. And I had a feeling we were going to be split up.

Al stayed at the far side of our group. Out of the corner of my eye I saw him creeping closer to the globe, his phone in his hand.

'Here you all are, then,' the lizard bird said. 'What a motley bunch you make.' She tossed her head dismissively. Then her eyes fixed on Toaster. 'What do you think you are?'

'I am a Servo-Furnishing,' Toaster said stiffly. 'I was built to serve human beings and help them during the settlement of Mars.'

'Not real, then?' flashed the lizard bird.

Toaster looked annoyed. 'Not quite.'

'I see,' sighed the lizard. 'I suppose you'll make an interesting toy for the people of the City Inside. They might not have seen your like before.'

I stepped forward, determined to be polite and calm. 'What is the City Inside? Who are these people you're talking about?'

The lizard ruffled up her golden feathers and stared down her long beak at me. 'You are Lora. You are the one who led everyone here?' She nodded at Vernon Adams. 'The oldest male specimen explained how you were the leader and not he. Well done, my dear.'

I wasn't about to give in to flattery from a lizard bird.

In the pause I heard an electric clicking noise, coming from by the globe. I realised it was Al taking pictures, far too loudly.

'What do you want from us?' I demanded, my voice going a bit shaky in all the echoes.

The lizard bird stood up and stretched lazily. She flung out her massive wings and then shot off into the air above our heads. She flew three times around us, spinning through the heights of the room. Her voice floated down imperiously:

'I am giving some of you in tribute to our enemies in the City Inside. I explained that much to your eldest male yesterday. The people of the City Inside need to be appeased and so, every now and then, we send them tribute. Things to study and look at. Things that might interest them. Now, you must decide which of you will go. Which three specimens should I send?'

The lizard bird seemed to laugh and it wasn't a nice sound, worse still when the ones hanging upside down joined in.

She alighted delicately on top of the blazing globe. I saw her direct a piercing stare at Al. She caught him in the act of snapping another picture.

'What about you? Will you volunteer to be brave?' she asked.

The rest of us were looking at each other. Ma hugged Hannah to her skirts. The Adamses were clutching each other, with Annabel pressed between them. Madame Lucille and Aunt Ruby stood separate and alone, with no one to cling to.

'I'll volunteer,' said Madame Lucille bravely, stepping forth. 'Why don't these enemies of yours take a good look at me? I'll give them something to learn from!' Her face gleamed with that mixture of defiance and brazenness that I'd come to admire in the bearded seamstress.

'Not you,' said the lizard queen. 'Someone younger, I think. They would think a younger human a better prize.'

Ma shrieked. 'Not my children. I will not allow you to take my children. Not one of them...'

'But you have three,' said the lizard. 'Surely three is greedy. Can't you do without at least one?'

Ma pushed Hannah behind her. 'No! Leave us alone ... please!'

The lizard queen sighed. 'I hate it when they get hysterical.'

'Can you blame us?' shouted Mr Adams. 'You're demanding ... sacrifice! You're trying to break us up. We've stayed together and worked together and come through so much... We don't want to be split up...'

'Enough!' squawked the lizard, flapping her wings. 'I

won't have excuses and whining. I need to choose three of you to send to the City Inside. No more quibbling. You!' She directed her gaze at Toaster. 'You are my first choice.'

'Very well.' Toaster stepped heavily forward. I tried to stop him. 'No, Lora. It's best if I go.'

'And one of the youngsters,' said the queen.

Ma cried out, as if pieces were being cut out of her. The jelly creatures advanced from the shadows in the corners of the room. They surrounded us, glistening with menace. We had no choice but to obey.

'Which is it to be?' shouted the lizard bird.

Ma looked wildly from Al to me and back to Al again. 'Take her! Take Lora! She's the oldest … she can look after herself…!'

I gasped, but I knew she was doing the only thing she could. Ma looked at me, her eyes filled with pleading.

'Good,' said the lizard queen. 'And one more. The youngest child. Hand it over.'

'Noooo!' Ma screamed.

'No way,' I heard Al shouting. 'You can take me instead. Leave Hannah with our mother!'

By then the lizard creatures were descending from the ceiling and the air was blurry with wings. There was a terrible noise as they flew about us. Our little party huddled together in the centre of the room, trying to block the creatures out. But we didn't stand a chance.

I felt someone seizing me by both arms and I thought

it was Toaster. Then I looked into a hideous lizard's face and it grinned at me. I heard Ma screaming and Al calling out for her. I heard all the other humans shouting after us.

It all became too noisy and hot very quickly and I guess I passed out for a few moments. There's only so much a body can take.

When I next came to my senses my body was moving of its own accord. I was running down a dark corridor of rock, and I was part of a small crowd. Our bodies were jostling along together in the confusion and noise. It was hard to tell who I was with and where we were going because the walls had lost their luminous glow.

I don't know how far we had run before I realised I was with Al and Toaster.

'W – where are the others?' I asked, when I could think straight again.

'They were taken off somewhere,' Al said. 'And we were pushed this way.'

'By the lizard birds?' I asked.

'No,' said Toaster. His voice was marvellously calm and reassuring. 'By *her*.'

I was about to ask who he meant when he pointed his palm at the creature leading us down the dark tunnel. A beam of yellow light shot out of his hand and suddenly we could see the long, patterned cloak our rescuer was wearing. She stopped and turned to face us.

It was Sook!

At first I could hardly believe it. 'How did you get here?!'

'Aren't you pleased to see me?' she smiled. It was the first time I had heard her speak aloud, and not just inside my head.

I was pleased, but I was amazed. I just stared at her.

Al was scowling. 'This is your friend?'

Sook gave a small bow. 'We should hurry. This tunnel leads to the outside…'

'But the others,' said Al. 'What are we supposed to do about them?'

'You must take us back, Sook.' I nodded.

'They will be fine,' Sook said. 'The birds have made their offering to the City Inside. They will not harm your friends and your family members. They will set them free again, and your people can continue their journey.'

Toaster looked alarmed. 'They will not survive in the wilderness alone. I will return at once.'

Sook reached out for his hydraulic arm. 'You can't, Toaster. You have been promised. You and Lora and Al. You must come with me. You must trust that your people will be able to look after themselves.'

I was staring at Toaster, then at Al and then at Sook. 'We are the tribute to these City people? You're saying that if we don't go, then no one will survive to go free?'

'That's right,' Sook nodded.

'How are you tied up in this, Sook?' I asked.

My friend wouldn't answer. She led us wordlessly as the tunnel started to rise and the walls became lighter, pulsing with that strange veiny luminescence again.

I struggled to walk alongside Sook.

'It has to be this way, Lora,' she told me. 'You'll see in the end that this is the best way.'

'But we were doing all right,' I said. 'I was leading them through the wilderness…'

'You did an incredible job,' she told me. She turned her face to me. I saw how smooth and fresh her skin looked now, as opposed to when I first met her. 'You should be proud. But your wanderings in the wilderness are over, for now.'

There was so much I wanted to know. I was sure she had the answers.

'It's just time, that's all,' she said. It was all she would tell me. 'It is time that you went to the City Inside.'

All of a sudden Al was walking level with us. His voice was hard and accusatory. 'You're Disappearing us, aren't you?'

'What?' I gasped.

'Your brother is naturally bewildered and upset,' Sook said.

'It's true, isn't it?' he snapped. 'This is how you Disappear people. You turn up all quiet-like and take them away like this…'

Sook didn't deny it. She went tight-lipped and

increased her pace. We hurried alongside her, with Toaster bringing up the rear. The hiss and clank of his joints was grating on my nerves.

'You're not going to eat us?' I asked. 'Are you, Sook?'

'No!' she cried, appalled that I could even think such a thing. 'You trust me, don't you, Lora? Look, we want to help you. That's all we want. No, we won't eat you. See – here we've got Toaster with you. We couldn't very well eat him, could we? With all his metal and glass parts. Don't you fear. This isn't about eating anyone. We simply want to help you.'

Daylight was filtering into the gloom. We were striding purposefully towards it.

'Really Lora, your mother and Hannah and the others will be fine. The lizard birds know they cannot harm human beings. They will be set free. You must trust me.'

'She can trust you if she likes,' sneered Al. 'But I don't.'

'I didn't think you would,' said Sook, and I knew she was smiling.

'You and Lora are old, old friends, aren't you?' he said, with that mocking note in his voice again.

Sook didn't rise to his bait. She said, 'These friendships are so important. Friendships between humans and Martians. It's all about learning to trust. And you, too, must learn to trust us, Al.'

'Never,' he said. 'You killed our Da. Our Grandma. You are responsible for…'

'Hush now,' said Sook, reaching out to touch his arm. He flinched away. 'This is the only way forward. Mutual trust, forgiveness and friendship. Now, look. The tunnel continues for only a hundred more yards. Then it is open to the sky. Breathe that air.'

The air was different. It was cooler, less stagnant.

'Now,' Sook commanded. 'You must take my hands. Toaster, hold Lora's other hand. We must all be linked.'

'But...' said Al. 'Where are you taking us?'

'The others!' said Toaster.

'You will see them again. They will be safe.' Sook started running and we had no choice but to be drawn along with her. 'You must come with me,' she cried.

We ran to the end of the tunnel and then...

Then we flew like I remembered we used to when it was just Sook and me. But this was the first time I'd flown by daylight.

Time passed and I realised after a while that we weren't flying through the Martian skies anymore. I opened my eyes a crack and I felt cool air on my face. Soft, refreshing air. And I was lying on damp soil. I was outside. No longer suffocating underground. Relief flooded through me.

I sat up and saw that I was in a field. At first I thought of the cornrows on the prairie that I'd worked in with Da. But of course this wasn't like those. This was a field of flowers. Orange-red flowers, swaying in the breeze. Endless flowers. Their petals like little rags at the top of tall, supple stalks.

Beside me lay Al. He woke with a yell. He sat up and looked straight at me. Neither of us said anything.

Sook was nowhere to be seen. She'd dropped us here in the field of scarlet flowers and she had taken off again. We had slept here, I don't know how long for.

Toaster sat up in the field of flowers and stared at both of us. His robot face seemed to shiver and flinch at the sight of us. He was relieved that we were all right. Then he put on his usual, implacable expression. When we asked him where he thought we were, he didn't have any answers.

When we stood up and gazed around, we saw that the field of flowers came to an end right on the horizon. And there was a City there. A City of immense towers, all of green glass. They gleamed in the sun.

'Is it the City Inside?' I asked Toaster.

'I suppose it must be,' he said.

Al came to stand closer to me. 'We flew. I can't believe that we flew...' He looked around at the horizon. 'How far has she brought us, though?'

'I don't know,' I told him.

In the daylight we looked so filthy. Our clothes were just rags.

Then there came a loud, frightening vibration through the ground.

Al saw them first, approaching at great speed from far away. He gasped in amazement and pointed frantically.

I could hardly believe what we were seeing.

There were about a dozen men on horseback thundering toward us. They were riding out of the City Inside and it was obvious they were coming for us.

28

The people of the City Inside fell in love with Toaster. They revered him. To them he was an astonishing survivor. He was a bona fide piece of the past. I think the people of the City were more glad to see him than they were to see Al and me. We were just two dishevelled, half-starved, bewildered-looking kids.

Toaster was fixed up by the City people. They dug out old manuals and they gave him a wonderful repair job. He received a complete makeover. They fitted him with reinforced glass plates and new bulbs. It turned out that no one actually made parts like his any more, so reinventing the sunbed was a unique challenge for the scientists of the City Inside. (Or, our hosts, our rescuers, our captors. Whatever we wanted to call them.) They were thrilled to recreate Toaster.

He came to my door and knocked and waited. Standing proudly to attention, gleaming as he waited for me to answer. Of course I could hardly believe it. Over the years Toaster had taken such a battering. Now he looked like he did on those really old photos of Grandma's that we'd left behind at the Homestead. He looked like he must have back in the days of the first settlements.

Toaster was the brightest thing in the apartment. He looked at the rooms that Al and I were living in and he tried to seem enthusiastic. The truth was, they were a bit bare and shabby. I guess, in the few months since our arrival, I'd not been concentrating on making the place pretty and homelike. I'd been working.

'What have you been writing?' Toaster asked, glancing at the heaps of papers and stuff on the long table in the dining room. There were pencil shavings and torn scraps of paper everywhere.

'About us,' I shrugged. 'About everything that we did, and where we came from.'

When we first came to the City Inside I spent time thinking about the books I'd brought with me. There we were, fleeing across the plains of Mars with our friends and family and a few belongings. We carried scraps of food and plaggy bottles of water. And I had an electric book that contained a whole load of the world's literature.

By 'world' I meant Earth, of course. I didn't know if anyone on Mars had written anything I'd like to read. Our Town was so small and isolated. I guess there might have been someone scribbling something down, somewhere on Mars. I guess Martian books were being written and I just didn't know about them. Someone, somewhere, would always find the time to write it down. Their stories, their feelings. The secrets that they were hoarding.

Our little town was so ignorant and lost upon the face

of Mars. Maybe every town had its own disaster and all the people had fled. Maybe all their written books got left behind, just as we left behind Grandma's photos and Aunt Ruby's tapes.

Now that we'd stopped running, and there was nowhere else to go, I'd decided to start writing. We were safe among human beings we didn't know and we weren't sure what they expected of us. All I could think to do was to start writing my book. So here I was. Writing down how it was, and what we had to do, and how we ended up.

I tried explaining this to Toaster and he nodded. 'I can help,' he said, and sat thinking hard. 'Though my memory cells are shaken up.'

I smiled at him. I already knew this. He had told me when they rode us into the City Inside. He said he had new portions of his mind missing, after all the hectic times we had been through.

We still didn't fully understand what had happened. All we knew was that we had been placed within this City and that we had lost our Ma and Hannah and the others and there was no going back. We prayed that handing us over as a tribute had been enough; that they had survived and that the lizard birds had set them free. We knew we were on our own in the City Inside. And several uncertain months went by.

My brother Al was changing. It was as if he had gone into shock. When we entered the City Inside, it was like getting to know a whole new person. His old, inquisitive, argumentative self had been driven away. He went quiet when we entered the City. He seemed smaller and wide-eyed. Overawed by the vast buildings and the complicatedness of everything.

Everything was strange to us. Our lives had changed utterly in the blink of an eye. But, surprisingly to me, Al started to settle in way before I did. He was keen to feel secure and cosy here. He was looking for stability and routine. He was looking, for the first time in his life, to fit in.

'Al's bringing his girlfriend round,' I told Toaster.

'His girlfriend!' he said, with a robotic chuckle.

'She works in the place where they found Al a job.'

'A job!' cried Toaster. He seemed amazed that so much had gone on while he'd been having his make-over and repairs. 'But he's only thirteen.'

'Fourteen, now. People start working early here, in the City Inside.' They had explained the whole thing to me. Everyone worked so very hard in the City, and that was why it was such a splendid place. If we were to settle here we must learn to be hard-working people, too.

'I'm not sure he should have been made to get a job,' Toaster frowned.

'It was driving him crazy, being in this apartment all day, with me just writing like this. So Al has got a job and he's met this girl, Tillian Graveley. It's amazing. He's fitting into this new life brilliantly. He's a child of the prairies, just like me, but I guess he's more adaptable … he always wanted to be some place else, didn't he?'

Toaster looked searchingly at me. He examined my face. When I looked in the mirror it surprised me. The sand and sun of the wilderness had changed my skin and my hair. It had scoured me and made me less soft. I felt older than just over fifteen.

'So,' I said, getting up and starting to clear away my mess. 'I've got to fix dinner.'

Toaster decided to help me. He said he had nowhere else to go. We prepared steamed greens and boiled chops and hot lava sauce. The kinds of food Ma used to make. Prairie food. It felt like keeping up a tradition, but truth be told, I didn't know how to cook much else. What did the other people eat in this City Inside?

When I was a kid growing up on the prairie we always knew where we were. This was our Homestead, these were our fields and our cornrows. This was the road that took us to town. Church, the school room, the meeting room, Adams' Exotic Emporium, Aunt Ruby's house, the Storehouse. Everything was laid out plainly, clear as anything. Our little, tiny world. It was all we needed to know.

That seemed so wonderfully simple to me. Imagine knowing your life was going to be limited like that. The limits of your town and the routines, seasons and festivals in the year. The winter and summer traditions; the reaping and sowing and storming; the celebrating and the slow eking out of supplies in the leaner times. The long, long days when the ground was frozen or covered in plagues of metal insects.

When I was a girl I used to ask, but isn't there any more than this? Is this really the whole, entire world? But I wished I could go back there now, to that small world of ours and our cosy limitations. I wished that we lived again in a knowable world.

This new world was much too big.

I'd read about cities in the old books, of course, and seen them on tapes and films from Earth. Cities that soared up into the sky, cities sunk into the sea. Ones built deep inside the Earth and others on mountain tops at impossible heights. Cities created on a magnificent scale. All for showing off. All just because the human race could.

Wasn't that part of the reason Earth got too hot and inhospitable? Weren't the cities why our great grandparents left and came to places like Mars? The cities were vast clockwork toys that expanded and expanded and ran out of control. They became too full and, in order to save themselves, drove their own people out into the wilderness.

The books and records always made the old cities seem so exciting. I would lie awake at night and try to imagine what the cities would be like. Where you could walk up and down in public and be a stranger. I would fantasize about being in a City one day. But I knew my dreams would come to nothing. Because there were no cities on Mars. It was too young a colony.

A City is what we had been brought to. A City had taken us in.

29

Right on time, Al arrived with his new girlfriend. I heard the jangling of keys in the lock and their lowered voices as they came into the hall. I was making a last check on dinner and wiping my hands on a towel. I wished I could hear what they were murmuring to each other. They sounded nervous, as if Al was bringing home a girlfriend for his parents to inspect. Then it hit me. Of course he felt like that. The only family he had left was me – and Toaster, too. Naturally he wanted this meeting to go well, and for me to like his new friend.

I met them in the drawing room, which was flooded with evening light. Our apartment was high up enough to catch the sun. We were told that this was a great privilege when we were moved here.

The young woman was blinking and smiling. Toaster stood by, taking her wrap and her bonnet. She was dressed in a formal tea-gown with a hooped skirt and laced bodice. She was very pretty and delicate-looking, with green eyes and gleaming, honey-coloured hair. She was a couple of years older than Al, I thought, maybe about the same age as me. Looking at the pair of them, it was easy to believe they were just kids playing dress-up games and pretending to be polite grown-ups in an old book or play.

Al was such a gangly boy and he'd always worn ragged outdoors clothes. Now he looked unnaturally smart in his grey work suit. He was holding his breath. This moment was important to him. So important that he had barely reacted to Toaster's amazing transformation. I knew the old sunbed's feelings must have been hurt by this. Instead, Al's gaze was fixed on this young woman as she extended her hand for me to shake. She wasn't nervous or over-keen to be liked, or if she was, she had the good sense to conceal it.

'Miss Graveley.' I smiled at her and found myself saying that I had heard a lot about her.

'Tillian, please.'

Al was too young for a girlfriend. He'd never shown any interest in girls before. I wondered what all this was about. He could be devious, my brother. Maybe there was a hidden reason for this, I thought.

We sat in the comfortable chairs by the picture window, overlooking the towers of glass and polished metal that surrounded our apartment block. Toaster went off to make us drinks in the coloured glasses that Al had bought at the Downstairs Market last Saturday, especially for this purpose. Miss Tillian Graveley was our first proper guest. It truly felt as if we were all playing at being grown-ups.

Tillian made gracious, admiring remarks about Toaster's refurbishments. She was amazed a vintage creation could look so new again. Of course, there was a spring in Toaster's step after this, as he left to check on our dinner's progress. Al blushed because he realised he hadn't admired Toaster enough. In his old age the Servo-Furnishing was increasingly prone to flattery. Tillian was soon musing aloud about interviewing Toaster for the newspaper that her father owned and that she and Al were working for. Tillian was that very unusual thing, she explained – a female reporter, forever on the lookout for curious subjects.

I wondered if that was all we were to this young lady, Al included? Were we just curious and unusual specimens? A hot topic for her newspaper, *The City Insider*. The wanderers who came from the wilderness. The survivors of the Martian plains.

But I had to stop being defensive and suspicious. This is what the wilderness had done to me. I didn't trust anyone apart from Al and Toaster. Everyone else I might have trusted or relied upon was long gone.

Then I realised that the smart, assured Miss Tillian Graveley was smiling at me. 'Dinner smells wonderful, Miss Robinson.'

'Lora,' I corrected her. 'Enough with all the formality. If there's one thing you people of the City Inside can't get enough of, it's all this damned formality.'

She smiled, but I knew she thought I was strange and rude for cutting through her manners like this. They all thought I was a wild girl. Here it was all elaborate sirs and madams and doffing of hats, and bowing, scraping and saying everything but what you really meant to say. I guess that life in the City Inside was so easy compared with what they called the wilderness. They needed all the courtly manners just to fill up their days. Like the way they paid visits to each other's homes and sat sipping tea or playing silent games of cards or doing weird, very slow formal dances. Nobody in the City Inside seemed to know how to let their hair down, or have a really good fight or a laugh.

Although the City Inside represented safety and a possible home at last, after more than two months I was finding it all a bit dull. Miss Graveley was a bit dull too, I decided.

But Al seemed to like her well enough. She and I had our stilted conversation and my brother's eyes went back and forth between us, his hands crushed together in his lap. He didn't have to worry, though. What was I going to do, even if I disapproved of his choice of girlfriend? In the City they regarded fourteen as old enough to work for your living and, if he truly wanted, he could afford to leave my care and the apartment they had given us, and take off by himself. My heart gave a tight squeeze at this thought.

Toaster served the meal. I watched it appear, dish after dish; this homely prairie food, steaming in its platters. I guess it seemed primitive and unsophisticated to a City girl like Tillian. But she hid those thoughts, if she had them, and beamed with delight at every forkful and unaccustomed flavour.

I tried to stop myself watching her like a hawk. This shouldn't have been a test. Toaster put some fancy music on the radio station and drew the blinds and lit the lamps. Between the songs, the voice of an announcer read out the names of districts of the City Inside, along with descriptions of what weather they could expect tomorrow. The names were like lists of strange, random words, and I remembered tuning in our radio on the prairie. So this is where we had been making towards, and we got here in the end.

'Lodger, Eventide, Kestrel, Softspot, Turnstile, Mousetrap, Stockpot…'

Al was talking. He was telling us about his work in the Archive Rooms of *The City Insider*. Already he had learned so much about how the data machines worked, and where everything was filed away. He marvelled at how much information was stored inside a roomful of machines no bigger than this apartment of ours. 'I'm talking about, like, everything, Lora. All knowledge. Everything that was ever known by human beings, going right back to the start. The sum total of everything!' His eyes widened and he looked so funny in his enthusiasm that Tillian and I couldn't help laughing at him.

He flushed with very Al-like crossness. 'But don't you think that's amazing, Lora? I sit there every day thinking, Why, I could find out anything. I could type in any word or phrase or name and the devices would rattle into action, think it over, and eventually they would tell me all there is to know about that particular thing or person.'

I asked him, 'And have you tried it? What have you looked up?'

'Oh, no,' he said, darting a glance at Tillian. 'All my time is spent looking up the things I'm told to. It's forbidden to go nosying through the archives for your own benefit. These are very expensive machines. Besides, there's a million things I want to know. Where would I even start?'

We all smiled at that as well, even Toaster, who was going round with dessert dishes. I found it a little sad, too, the thought of Al wondering what it was he most wanted to know about. I guess, high up on that list would have to be what had become of our mother and our sister. But I didn't know how much he thought about things like that, did I? Sometimes Al was like a typical fourteen year old. His feelings were a closed book to me. He might just have accepted the fact that the rest of our family were lost to us. We couldn't bring them with us. They only made it so far. Only we three came to the City Inside. Somewhere on Mars they were still wandering through the wilderness.

Whenever I pictured them, alone, still struggling through the desert, I knew what I must do. Even if Al found a new home and settled down, I knew I couldn't settle here in the City. I had to find them. I had to do something about finding my folks.

30

Next morning at breakfast Al wanted to know what I thought of Tillian. We were eating grapefruit segments that Toaster had brought for us. I didn't think I'd ever get used to all the fresh fruit they had in the City Inside. I'd had a lifetime of dried, salted, and pickled foods and the glass gardens I'd been told about, where they grew amazingly juicy and colourful vegetables and fruit, were mind-boggling to me.

Al was looking at me earnestly, so I told him that Tillian was a very polite and attractive young lady. He blushed.

'Aren't you a bit young to become so attached to her?'

He glared mutinously. 'I don't see why.'

'It's just all a bit sudden. You're my little brother, and here you are with a job and a girlfriend who seems so...'

'Seems so what?'

'Well, sophisticated, I guess.'

'That's how it is here, Lora,' he told me, very seriously. 'Everything's better and more sophisticated than we're used to. We've gotta fit in with them. That's what I'm doing.'

'Are you happy doing that?' I asked him.

'Yeah, I am,' he said. 'Now she wants me to meet her parents. They live in the Darwin District. Sorry if I'm snappy … it's because I'm nervous. They do sound … rather grand.'

I smiled ruefully: 'rather grand'! Al was already starting to talk like one of these City people. I guess he was going to have to, if he really wanted to fit in.

Too late for me, of course. I'd be a farm girl and a prairie girl all my life.

'Al, they'll love you. Why wouldn't they?'

He pushed his unfinished fruit away. (The waste! I thought. That was something else I couldn't get used to. At the Homestead nothing – not a single scrap – ever got wasted.)

'It's the…' He lowered his voice and looked away from me. 'It's on our Martian Thanksgiving, Lora.'

'Oh,' I said. If I added anything he'd think I was angry and envious. But really, how could he even consider it? No one else in this City would celebrate or even know about our Thanksgiving. It was nothing to do with them. Only we could celebrate this important day together. We only had each other. Would he really leave me alone on that day? Alone in a City where I couldn't even find my way around? I couldn't even work the public transport system. Al could get around fine, of course. He was slotting into life so easily. Too easily.

I was going to be stuck here. A prisoner in this small apartment on one of the most important weekends of the year.

I brightened my voice. 'Don't worry about that.'

He looked at me again, smiling. 'Tillian said it might not be the right thing to do. Leaving you alone. We haven't been in the City Inside very long and … well, she said you might get lonely without me.'

'That's very thoughtful of her,' I said.

Al laughed. 'I had to tell her, "You really don't know my sister yet, Tillian. Why, she's the toughest young woman you're ever likely to meet. Why would she care two sticks about being alone? She's not scared of anything. The things she's done in her life!" I told her that she wouldn't believe even half of what you've had to face up to. The way that you took charge of us all and led us and made sure we kept together through the wilderness…' Al shook his head and whistled.

I was touched by his words. He gabbled away and I was pleased that he had explained me like this to his girlfriend. In the past Al had never had a good word to say about me. At the same time I was thinking that I really did mind about being left alone, but I didn't want to worry him. He needed more than I did to find new roots, and going out to visit Tillian's family was a big step.

Al got up cheerfully to go work in his archive. Carefree, he seemed. Who would have thought that? After all the dangers and disasters and nearly everyone we knew being dead and all? Who'd have thought Al would turn out to be so happy?

Before he left that day he said, 'I'm thinking of doing a search with the machines at work. I'm sure they won't mind too much, if I do it in my lunch hour, say.'

'What will you look up?'

'I want to know more about old Earth. Things I don't really understand. Like kangaroos or pizza or Alexander the Great or the Great Barrier Reef … things you used to read about in books. People in this City get kind of snobby about knowing all about old Earth.'

'I guess they do.' I had noticed this too. Al had always been a bit snobby about old Earth stuff, too. I remembered his games when he'd pretend to be a prince of Earth, on a yacht with a cloak and everything.

'Anyhow, I think I'll look up someone specific. I'll find out if they have anything in their Archive about Grandma.'

I was surprised by this.

'Except I'll need to know her full name, Lora. I don't think I ever knew what it was. She was just Grandma to us. Names seem to have been so complicated, back on Earth. I can't just type 'Grandma' in, cos I guess I'd find – why, maybe thousands of different Grandmas!'

'It was Margaret,' I told him. 'She was Margaret Estelle Robinson. But I don't think…'

'I'll find her.' Al smiled, and then whirled out of the apartment.

Toaster was clearing up the breakfast things. His electronic ears had perked up at the mention of Grandma.

'Al wants to go digging into the past,' I said.

'Very laudable,' he nodded. 'Too much of our history has been lost. The things we left behind. My memory being burned out in patches. It would be good to remember more.'

'Would it?' I grimaced.

Toaster stared at me calmly. 'I really don't think Al will find anything in the Archives of *The City Insider* though.'

'Why's that?'

'Because I don't think this is a real City,' he said.

He bustled off with all the dishes loaded up in his arms and vanished into the kitchen. He didn't say what he meant. Not yet. Toaster was still thinking it over.

Thinking too much was never really in my nature. I slung on my new hat and coat and decided I'd ride the elevator downstairs to get some air. I secretly loved the elevator and used any chance I could get to have another go in it. Of course we'd never had anything like it in Our Town. That wonderful arrangement of metal ropes and gears and cogs, all chiming and clanking away, pulling that cage up and down, up and down all day. It was like being inside some wonderful clock.

Toaster made a few concerned noises about coming with me, but I decided that I wanted to be by myself. He looked woeful and I laughed. 'Really, Toaster. It ain't dangerous out there.'

Actually, some of the looks he'd been giving me lately – equal parts wary and worried – reminded me of how he would look at Grandma back in the day. As if at the grand old age of nearly sixteen I'd turned into a crabby, crazy lady.

He was just trying to help, though. It was what he'd been programmed for, after all. He was built to look after the members of our family, no matter what. It just about destroyed him to see what had become of us all.

I got aboard the empty elevator. We were on Storey 202. Pretty high. Dazzlingly high. I couldn't even conceive of the distances and forces involved in building and living so high. The metal grilles slammed and I gave myself up to the gut-wrenching lurch of its rapid descent. I spared a glance at myself in the highly polished mirror. My hair was up under my shapeless hat, my dress was plain, but tidy and pressed.

Al would tell me that I ought to dress up more. People in the City Inside noticed such things, he'd said, once or twice. He said that I made a habit of dressing like a servant. Well, that suited me fine. I'd no desire to go putting on airs. Al needed to wear fancy outfits and suits more than I did. He seemed so pleased to wear the ancient, old-fashioned stuff that the City people preferred. They put me in mind of the folk in my old electric books.

When we first got here I thought we'd gone mad. The women looked just like the etched illustrations in the Brontes and the Dickens. I thought we'd flown with Sook into a world of madness. But this kind of dress turned out to be normal. It was how people had been living here for just about forever.

The elevator deposited me in the wide foyer of our building. It was all mellow, gleaming sunlight down there. The Downstairs Market was held here everyday, and the place was all hubble bubble with folk milling about. They came from the residential apartments above and from the other buildings in our district, which was called Stockpot, of all things.

Multi-coloured awnings stretched over rickety booths, where City-dwellers of all kinds plied their wares. It was a shambolic place, a little bit rough and ready. You could hear accents other than the refined talk that my brother was trying so hard to imitate. In the Downstairs Market you could hear all kinds of surprising things.

I had my basket and a pocket full of credits and I was checking out the fresh produce. Weighing fruits and vegetables in my hands, squeezing them, smelling their firm, plump skins. It was all luxurious to me, after some of the rubbish we'd had to eat in the desert and the deep canyons of the wilderness. I'd never forget the taste of rat or blue Jack Rabbit or those dreaded dried capsules Aunt Ruby loved so much.

I couldn't believe the gorgeousness of the colours and aromas that they took for granted in the City Inside. I drifted over to where some old guy was stirring a huge pan over a naked flame. Yellow rice, chunks of sizzling meat and tiny baby squid. The smell was irresistible.

Sometimes I wondered what Da and Ma would make of this place. I didn't suppose either of them could have imagined a City like this. Towers of a thousand storeys and everyone living in vertical harmony. The vastness of the numbers involved were hard to imagine, even when you were right in the middle of it all.

Funny, that I was thinking about my parents as I moved through the market. Just about then I heard one of the songs that would always remind me of them. One of the old songs Ma used to play on her harp.

I could still picture her pale, slender fingers rippling at the tall, taut strings. It was the same song: 'Show Me the Way to Go Home.' It was being played just the same as she always played it. I could hear the liquid notes of a harp, drifting over the crowd's heads.

Suddenly I was being pushed backwards through time. I was back in the Homestead, in the days before we fled. Before anyone died or was made to Disappear. I was hearing Ma play her harp by candlelight.

Then the moment of disorientation ended and I was

back in the Downstairs Market. Ladies and gentlemen in their elaborate clothes and bustled past me. Thieves and ragamuffins went about their business. No one took any notice of the sunbaked teenage girl in the plain dress and messy hat as she stood there having a reverie about an ancient song from planet Earth.

I saw a gap in the crowd and where the music had come from. A young man stood beside a newspaper stand. He was filthy, unwashed, with dreadlocks and a terrible red jumper that hung to his knees in tatters. His music was finished for the day, and he was manhandling a golden-stringed instrument into its case, stowing it away with infinite care. At his feet, beside a hatful of tossed coins, was a small black creature. It was hard to say whether it was a cat or a dog.

31

I was drawn to them, in the whole crowd. I don't know why. The harp music was still filling up my head, even though he'd put the instrument away.

The boy said his name was Peter, and the cat-dog's name was Karl. I dropped a couple of coins into his battered hat and I flashbacked onto Old Man Horace, the kindly hobo of Our Town. The man who blew away out of town when the big storm hit. He was the first of our Disappearances. But this was a much younger man.

I knelt down to pat Karl, and still couldn't tell if he was a cat or a dog, but he liked having his ears tickled all the same. He was malnourished, and so was Peter.

'I know you,' Peter said. He was staring into my face as I straightened up.

'I don't think so.'

His thin face and straggly beard weren't familiar to me.

'I've read about you,' he said, becoming excited. 'In the newspaper. I'm sure of it!'

Oh. Oh yeah. My two minutes of celebrity. When we were featured in a few articles in *The City Insider*. It was how Miss Tillian Graveley had first come into our lives, despatched by her editor father to get our story. They wanted to know where we had come from, and how we had found our way to their City.

I remembered the terrible photos that had accompanied those articles. Al, Toaster and I looked wild and beaten up, like we'd been through hell. We were filthy and completely bewildered-looking. The photographers' crystal bulbs were going off and they crowded us. Al was scared and aggressive. Like the gallant old protector he was, Toaster powered up his laser blasts and was ready to fight the strangers to the death.

But all they wanted to do was grab our pictures and talk to us. They wanted to hear about the girl, the boy and the robot who had wandered out of the impossible desert, from the wrong side of Mars.

'It was some story,' Peter the harpist was saying. He had a disconcerting habit of staring straight into my face. He was so handsome, I wanted to flinch away from looking at him. It was like looking into the sun. All I could think was that he would see the flaws in my own face; the dried-out skin, and the half-truths I had told about our prairie past.

He said, 'I guess you think a vagrant doesn't keep up with the papers, or know everything that's going on. But this vagrant does. I spend my mornings in the City Library, you see. Reading everything I can lay my hands on. It's good there, in the public reading room, though it can get rowdy at times. They even let Karl come in with me. They know he's old and sensible, and can be relied upon to behave himself. Also, he's an avid reader.'

I patted Karl on the head again, and it looked like the cat-dog was grinning at me. His mouth went right around his head and it was like he was one great big, panting smile.

I turned to go.

'Wait,' said Peter. 'I want to hear more about your story. I bet those newspaper articles didn't cover the half of it. They always smooth over the real truth of things, don't they?'

He was right enough about that. Even the inquisitive Miss Tillian Graveley wasn't interested in the more gritty and gruesome stories we had to tell. She and the other reporters just wanted the big story. They wanted to know about a triumph over adversity. A testament to the spirit of man. Stuff like that.

I stammered at Peter the vagabond, 'Actually, I don't want to go over all that again. You see, we're trying to make a new life for ourselves, my brother and I. And it's all starting to fade, anyway… It's nearly three months now since we arrived in the City Inside…'

Why was I gabbling at him? There was something kind and tender about his face. It made me feel he deserved an explanation. Anyone else and I would have turned and gone.

'I understand.' He picked up Karl and hugged him close. 'You want to leave your old life behind. Too painful. Well, I can roll with that.'

I smiled at him.

'But you live here?' he asked. 'In Stockpot?'

'We're in this very building,' I told him.

'Then I'll look out for you in future,' he promised. 'This is my new patch for busking. I was just trying it out today. But we like the market, don't we Karl? The people have been pretty friendly. So I guess we'll see you again.'

'My name's Lora.'

'I know,' he nodded. 'I read all about you. How you journeyed all the way from your little town in the back of beyond. How you left your Homestead on the prairie. I read all about it. All those thousands of miles you travelled with your people, with no idea of what you were heading towards. With no idea that you would wind up here.'

As he talked, I was aware of the dryness of my skin again, seasoned by the hot winds. My hair was bleached white by the sun. I was aware of my rough talk and how I hardly knew how to hold polite conversations with City people.

I said quick goodbyes to both Peter and Karl and I hurried away. I put them out of my mind as I bought my groceries, hunting around the intricate by-ways of the Downstairs Market. At the same time my heart was thrumming with the thought that I might have made some new friends. Even if one of them was only a cat-dog and the other a messy boy with a harp.

When I wandered by with full bags a little later, their

spot was empty. They'd gone wherever they went when they were done with busking.

I headed to the elevators and Storey 202, where it was my turn again to cook supper. I still wasn't over the novelty of cooking fresh food, things I hadn't had to forage or loot from abandoned stores.

Soon pans were steaming, I was chopping up vegetables, and Toaster was trying to engage me in conversation. He had been hanging out with other Servo-Furnishings from this building. One of his shocks in the City Inside had been learning that he wasn't the last of his kind at all. He was unique, sure, in his design, but it turned out that in this City nearly everyone could afford to have domestic appliance help.

Toaster would bump into these guys when he was doing the recycling or the laundry in the basement. He found them all fascinating and, because they were all much more primitive designs than himself, he was pleased and flattered by their attention.

So Toaster was burbling on about his conversations with the other robots that afternoon. It was all who said what about who else, and what their human beings were like to live with. Then he said something strange, which snagged my attention.

'What was that?' I asked him, with my chopping knife raised in mid-air.

'I said that I was trying to learn from the other Servos

more about where the City Inside is actually located. I wanted to know if they knew any geography.'

'And?'

'They couldn't tell me. They said that the City Inside is the only place they know. It's all anybody here has known. No one goes anywhere else.'

Toaster and I looked at each other. He had a strange expression on his face. I said, 'Toaster, earlier you started telling me that you didn't think this place was real…'

He nodded firmly. 'I'm becoming more convinced of it, Lora.'

'But what does that mean exactly?'

'I don't know yet.' He looked uncomfortable. 'I think … I think we are inside the globe: the globe of Mars that the lizard birds had in their throne room. I think we have been placed inside a miniature City Inside. Like people used to put ships in bottles.'

I couldn't believe what I was hearing. It wasn't like Toaster to be fanciful. He wasn't programmed for it. Had his circuits been shaken up so much that he could believe in such weird thoughts?

'You mean we've been shrunk and put inside a model City?' I started to laugh.

'Yes,' he said, looking stung by my laughter. 'That's what I've been thinking about recently. Yes.'

32

The apartment door crashed open and Al came bursting in. He was carrying armfuls of paperwork, with his cravat untied and his smart jacket slung over one shoulder. I smiled to myself, thinking that he'd never be the proper, stiff little gentleman who seemed to be all the fashion in this City. The formality and all that decorum couldn't quite contain my brother.

As soon as he was in the kitchen he was gabbling away about his day at work. Who he saw and what was going on. He loved the whole business of breaking news coming over the wire. He said that his morning was spent in the Archive Rooms, polishing the expensive cherrywood cabinets that housed the computers. He had to gather up the great long threads of tickertape that came spooling out.

Then he was keen to get to his biggest story of the day. 'It's about Grandma,' he said. 'Mrs Margaret Estelle Robinson.'

'Did you look her up?'

'I went to the machine that is supposed to know everything about everyone who ever came to Mars. And it does, Lora. It knows everything. And guess what? I found thirty-eight Margaret or Estelle Robinsons or combinations of those names. I found thirty-eight Grandmas!'

I couldn't take this in. How could there be thirty-eight of her?

Al said it only took ten minutes of his lunch hour. Ten minutes of that wooden computer grinding its teeth and cogitating over the old records. He anxiously kept an eye on the door while it worked. Then a great long thread of tickertape came spewing out with the details of thirty-eight women called Margaret and/or Estelle Robinson. The machine chattered and whirred and Al ravelled the paper up, wrapping it round and round his wrist like an endless strand of wool.

Now he passed it to me. I squinted at the tiny print. It was in some kind of code. Somewhere in all this tangled information was the life of our Grandma. The grand old lady of our family. I glowed with pride for only a moment before I was thinking, how would they know about her? With all the many thousands of people in this City Inside? How would they ever know about a Grandma on a prairie that was so far away?

And if Toaster was right, and all of this place was miniaturised and trapped inside the globe – then the City Insiders couldn't know anything at all about the world outside, could they?

But Toaster had been talking crazy. No way could his theory be right. Could it?

Al was looking at me strangely. He tapped the spool of paper. 'They know who Grandma was. They know who we are. They have all that information in their machines. They already know all about us, Lora.'

I frowned. I admitted to myself that I hadn't expected the computers to find anything. I didn't expect all this information – whatever it contained.

I gave the spool of paper to Toaster to see if he could make anything of it. He held it up to the light, frowning. 'I think I can learn to read this code. I could feed it through my circuits and I'll tell you what it says.'

'How long will that take?' Al asked.

'Not long.' He looked eager and I remembered how attached to Grandma he had always been. He'd known her all of his life, since the very beginning. 'One of these thirty-eight women has to be her,' he muttered.

'Toaster,' I said. 'How do you think the people here know about us?'

He didn't answer. But he looked perplexed.

That night I had some trouble going to sleep.

I thought about the starvation and the hardships that we endured on the prairie. The Disappearances and everything we suffered, and how we had only just survived. Did these City people know that we were there all along? Did they know what we were going through?

Why did they never come and help us?

Did they know that the rest of our people were still out in that wilderness?

Could they help me find them?

It was the question I had longed to ask someone since I had arrived here. But so far I had never found anyone I could trust enough.

I lay awake most of that night. Through my bedroom wall I could hear Toaster clumping about in the drawing room. Just as I was on the verge of sleep I thought I heard his electronic voice, muttering away to himself. Then it stopped.

The sunlight poured through the wooden shutters. It was a watery, thin light here, even on Storey 202. Back at home the dawn light was much more spectacular. Shimmeringly beautiful, waking us rudely each morning to another day's hard work. Here life was easier and the light was more dull.

That morning brought two things. Both unexpected. Both were official notifications. The first came for Al, who was soon banging on my bedroom door and looking tearful when I let him in.

'Tillian just telephoned,' he said. I never heard it ring, I realised. I must have fallen asleep, after all, in the hours before dawn. Al was sobbing and trying to hide it. I wanted to hug him or something, but I knew he'd never allow it.

'What's the matter?'

'They don't want me to return to the City newspaper offices. Tillian says I'm suspended from work.' He shook with anger. How dare they make him feel like this, I thought. 'It's because I performed an unauthorised search. Of course they discovered what I had done. Grandma's name tripped an internal alarm. The machines are too precious for junior staff members to mess around with.' He snorted back his tears and looked at me defiantly. 'It was awful, Lora. Tillian sounded so angry with me. Like she couldn't believe I'd done something so terrible. She says her father is apoplectic, whatever that means.'

I touched his arm and he shrugged me off. 'I'm sure that it's not as terrible as all that. Look, they haven't fired you. It's just a suspension. They'll let you go back to work.'

'Tillian sounds so disappointed in me.'

I placed my brother in the care of Toaster, who flapped around him in concern. I showered and dressed, all the while thinking I should punch Tillian's face in. That girl had no right making Al feel bad just for being curious. The rules of the place obviously hadn't been made clear enough to him. He probably hadn't known he was committing such a great sin. I reckoned that young madam Tillian was gonna have to explain herself to me.

Al drank some hot chocolate, and decided he might as well go back to bed. 'What's the point of staying up? I

238

don't have a job anymore.' A hint of that surliness he often had as a little boy was back in his voice.

I let him go to his room and turned to Toaster. 'They really didn't want him to extract that information about Grandma, did they?'

'That would seem about the long and the short of it, yes,' he said, carrying the mugs and plates back to the kitchen. 'I must admit I didn't get very far decoding that print-off last night. It's such an arcane code. It will take a little extra work on my part. But I should be able to crack it.'

I nodded. 'Would you work on it today, Toaster? Just leave the cleaning and stuff. I can do that. I want to know why and how they'd know about Grandma, and not want us to know about it.'

Toaster smiled at me. 'Ah, I'm not sure if it's as sinister as all that.'

I refused to be cheered. 'You said yourself there was something queer about the City Inside. You said it was all fake.'

Toaster sat down heavily. 'Yes, I did, didn't I? That's how I felt about it. I felt … disoriented. As if we weren't even on the same plane of reality anymore.' He shrugged, realising he was talking gibberish. 'I think my refurbishments have done something strange to my logic circuits. I need to concentrate on something meaty. This decoding task is just the thing.'

Then came the second official thing of the morning.

It was a letter on a very fancy, heavy paper. It was from the Dean of the Department of True Life Stories at the University of the City Inside. Dean Swiftnick, he was called. At first I thought it must be a mistake. What would the university want with me? My mind flashed on the old books I'd read. That's where scholars went. Jude the Obscure, he went there, didn't he?

I stared at my name on the letterhead. It was the most exquisite, scrolling handwriting. Dean Swiftnick urgently requested my presence. My story was required. And he was inviting me to donate it to their storehouse of knowledge.

33

I went to the Downstairs Market with my basket and a list and my head swimming. Now they want paying back, the people of this City, I was thinking. They gave us a place to live and they've looked after us since we arrived. We assumed they were generous and cared for our welfare. But now it was payback time.

I supposed it wouldn't be too bad. Telling them our story for the sake of their records. Why, we'd already told the main points to the newspapers, hadn't we? And maybe it would be a good thing to do. Maybe I wanted it all to go down in their archive. They should know more about Our Town, our family and the Homestead. Those things would all want to be remembered by someone.

Little though we were, we were still a part of the story of Mars.

The marketplace was less busy that day. It was easier to get a good look at everything. I paused at a stall of pets in wooden cages, all kinds of beasts. I wasn't sure I'd want any of these monsters set free in my home. A large Jack Rabbit sat there, bulging its eyes at me.

Just then I heard the rippling music of the harp.

I went to the same spot beside the newsstand. Peter the vagabond was back. His tune was downbeat – even sombre – and fewer passersby were stopping to listen. I could hardly blame them. I saw what the cause of his mood must be.

'Karl's gone,' I gasped, staring at the space where the cat-dog had been sitting last time.

Peter nodded glumly. 'Don't worry. He hasn't run away from me or anything. He just isn't very well. I didn't want to bring him out today. He was throwing up and stuff. Didn't look like he could face coming out.'

'Is someone looking after him?'

'Everyone's got their own thing to do,' he said. 'There was no one I could ask to keep an eye on him. All I could do was make up his little bed out of his hairy blanket in my alcove, and tell him to keep quiet so no one notices him.'

It was obvious Peter was fretting desperately. All that anxiety was seething through his music, and it had cast a pall over the market stalls all around. Maybe his moody tunes were the reason the Downstairs Market was so much emptier today. I asked him how long he'd been there.

'Since first thing.' He glared down at his hat, which held less than a few credits. 'It's a slow day.'

'I reckon you should go home to see Karl,' I told him. 'Take him some treats. You're doing no good here. Your music's dreadful today.'

Peter seemed glad to take my advice. It was as if he needed permission to pack up his harp and leave his patch early. He used his handful of coins to buy a bagful of gristly lizard bones at the nearby butcher's stall and then he turned to me. His handsome face was bright with a new idea.

'Lora, you could come with me!' He had the most infectious grin I'd ever known. Something about Peter made me want to hug him. It was ridiculous.

'Come on,' he urged. 'You'll be interested.'

He grasped my hand and dragged me along. He was completely encumbered by the harp, the bag of bones and me. I struggled feebly as he led us towards the revolving doors.

The fact was, I hadn't been out of the building much since we'd moved in. There wasn't much need. Truth be told, I found it all a bit overwhelming out there. The tallness and the pressed-in-ness of everything. And the buttoned-up businesslike way all the City Inside people went moving about.

We were outside now, though. There was a misty fall of snow coming down, which made me catch my breath. Of course, it was something exceedingly rare on the prairie. I wanted to stop and stand in it, and marvel at the colours, but Peter urged me on, laughing. The flakes were soft and cinnamon-coloured. So cold, they made me feel like my skin was burning hot.

We crossed an open space – a park, Peter called it – that I remembered seeing the first day we came here. I had meant to come here, to sit by the lake in the sun, and somehow I had forgotten all about that. I got used, very quickly, to living 202 storeys up. There was no time to sit today, apparently, and besides, it was too cold.

Next, we were heading towards the train station. All the while he was telling me where he lived, how it was all an amazing secret. Something the Authorities must never know about. The Den was located at the end of the railway line we were about to ride. We joined a large crowd – lots of crinolines and topcoats and brollies covered in downy pink snow. I felt such a drab disgrace in my clothes.

'Perhaps you shouldn't be telling me,' I warned Peter. 'Why are you telling me your secrets?'

He shrugged and smiled as we edged around the crowd together. Then he was coaching me how to jump the turnstiles so that we could travel for free. The City trains were known as the Pipeline. I knew that Al used them every day. I tried to imagine him walking about, all confidently, in this echoing, fumey place.

Next thing we were dashing down an escalator – a moving staircase kind of thing – that sent me dizzy first time.

We were in a tunnel, deep underground, under flickering light from an electric chandelier. Others waited with us, no one speaking. The tunnel streamed with approaching noise and slow, warm gales.

'I trust you, Lora,' Peter told me. 'I know that you don't come from this City. You come from your prairie. Your Homestead. I remember that, from what you said in the newspaper. I thought then that I liked the look of you, and the sound of you. You had a great, plain, wide-open face. Haven't you noticed the faces here?' he gestured along the platform at the others waiting. 'They're so closed-in and sly-looking.'

Now that he mentioned it, I did think the folk of the City Inside shared a certain expression. I wouldn't have called it sly, though. It was more like they had a dozen things on their mind at once, and when they were talking to you, their thoughts were wandering elsewhere. Sometimes they didn't seem altogether sincere. But what did I know? Peter knew what these people were really like. He'd lived here all his life.

'I hate the way the City Insiders are,' he told me, quietly, stepping closer. The harp case rested between us like a small black coffin. The reek of the lizard bones was making me nauseous. He went on, 'So I live in the Den, way underground. And we look out for each other.' The train came rattling out of the tunnel, and I stepped back in alarm as it dashed up to the platform.

All aboard was plush red and polished wood and glowing brass lamps. We sat down. A woman with a high bosom looked repulsed by Peter and the sweetish smell of the butcher's bones. Her husband glared at the pair of us, as if we had no right to be there.

The train tooted and howled busily through the jerky tunnels. Yellow smoke leaked through the black windows and smelled deliciously toxic. We hurtled to the end of the line, to some sector of the City Inside I'd never been to before. And I knew – as Peter took my hand again and we hopped out of the Pipeline – that I was thrilled and excited in a way I hadn't been for months.

He took me to the corner of another park. I'd never seen so much green in one place. I felt like the grass was kissing my feet as we ran across the bumpy lawns. The reddish pink snow was falling, thicker now, slowly blotting out the green.

Peter breathlessly explained that the park was rarely used nowadays. People preferred more dynamic entertainments. What did the park have to offer? Some stone dinosaurs lurked amongst the trees, boggling their blank eyes at us. They had a look of Molly and George about them.

Peter took me to an old bandstand, where music used to be played on summer days. 'You've got to be able to keep a secret. They aren't to know that we live here, underneath the park. The Authorities, I mean.'

I agreed. Why would they be bothered? It all sounded a bit paranoid to me but I thought I'd better humour my new friend.

Beneath the bandstand was a mildewy door, hidden by snowy ivy, which opened onto a tunnel. Peter lit a match and took a candelabra from a side table just behind the door. The walls were covered in layers of newsprint from decades ago. The print was almost rubbed off. Peter closed the door behind us and I followed that naked flame as it bobbed ahead.

We went downwards. I don't know how deep under the park we went. It was quite steep. I was quite content, though, even as I held my breath and my heart hammered. This was adventure and life once more. I realised how hemmed in I'd been feeling in that flat on Storey 202.

Soon there was noise up ahead. Voices.

'Everyone's friendly,' Peter told me, his face pale in the torchlight. 'Don't worry.'

We were in a widening corridor. Then in a gas-lit street with cobbles underfoot. Through gaps in the drizzly mist, I could see brick dwellings that seemed to rise out of the ground.

We passed a few people and they nodded acknowledgement at Peter. They were dressed in less buttoned-up styles than the people above ground, perhaps. Shabbier, but more colourful.

Everything was cramped, even when we emerged into a kind of town square. I had to duck to avoid banging my head on the ceiling of wet rock. Then Peter squeezed my hand and led me into a mean-looking building with narrow windows. Inside there were dormitories and small alcoves, like cupboards, and I realised that this stuffy, musty place must be where he lived. When we were both inside his alcove, he pulled a curtain across a rail and there was hardly any room for us both. I perched on the unmade bed.

'I'm sorry it's so … awful,' he smiled.

He manhandled the harp into the corner of his tiny room and, as he did so, I noticed a squirming bundle of black fur in a nest of blankets on the bed. It was Karl, who had woken at the sound of our voices. His eyes shone like he recognised me. He tried to get control of his awkward, trembling limbs so he could come and sit on my knee.

'Didn't do so well busking without you, boy,' Peter laughed. 'But look what I brought back anyway!' At first I didn't know whether he meant me or the sack of bones, which he quickly opened for the cat-dog to see. Karl was sniffing crazily, leaping about the confined space, bumping into everything.

It struck me that this was it. This tiny corner of a room, curtained off from a whole load of similar alcoves, was the full extent of my new friends' lives. I thought about everything that the Authorities had given to my brother Al and me when we came to the City Inside. It hardly seemed fair. I felt ashamed. What was so special about us?

I could hear shuffling, mumbling noises behind other curtains, so I kept my voice low. 'How come you have to live like this?'

Peter looked offended by my question as he sat watching Karl nibble and paw at the bones. 'Hey, there's nothing wrong with this place. I like it here.'

Karl settled back on the bed, his limbs all over the place, chewing noisily.

'But it's so dark and dirty,' I said, the words out before I even knew it. I sounded like such a prissy housewife. In our Homestead, and in my apartment, everything was scrubbed clean and kept immaculate. Even on our journey through the wilderness we never let our standards slip. But it was rude to judge other people like that.

Peter's face darkened. 'Some of us don't have any choices,' he said.

I remembered that I was stuck down here in this place he called the Den. No one else knew where I was. He could do anything. Though I was sure he wouldn't. I was sure he was a good person.

'We can't all live in Stockpot District.' He pulled a face at me to ease the tension.

I tried to tell him, 'Hey, Al and me, we've got nothing, either. We came to the City Inside with absolutely zilch.' I could feel myself flushing with indignation. My embarrassment was making me defensive. 'So you needn't act the poor boy with me. You never had to walk across half the planet, did you? You never had to flee from the Martian Ghosts? You never had to fear being eaten or lose half your family...'

'Hey, hey,' he said, taking hold of my shoulders. I shrugged him off. 'It's OK. You needn't get upset.'

I was getting worked up. Somehow the things I said to Peter and those he said to me felt important. For the first time in ages I'd met someone I wanted to explain everything to. Everything I'd seen and lived through.

We sat on the lumpy-bed with his little cat-dog between us. Karl was making lip-smacking noises.

'You're an asset to the Authorities,' Peter said. 'They want you here. You and Al and Toaster – they stand to learn a lot from you. You're the people of the future.'

I stared at him. 'How can that be? You all live in this totally magnificent City. We lived in a shack on the prairie…'

Peter shrugged. 'Maybe. But tell me, Lora. When did your people first leave Earth?'

I answered automatically. We learned all this stuff by rote in the school house. '2094 was the year our first Settlers came to Mars. Grandma and Aunt Ruby and old Toaster were on the first wave. Aboard the *Melville*.'

Peter whistled at this. Then he looked like he was about to tell me something I'd find surprising. I braced myself. 'And do you know when this City Inside was first built?'

This had been puzzling me. I'd asked Toaster about it, but he kept saying his circuits were damaged and thinking was coming hard to him. I lay awake in our new apartment sometimes wondering how the City Insiders could have all this. These towers and pipelines and all these riches. How could they be as civilised as this?

'When was the City Inside built?' I asked Peter. I wasn't sure I wanted to hear the answer.

'1900,' he said. 'It's been here over 250 years.'

34

When Al and Toaster and me woke up in the City Inside, we didn't know what we had fallen into. We stumbled into the streets and we couldn't understand why everyone was wearing such old-fashioned dress, why horses pulled carriages, why men wore hats and women bonnets, and why everything seemed to run by clockwork. We thought we were dreaming. I thought we had fallen into one of my Victorian books that had got so mashed up in my electric machine. All the belching chimneys and the clattering hooves – surely we'd fallen down a rabbit hole and come up in the past?

But the sky between the blocks was pink and orange and the dirt underfoot was good Martian dirt. The horses stamping impatiently through the traffic were green and reptilian. This was still the world we had known, but it was the human beings who were the mystery.

They were surprised and delighted by us. They took us in and gave us medical examinations and they fixed up Toaster, so that he looked better than he ever had. But they couldn't fix his memory circuits. The technology bamboozled them.

The Authorities were astonished by us.

And now I knew why.

We came from a planet 250 years after they had left it behind. They were the secret City Inside, somewhere on the other side of Mars. No one on Earth in our time knew about them. But somehow they had thrived.

That afternoon in Peter's musky-smelling alcove in the Den, the two of us sketched out a history of his people and mine.

'So ... other people came to Mars before we did,' I said.

'Many more,' said he. 'We came from England. Well, our ancestors did. In the last millennium. Sorry about that.'

I gawped at him. In our town we were settlers. I was part of the third generation. Mars was new and uninhabited. We were holding on by our fingernails.

But before Grandma and Ruby grew old on the prairie – almost two centuries before them – the British were here. Drinking tea and all the other strange things they do.

They came from the late Victorian period, Peter explained. He brought out albums, showing me scratchy pictures and dim photographs. He had books piled up, dusty under his messy bed, and he yanked them out excitedly.

'How did we not know?' I kept saying. 'How could we be such fools?'

Several thousand human beings absconded from planet Earth and came to Mars between 1885 and 1902.

'Oh, it wasn't very widely publicised,' Peter told me. 'It was all quite clandestine and hush-hush.'

They came in bunches of several dozen, in spacecraft no larger than a motorised lorry, which were built very quietly in Newcastle-upon-Tyne docks. These 'Celestial Omnibuses', as they were called, were manufactured in the North, away from prying eyes. The people who were leaving all belonged to a secret society. They were 'Insiders'. None of them were very pleased about the way life on Earth was heading. They were convinced man was about to do irreparable harm to himself and his planet. Well, that turned out to be true, though not for a while yet.

They signed up and paid extortionate prices by monthly installments. All of them were convinced they were going to be happy colonists on a new world, creating a better life.

Just as we were, almost two centuries later, when we settled thousands of miles away, across the supposedly barren surface of Mars.

They came here, all that time ago. They landed their brass and lead-lined spacecraft here in the dust bowl and set about making their towns, to plans laid down by the geniuses in charge of the exodus. The Mars Exodus, the Insiders had called the whole enterprise, Peter told me.

And so the City Inside grew up over the decades and centuries. They were secret and independent of Earth and soon completely forgotten by everyone down there, apart from surviving members of their secret society and the custodians of their papers and affects, who – it was rumoured – would secretly keep them abreast of some of the useful technological advances on old Earth. Their colony expanded and settled in and grew hugely. Filling out this whole, magnificent City.

By the time my grandma and her generation of settlers left for Mars, they knew nothing at all about the Victorians far across the vast deserts.

Perhaps that was just as well. How would Grandma and Aunt Ruby or even Da have reacted to this? Would they feel foolish and amazed like I did? Would they have felt tiny and futile, building their dust-blown towns and never knowing about the City Inside?

I didn't know. I just didn't know.

I was sitting in an underground Den on a snowy day with a boy and his cat-dog. I was learning all this stuff, where I came from. I was having my mind blown.

'OK,' said Peter at last. 'You're reeling, aren't you? We can stop talking about all this cosmic stuff, and time and civilisation and everything for a while, if you like.'

'But it's important!' I burst out. 'I need to understand. No one's ever gone from one civilisation to the other, have they? Me and Al and Toaster – we're the first, aren't we? The first to understand.'

'I guess so,' said Peter.

I thought about that Dean of the University. Dean Swiftnick. Yeah, no wonder he wanted to talk to me. If the Authorities knew what me and Peter had just pieced together – I guess I had quite a few things in my head that they'd want to know about. I had about 250 years of Earth history and advances locked away somewhere inside me. Valuable stuff they knew hardly anything about.

I must have looked completely freaked out by now. Peter jumped up off the bed. 'Come on. Enough now. I'm taking you to the pub.'

Karl went happily into his walking harness and, even though he could only manage about ten yards under his own steam, he was glad to get some exercise. Peter carried him the rest of the way through the dark streets. A sulphurous drizzle had started up. I couldn't imagine why anyone would prefer to live down here to up above, amid the green glass towers.

Then we arrived at the pub – a dingy, neon-lit place where people huddled around strange-looking pipes that bubbled as we passed and emitted multi-coloured smoke. There was music like nothing I'd ever heard before – jangling and discordant – and somehow it got under my skin straight away. I loved it.

Peter put Karl on the busy bar, and the cat-dog drew attention from the men standing on either side. The animal didn't look so sickly as he sat there while Peter ordered some drinks.

We sat at a small table and I found myself telling him about Al's problems at work.

'They're not used to people breaking rules,' he said. 'Poor Al. There are rules everywhere in the City Inside and the Authorities are used to people who would never dream of breaking them.' He sipped his drink and grimaced. He dribbled a little into a clean ashtray for Karl to lap up, which couldn't have been good for him. The stuff was spirits. I pretended to sip mine in a grown-up fashion but didn't like the taste much. 'They're very precious about the bits of technology they've managed to cobble together over the years. Only a very few geniuses know how all these miraculous things work.'

'They certainly don't seem to want people to use the archive computer for personal reasons,' I said. 'Al should have thought it through. He's been brought up to think he can't do anything wrong. He was always pretty inquisitive as a little kid.'

Peter was paying close attention to me and seemed about to say something, when the lights plunged even dimmer and much louder, aggressive music came on. All eyes were on a single figure standing under a sodium light. It was a man, I think, starting to dance. He was dressed up as a robot. But a robot in a tutu and tights, with loads of make-up slashed across his face and a white wig hanging in tatters. He moved his mouth to the words of the song and moved his body to a pounding beat. I thought I recognised the song, but couldn't put my finger on it. He slung a feather boa around his shoulders and made the crowd laugh and howl with drunken appreciation.

Peter was watching my face as I stared, mouth open at the performer.

He reminded me of Madame Lucille, the dressmaker. I was remembering how she'd danced so outrageously for us, lit up like a star on the sand dunes that night. The night she'd made us all dress up.

Down in the Den there was no telling how late it was. Soon enough I felt tired. I should have been home hours ago. Al would be wondering where I'd got to. He went on like he was tough, but I knew he hated being in the apartment without me.

I asked Peter to show me the way back out to the surface, and tell me how to get back to Stockpot District. He just needed to point me in the right direction, and I could find my own way. I knew at once he was disappointed. By then we had watched a number of dancers come and go, each more elaborate than the last.

That crazy-looking cat-dog was sitting in Peter's lap with his deformed limbs sticking out in a tangle. Karl seemed to be looking at me disappointedly, too. I didn't know what they wanted from me. Did they want me to stay here with them?

Soon we were out of the bar and moving through the dim streets. I was feeling woozy from the drink I had ended up finishing. There were more people about, coming and going like it was rush-hour, many of them got up in their finery.

Soon we reached the doorway, the curtain of ivy and, beyond that, the untended park. We emerged from beneath the bandstand to find that night had fallen and there was a layer of crisp, blood-coloured snow over everything. It looked surprisingly gruesome out there.

I patted Karl and Peter didn't make a fuss insisting on coming any further with me. I was grateful. I just needed to do some walking by myself.

Pretty soon I was lost.

I found grand arcades and fancy streets crammed with shops. It was all emporiums here, in this part of town, beyond the wild park. The windows were lit up, filled with gorgeously colourful displays. Hordes of shoppers flitted to and fro with parcels. Lizards clopped by in the roads, the wheels of the carriages turning the snow to bloody slush. For the first time it hit me that we had both Martian Thanksgiving and Christmas coming up. Except the people here didn't have Martian Thanksgiving, did they? What they had, it seemed, was a full-on Dickensian Christmas. Ding-donging merrily on high and with more trimmings than I'd seen in my life. Something gripped me deep inside my stomach.

That pit-of-your belly Christmas feeling that I hadn't had in years.

I remembered how we used to think that Adams' Exotic Emporium was the last word in festive displays. Their windows and well-stocked shelves were the highlight of our town's Christmas. Why, that whole shop would have been lost and insignificant in the City Inside. Everything in it would have looked tawdry and poor by comparison.

I succumbed to a moment of tearfulness. Just the thought of being back in Our Town made me catch my breath. I thought about Da steering our hovercart into town with Al and me, our pocket money clenched in our gloves, ready to pick out gifts.

Why was I thinking about that now? Standing in the cloying, noisy heat of the entrance to a fancy store, deep in the heart of the City Inside, I was brimming with tears. My clothes were shabby and plain and wet through. Some of the fancy-assed people going by on either side of me were giving me nasty looks.

I checked my purse to see what money I had. It would be great to surprise Al with a small gift. Cheer him up for losing his job. I looked at all the colourful silk shirts that were on display in great, billowing profusion. I could picture him in something with flowing sleeves and ruffles, like a buccaneer or a pirate. But all I had in my purse and my basket was a handful of coins.

35

I returned home with my shopping basket stuffed with several silk scarves, an expensive shirt and more bottles of cologne than Al could ever use. I had walked the cold streets of the City Inside carrying hot merchandise, and it felt good.

Al was asleep on the sofa. Toaster was bustling about, complaining that dinner was dried up and ruined.

'Where have you been?' my brother scolded me.

'It's so Christmassy out there,' I said. 'The stores are incredible. We need to go and see them together, Al.' In the meantime I had brought Christmas to our apartment. I produced the silk shirt and the scarves and laid out the bottles of cologne on the table. He was delighted, despite himself.

I asked whether he had heard from his young lady.

'Oh, Lora. She's so mad at me. She can't believe that I got myself into trouble at work. She's actually shocked. She's never been in any kind of bother in her life.'

I nodded sadly. 'Maybe that's why she's so dull.'

'Lora!' He clapped a hand over his mouth, starting to laugh.

'Well, it's true. She's a lovely looking girl and all, but she's a bit prim and boring, isn't she?'

Al sighed, fiddling with his new shirt. 'Maybe.' He was wistful about losing his job with the newspaper. He had loved working there and being treated like a grown-up.

'Don't you wish we were still refugees?' I asked him impulsively. From the kitchen there came the clanging of Toaster trying to rescue our dinner from the oven. 'Just imagine. When there were no rules at all. When all we had to do was make sure we survived.'

Al surprised me by looking scared. 'Promise me we won't ever have to go back to that. We can stay here in the City, can't we? We won't ever have to leave?'

'Sure, yes, of course,' I said. 'Our lives are here now. But was it so bad when we were in the wilderness? I looked after you and kept you safe, didn't I?'

He nodded. 'Of course you looked after us. You saved us. Tillian says it was a miracle we came through all that.'

'Does she now?'

Toaster appeared with a stiff expression. Tillian's father, Mr Tollund Graveley, was on the telephone, he announced, and he was terribly eager to have a word with Al. My brother brightened up straight away. Toaster brought out some plates of horrible, blackened food, like he was making a point.

Al returned after only a few minutes, looking pleased with himself. Mr Graveley had apparently forgiven my brother personally for his indiscretion with the Archive Machine. Furthermore, Tillian's father had renewed the invitation to Al to visit their family home in Darwin Sector the following evening. Martian Thanksgiving, as it would have been, back in our old life. He told Al, as if in passing, that I was invited, too. The Graveley family was eager to make my acquaintance. Having read a couple of newspaper articles about me, they were intrigued to meet the girl who had led her family and friends through the wilderness.

As Al told me this I groaned aloud. I wanted nothing less than to spend an evening being quizzed by people about our adventures.

I saw that Al was looking perturbed again.

'Are you dreading it as well?' I asked.

'It isn't just that,' he frowned. 'Mr Graveley passed me onto Tillian for a quick word. She was whispering down the receiver so her father wouldn't hear. She says she has a package for me. Something she must smuggle out of work tomorrow. She said that she's going to do it for my sake, at great personal risk to herself.'

I was surprised to hear it. 'What's in this package?'

Al said, 'It's got something to do with Grandma.'

I spluttered out the water Toaster had brought with my singed dinner.

'It seems that after I typed in my search request and then got found out and sacked, the Archive Machine carried on doing what I'd asked it. It continued to go through all the records of women called Margaret Estelle Robinson. And it printed more stuff out.'

'What stuff?'

'Tillian found the evidence today. Piled up in a tray no one had noticed.'

We set off late in the following afternoon. Of course Tillian had given us very precise instructions for getting to her parents' apartment in the Darwin District. Now we had to cross the City and meet these strange, grand folks. But we were the kids who had crossed half of Mars together! The evening shouldn't have held any worries for us.

I was pleased to see that Al was wearing the cream silk shirt I'd pilfered for him. One of the scarves, too, which was vivid orange against the deep crimson of his new woollen coat. He'd always loved bright, clashing earth tones like that. He had always been more interested in dressing up than I had. I was wearing more sombre and respectable clothing. I'd bought myself a frock with only minimal constrictions and ruffling, but at least I was branching out into that Victorian style of theirs. Now I knew why they favoured it. They were actual Victorian people, living in space, according to Peter. I hadn't told Toaster or Al any of that yet. It still seemed so unreal.

For the hundredth time Toaster asked whether we

wanted him to accompany us. I told him we'd be fine, imagining their reactions if we turned up with our sentient sunbed for a chaperone. Toaster didn't appear to mind the snub. He admitted that his thoughts were elsewhere. He was busy imagining what information about Grandma the computer at *The City Insider* had apparently found.

'It is her life story, I am sure of it,' he was burbling as we prepared to leave. 'I can't wait to find out. Why, she was a Historical Personage, and even people from the City Inside must know of her. That seems likely now. We are going to be able to read about her true story! Her past will be returned to us! And with it, mine too! Everything I have ever forgotten!'

We left him in the dizzying throes of his new obsession.

I didn't buy it, though. If, as Peter had told me, the people here were descended from humans who had left Earth just prior to the twentieth century, and if there had been no traffic or communication between them and our own folk, then there was no way they could have any knowledge of our Grandma whatsoever.

All the while I was wondering ... well, what if the City Insiders *did* know about us all along? They had telescopes and stuff, didn't they? They must have watched the skies and seen us landing. How come they never came offering their help? They had so much here, so many resources. It would have been so easy for them to help us out.

And, come to that, when Grandma and her people

crash-landed in the *Melville*, the *Hawthorne* and the *Dickinson*, how come they never saw this place on the horizon? How come they missed seeing a whacking great big Emerald City like this?

Our ears were popping in the elevator and I found myself once again enjoying the sensation of falling through all those many storeys.

'Al, do you still have those pictures on your phone?' I asked. 'The ones you snapped of the globe in the lizard queen's throne room?'

He frowned at me, his thoughts a million miles away. 'What? I suppose I do. Toaster fixed the charge for me once before. Maybe he could get it going again.'

'Could we take a look at them?'

'I guess so. How come?'

'I was thinking about our lost relations and friends. They're somewhere out there…'

'Oh, Lora,' he sighed. 'We have got to start thinking about the future, you know.'

This sounded unnecessarily heartless to me.

We emerged from the elevator into the Downstairs Market, where there were paper garlands and swags of tinsel and candles burning everywhere. A group of men were hauling a colossal fir tree into place. Me and Al paused to marvel at the livid green foliage.

Passing through the market, I was listening for the sound of Peter's harp. I would love to introduce Al to him, and to show him Karl. But my new friend wasn't there. His spot was taken by a mime artist that we hurried past.

Al and I rode the omnibus from the corner of our long street. It, like the Pipeline train we caught next, was packed with commuters. Even at the close of a busy day, the people looked immaculate to me, in their high buttoned-up collars and waistcoats, the women in long dresses that dragged in the melting red snow.

Al led us to the platform where we were to catch the final train into Darwin District. He was completely in charge of us now.

36

The Graveleys owned an entire storey of their tower block, and there was no noisy Downstairs Market in their foyer. Just a fancy little shop for last-minute gifts and tasteful music and tasteful just about everything, as a matter of fact. I hated it straight away.

'They can trace their family back to the first generation in this sector of Mars,' Al told me. 'That's why they're so rich and respectable. That's what Tillian told me.'

Their apartment on the 86th storey was furnished beautifully, with genuinely ancient fixtures and fittings. Everything smelled wonderfully of beeswax polish. Wooden furniture gleamed in the lamplight and the carpets felt about a foot thick.

An extremely delicate Servo-Furnishing guided us to a worn couch and offered us the teeniest glasses of sherry. He was a grandfather clock and it was easy to believe that his steady ticking had been going on for centuries.

'Very plush,' I hissed at my brother. I sipped my drink and almost gagged. It was way too sweet and thick as molasses. 'Whoah. You've brought us into Dickens or Jane Austen.'

Al frowned at me. He was never big on reading so he didn't really know what I was talking about.

There was a delicate 'harrumph' and we looked round to see Tillian entering the room with her parents. The old man was wearing some kind of army uniform with epaulettes and medals and even a ceremonial sword strapped to his belt. More dressy up, Aunt Ruby would have complained. Tillian herself was in quite a plain, straightforward gown of a pale blue fabric, which was very becoming. The mother came behind them, weighed down in layers of lacy fabric, yellowing with incredible age.

'Tillian informs us that you made a most remarkable journey, Miss Robinson,' said her father. His voice was kind of muffled by his elaborate moustache and sidewhiskers.

'You walked, didn't you?' her mother smiled through her ratty veil. 'You walked through the wilderness.'

'Most enterprising,' said the father.

'Extraordinary,' said the mother. 'Really, most extraordinary.'

'Yes, extraordinary,' added the father.

'But, why?' Tillian's mother asked. 'Why did you ever do such an extraordinary thing?'

I could feel my face burning up. Al was glancing at me sideways. I knew what he meant. Don't kick up a fuss.

I kept my voice light and sweet as I could when I replied. 'Well, you see, Mr and Mrs Graveley, it was a question of survival. Our Town and our Homestead were no longer habitable. We all had to leave, quite suddenly. Things had been going wrong for some time. Storms which destroyed our crops, and then there were the Disappearances and all. We knew that hostile lifeforms were watching us and meaning us harm.'

I saw that I had all three Graveleys hanging on my every word. Even the robot clock.

'Extraordinary,' said Mr Graveley.

'So, things happened quickly. Grandma vanished. Our father was killed. And I decided that we had to go. I had to take charge of our family and get us to safety.'

Mrs Graveley looked astonished. Her eyebrows rode up her lacey scalp. 'And you are how old, child?'

'Fourteen, when we started out,' I said, sounding gruffer than I meant to. 'My brother Al here was thirteen and my sister was three. That's how old we were when we struck out into the wilderness.'

Tillian was sitting close beside Al. 'It must have been terrifically difficult for you all. And I can't imagine what it must have been like to lose your sister and your mother, and all the others.'

With surprise, I saw from her expression that her feelings for him were absolutely genuine. She actually had feelings for Al, it was plain as anything.

'It was pretty tough,' Al said.

They sighed meaningfully as they listened to him. The

Graveleys were imagining the hardship, poverty and tragedy we poor children must have endured.

'Well then,' Mrs Graveley said kindly. 'There's plenty of time to hear about your extraordinary escapades, I'm sure. In the meantime, Mrs Gallagher the cook will be keen for us to eat the dinner she has prepared for us. Shall we go through?'

Though we never saw Mrs Gallagher the Servo-Furnishing, we did see her food, and it made all the torture worthwhile. A whole retinue of robots brought it out on silver platters. Each course consisted of seafood and, as the shining dishes came and went, the fish got bigger and bigger. We began with golden sprat fried whole and served with triangles of toast, through pink fish with golden coins for eyes and eventually to a many-legged creature baked in a savoury crust and brought in upon the shoulders of the servants as if it were an infirm guest.

As children of the prairie Al and I had never seen so much fish. Sure, we'd tasted it before, preserved in tins and sold over the counter at Adams' Exotic Emporium, but that was never fresh. All these specimens of fish came from somewhere incredible in the south that they referred to as the Suspended Sea. Everything we were eating was extremely expensive.

Tillian's family seemed barely to notice. They sat with miraculous aromas wafting about and didn't appear to care. Mr Graveley was telling us of a story about to break in *The City Insider*.

271

'Turns out that these Antique Hunters were a good deal more sinister than you'd think. They went to every auction they could find and between them filled a vast warehouse chock-full of clapped-out Servo-Furnishings. You might suppose they were about to recondition the things and sell them on at a profit, but that wasn't their idea at all – oh no! What these chaps were doing was much crueller.'

Tillian and her mother leaned forward in polite interest. 'And what was that, Father?'

'They tarted up the Servo-Furnishings just enough to get them moving again, and then shipped them to some bleak, godforsaken prairie a hundred miles from the City Inside. They set them free to run as fast as they could, and then they hunted them with guns. BANG BANG BANG! Shot them to smithereens!'

Mrs Graveley's watery eyes went wide. 'How unutterably nasty!'

'It's despicable,' Tillian's father said. 'The worst thing is that it isn't even illegal. One of the Antiques Hunters was injured in a horrible rifle accident and that's why it's about to be in the newspaper. But in terms of the law, they aren't doing anything wrong.'

I looked at the grandfather clock, who was going round the table with a bottle of white wine. He tried to look as if he wasn't listening to his master's tale, but I could see the trembling in his wooden fingers. I thought about Toaster at home. How long would he last if he had men with guns coming after him, intent on blowing him to bits for fun?

My brother excused himself and slipped away after dessert. Mr Graveley passed around a boxload of fancy bonbons. Al had been gone for a few moments when Tillian stood up sharply and declared she'd go and find him. He must have got lost somewhere in their vast apartment. Mr Graveley chuckled indulgently, observing to me that the youngsters were clearly grabbing a few private moments to canoodle.

'Darling!' protested Mrs Graveley.

'They're young!' he laughed. 'Like we were once, remember?' Then he looked directly at me. 'Why, you are very young, too, aren't you, Lora, my dear? Isn't there a special young man for you? Surely someone here in the City has caught your eye?'

I shrugged helplessly, feeling foolish and mildly dizzy from the wine. I didn't dare explain that I'd spent the months since our arrival mostly in our apartment, venturing out only occasionally for supplies. That only very recently I had met someone I got along with and, under his influence, explored further this bewildering place.

Peter. Yes, I had met a nice young man. But he was no good for me. Not in the way Tillian's father meant. But I thought that he could turn out to be a good friend.

Mrs Graveley turned a quite serious expression on me.

'Yes, we must see what we are to do about you. Many ladies of my acquaintance have sons of good prospects. Men who need a woman to show them the way and domesticate them and tame them. It's very important for your health and mentality and your social standing, you know, to marry well and to bear children. Then you can become part of the Great Martian Project. The ongoing Mars Exodus. Populating this barren, empty world with new life. Why, it is the single most important thing that we can do.'

Clearly the old woman thought that I must be made respectable.

For a fleeting moment I thought how marvellous it would be to run away to a place underground like the Den.

I found myself saying, 'But Mars isn't a barren, empty world.'

'Hm?' Tillian's mother smiled vaguely at me. 'Pardon, dear?'

'It isn't empty. We needn't feel so keen to fill it up with human babies. It's never been an empty world.'

Mr Graveley heard the tension in my voice and he laughed warmly. 'Old wives' tales and stories to scare the children! Mars is a dead world, my dear. It is stone dead, save for all the human life we have been blessed enough to have created here.'

I forgot my manners completely. 'You don't know anything! You've only ever lived in this City. You've never really seen Mars at all. Not like I have!'

Mrs Graveley dragged her veil away from her face and snapped frostily, 'Oh yes. Of course, we bow down to your superior knowledge and experience, my dear. Of course we do. Forgive us for not having been born in the back of beyond. I am sure you are right, and that you have met with many kinds of extraordinary beings during your adventures in the wilderness. I suppose you have even met with the fabled Martians!'

She and her husband chuckled nastily together.

I glared at her. And at her husband. They wanted me to feel ridiculous. They wanted me to start thinking that I was crazy. It would suit them if I had started babbling and shouting and kicking up a fuss. They would adore that. But I wasn't about to give them the satisfaction.

I bit my lip. I smiled at them. 'Yes, I've seen all kinds of strange lifeforms in my time.' It was all I said. But I looked at them as if I was including the pair of them in my list.

At that very moment I noticed something odd about Mr Graveley's eyes. They were moving round and round. The pupils and irises were whirling in circles. Now they were lilac-coloured. They were moving like kaleidoscopes.

'*Heee heeeee heeeee…*'

Was he laughing? No, it was his wife. She was grinning at me and her teeth were showing tiny points, and her eyes were spinning too.

Now both Graveleys were laughing at me. Giggling at me.

'*Hee heeee heeee heeeeee…!*'

I sat there absolutely frozen still.

Then I blinked. And everything was back to normal.

Tillian and Al came strolling back into the dining room. They looked a bit dishevelled and flushed, as if they had indeed been kissing hurriedly elsewhere. Taking advantage of every moment they had alone.

Mr and Mrs Graveley snapped back to attention, smiling warmly and starting up their genial chatter again. The evening flowed on in a good-natured blur, and they mostly forgot about me. I sat, saying very little.

I knew what I had seen and heard.

But had I? Could it be possible? Hadn't I just … maybe I'd just … I was over-tired and nervous and out of my element. I must have just imagined it. Surely?

Al had in his lap a parcel, tied up with ribbon. It looked exactly like Tillian had given him a box of fancy chocolates. He looked very pleased with himself. I reflected that people had always spoiled Al.

Soon enough – though not before time – we were leaving. Farewells and pleasantries were said in a very formal, ritualised way. There was warmth, though, in the way they talked to Al. They saw him as a decent boyfriend for their daughter. Al, it seemed, had passed some invisible test.

The Graveleys were far chillier kissing me goodnight in their apartment doorway. The feeling was mutual.

In the elevator I closed my eyes exhausted as we plummeted to the foyer. I pictured those revolving, purple eyes. Yes, I knew what I had seen. I didn't think I was mistaken.

It was very late by then. We exited the building and were hurrying through the Darwin District, where the streets were safe and swept clean. We had a long trip home ahead of us and I hoped Al could remember all our connections on the Pipeline, 'cos I surely couldn't.

My brother was in a trance that he didn't emerge from until we were aboard our first train. The gas lamps spluttered and fizzed. We were alone in there, rattling through the underground night. I pulled the window shut. The room was still filled with curls of greenish smoke.

'You're very quiet.'

He smiled. 'Wasn't it lovely? The food, the apartment. The way they live.'

'I guess so.' I studied him and could tell he was anticipating spending the rest of his life in such beautiful trappings, and among such people. I'd wanted to warn him all evening – just because they've got nice manners and just because they smile and simper over you, it doesn't mean that they really like you any. Those kinds of people could put their true feelings aside, so that you never knew what they were.

But now, since their masks had slipped off – my thoughts were even darker.

'Heee heeeee heeee…'

I had heard them, hadn't I? I had seen their teeth and eyes.

But how was that possible? How? Could they really be Martians? Or were they some kind of horrible hybrid creatures, even? Or was I simply crazy? Maybe everything had been too much for me and my mind had cracked at last.

Al said, 'Thank you for coming along tonight, Lora. I know it was hard work for you.'

'Hey, it was OK.'

'I know they're not your kind of people.'

I smiled and shrugged and then I was thinking, why don't I just tell him? Why can't I simply blurt it out? It's not just that they're not my kind of people, and it's not just that I didn't like them. They're dangerous, Al. I think they're … I think…

No. I had to be imagining things.

It had been so hot and cloistered in there. The wine fumes and the rich food. All of it conspired to send my senses funny for a few moments.

About an hour later we arrived at the Stockpot District and our tower block. Al dug around in his jacket pockets for his keycard and tossed me the ribbon-wrapped parcel Tillian had given him when they were alone.

37

I stowed it away in my bedside cabinet, ribbon and all. Grandma's secrets – whatever they might be – would wait there until I could devote proper time to them.

I lay awake exhausted that night. I felt the pressure of the past few days behind my eyes. I was dazzled by the weirdness of it all. There was too much to think about.

First thing the next morning Toaster demanded, 'What was in the parcel? What secrets did the Archive find inside itself? Have you opened it yet?'

He was serving me breakfast. Grape jelly on wholemeal toast. Every scrape of the knife was war on my nerves. I couldn't give our sunbed adequate reason for not opening the box yet.

He kept asking, several times a day, in the days that followed. His voice became grating and impatient.

Once, I distracted him by asking, 'Toaster, did you ever think more about your idea? About this City not even being real?'

He stood there, face frozen, hefting a large basket of laundry he was taking to the basement. 'Did I say that?'

'Not so long ago. You said you thought this whole City

might be inside the living red globe that the Queen Lizard showed us.'

Incredulity was plain on his face. Toaster looked at me like I was making stuff up. 'The what? Who... Why would I think something so peculiar?'

I shook my head and dismissed him. Then I thought again. 'Toaster, would you try to get Al's phone working for me? I want to look at his pictures of the globe of Mars. Maybe I can find the City Inside on the globe and then...'

But Toaster was looking highly annoyed. 'Is that all I'm good for? Charging up phones?' He stomped off with his laundry basket. He'd be away with his robot cronies in the basement for hours.

If I looked at those pictures of the globe, I thought, maybe I could find this City and also the ravines where we last saw Ma and the others. I could work out how far away they were. I could find the prairie and everywhere we'd been. If I could see it all together on a map it would all seem logical and laid out somehow. It would all make sense. And then I could start to make plans.

More days went by, and outside our apartment the City Inside became noisier and more Christmassy. Al came dashing in, clutching parcels and bags, excited and pleased with himself. Sometimes he went with Tillian, other times with Toaster, who privately told me that he was spending credits like there was no tomorrow. Al had never had so much money in his pocket before.

He reminded me of my promise to go Christmas shopping with him. I'd been keen enough the night I came back and brought him a shirt and those scarves and cologne. The truth was, I no longer felt like it. It just didn't feel like real Christmas to me.

Tillian came to our apartment one or two times, and I watched her warily. Just to check that nothing crazy went on with her eyes. I listened hard for that tell-tale giggling.

A creeping thought obsessed me in the run-up to Christmas. Could human beings from Victorian times have mated with Martians? Could their descendents be living here today? Most of the time they were normal. But sometimes – just sometimes – when the light caught them strangely or when they were turning on you with sinister intent … you could see it in their eyes. You could see who they were underneath. Neither human nor Martian. But something worse than both.

I couldn't shake this ghastly thought. It went whirling on and on round my head.

'My parents were very impressed by you,' Tillian told me, during one visit.

'I can't see why,' I frowned.

'They're very grateful to you, actually,' said Tillian, in her refined City accent. 'For looking after Al and seeing that he has turned out to be such a fine young man. You must take the credit, you know. He tells me he was a wild ragamuffin at one time. I believe you are responsible for taming your brother. And so I thank you, too.'

'I can't take any credit for how Al's turned out. He's his own man.'

Yes, I thought. He's a young man, now. He was taller and smarter, but also more calm and thoughtful. Nothing like the endlessly questioning and cross little boy I once knew. He seemed alien to me. I no longer knew what was going on behind those quicksilver, sparkling eyes.

During Tillian's visit that morning there was a funny thing with Toaster. The sunbed was in a flustered mood when he brought in our mid-morning tea. When I asked what the matter was, he was evasive.

Then there was a knock at the door and it was two repairmen, who showed me their identification badges and told me they had come to collect Toaster.

'Collect him?'

'His memory circuits, miss. When he filled out his evaluation form he complained that we hadn't been able to do them much good during his recent refurb.'

Toaster appeared at my elbow. 'That's right. I'm here. I'm ready.'

They were taking him away again. When I watched him gathering his few necessary things, I felt a clutch of fear.

'It's all right, Lora. They did a good job on me before, didn't they?'

Al appeared, dressed for going out with his girlfriend. 'Oh, Toaster. Are you off?'

So he knew about this!

'Now,' Toaster said. 'I won't be gone for long, Lora. I've made these gentlemen promise to return me home on Christmas Eve at the very latest. Don't fret! I shall be here to cook your dinner for you on the big day!'

It wasn't that. It wasn't as a servant that Toaster was important, and I hoped he knew that. He looked at me earnestly and said softly, 'Imagine if they can reboot my whole memory? What then? We shall know everything then, won't we?'

I nodded and tried to smile. Then the two repairmen took him away.

Al and Tillian thought nothing of it. They were soon ready to go out themselves. Today Tillian was going to take my brother to Eliot District, where the most wonderful stores were to be found.

'Are you sure you won't come, Lora?'

I told them I had things to do in the apartment.

Once they were gone, I went straight to my room and opened the little door in my bedside cabinet. The box was waiting there, just as it had since our night at the Graveleys'.

I put it on my knee and tugged the pink satin ribbon free. It felt heavy enough, as if it had a hard-backed book inside, or a whole ream of computer paper. When I opened the lid, I saw that it did. Inside a wrapper of frayed grey silk there was a stack of perhaps five hundred pages. Five hundred very clean, white pages of paper.

They were all blank.

My heart rate went sky high as I leafed through, faster and faster. Why would Tillian bring us this? What was she playing at? Each page was attached to the next by little perforations. The whole lot flew out of the box and concertinaed around me.

Nothing. Nothing. The box of secrets had nothing whatsoever inside.

Except. On the very last page. In the smallest possible type, there was this:

536 / Appt D
Bolingbroke District
900044 NNVX

'It's an address,' Peter told me.

'Well, I can see that,' I snapped.

He looked at me, hair falling into his eyes. I'd hurt his feelings with my brusqueness. I ploughed on. 'Can you find it? Can you help me get there?'

'Sure,' he said. 'Easily. Actually, it's not too far from the park and the Den. You've been quite near the place yourself.'

'I have?'

My palms were sweating against the greasy oilcloth of our café table. We were having frothy coffee at a stall quite close to Peter's busking spot. After I opened the box and found the address in that heap of computer paper, I knew I had to go straight to the Downstairs Market.

I'd been so relieved to see Peter standing there, playing one of the old tunes on his harp. Folk were buying papers and walking by him, tossing him coins, as he concentrated on drawing that golden music out of the strings. Christmassy music now, of course. Pure. It bubbled over everyone's heads and drew me to him with my scrap of paper with the address on it. The address that had come out of the archive when Al had punched in Grandma's name.

Sure, there were thirty-two women of that name on the list. Why was I so keen on finding a namesake, or even a distant relative?

Now we were in the smoky café drinking coffee together, I realised that I'd neglected Peter for a few days. He casually suggested I was keeping my distance since I'd learned he lived somewhere as grotty as the Den.

'No!' I said. 'Not at all! You must never think that.'

He nodded. I looked at Karl, who was bundled up on the bench in Peter's coat. The twisted cat-dog was trembling worse than ever, but his tongue was pink and he shuffled forward to be petted by me. Whatever was wrong with him seemed to be getting worse, I thought.

Karl wagged his stumpy tail harder, but couldn't manage to jump up at me.

The waitress brought us coffee refills and slipped the cat-dog a tough biscuit to chew. Karl poked it with his dry nose, but didn't eat it.

'It's just a touch of cold he's got,' Peter told me. 'It's since the weather's been worse. It's kind of damp in the Den.'

I thought about the dinginess of the place they lived. I still didn't understand why they had to live there.

'We could go to this place this afternoon if you like,' Peter said. He flicked at the paper with the address on.

'Not yet. I've another appointment today,' I said nervously. 'At the university.'

38

Dean Swiftnick didn't seem to be in a great mood. He was grumbling from the minute I first saw him.

'You'd think they'd be more interested,' he was saying when I walked into his book-lined office. 'After all, they chose to do this course and they paid for it. Can you believe that? Out of the whole group only three had finished the set text and none of them could say they actually enjoyed reading it.' He was waving what looked like a very old soft-back book at me.

The room smelled of books. It was like a blend of fallen leaves, vanilla extract and stewed tea. And tobacco, too, for Dean Swiftnick was smoking a pipe that had, over years perhaps, turned his hair and beard yellowish.

'What was the book?' I asked. He blinked at me owlishly and tossed the very delicate article to me. An actual book! It was called *Our Astounding Voyage to Mars* by G.E Watson. A subtitle ran: 'How Earth Insiders Invaded the Red Planet'. I had never even heard of it, but I coveted it at once.

Dean Swiftnick sat down heavily at his messy wooden desk. 'How I wish I was reading Mr Watson's firsthand account for the first time like my lucky students ought to be, and not for the twenty-ninth. I think I am growing just a tad jaded…' He plucked off his spectacles and rubbed his red eyes with dirty cuffs. Then he glared at me. 'Am I expecting you, young lady? Do we have an appointment?'

I hugged the book to me, wondering if the old professor would notice if I slipped it into my shopping basket for later perusal. I was in my bonnet, clutching a basket, duster coat over my dress. I knew I looked like a girl dressed up in her mother's clothes, or perhaps the cleaner come to deal with the impossible task of tidying this office.

But I had been invited. I was supposed to be there, in the Department of True Life Stories. I told him so.

The Dean's eyes widened and he came scuttling around his desk to grasp both my hands in his own. 'Oh, you're here! You are here!' He beamed at me. 'You found us all right, then?'

'Oh yes,' I said as, with a showman's flourish, he pulled out a chair for me.

Peter had shown me the way. The University of the City Inside sprawled within the square mile of Ruskin District. There were a bewildering array of orange-bricked edifices, surrounding the verdigrised dome of the Central Library and Royal Planetarium. Peter had surprised me by confiding that several years ago he had begun a degree in the very department where Dean Swiftnick taught. But he had been thrown out for reasons he didn't go into, one term short of completing his qualification in True Life Stories.

'Ah, it was all just gobbledegook and bunkum,' he said, as he led me through the dark warren of streets. We had to squeeze past crowds of begging students. 'It was much too theoretical. It had hardly anything to do with real or true life. And yes, I remember old Dean Swiftnick!'

It seemed that being close to the university and talking about his days there put Peter in a very odd mood. Like he was going back to a part of his life that he'd rather forget about.

For me, I was amazed to be there. In that 'august seat of learning' – which was the kind of thing they used to say in the novels I'd read. I didn't mind the dirt and slime in the alleyways, or the coughing and sickness of the students all around me, or the shouts that rang out as we went by. All I knew was that one of the esteemed professors up in those towers, in one of those hidden offices, wanted to hear all about my True Life Story. Through him, my life was about to go down in the records. It would become a part of History.

Even though Peter had looked sceptical about the whole visit, he led me into the reception of the True Life Stories Department and saw that I was taken to the right place. 'I'll wait in the little quadrangle outside,' he'd said. He had Karl bundled up in his arms. Karl was trembling harder than ever.

I couldn't help thinking Peter should have left him home at the Den today, damp though it might be.

I came out of my reverie with a jump, realising that Dean Swiftnick was talking to me. He was leaning earnestly towards me. His voice sounded so kind.

'There will be consent and copyright forms, of course, and then other things to fill in, to do with insurance and indemnity, liability and so on. Naturally! And then evaluation sheets to complete. But I'm sure that we can cope with all of these in due course. The main, important thing, my dear Lora Robinson is, that you are ready to pass on the tale of your most fascinating and, may I even say, historically significant life?'

I smiled at him. 'Yes, I am.'

I imagined he would transcribe what I had to say, very carefully. In fact, I had even started rehearsing in my mind how it would be. In my basket I'd brought the sheets of paper with my scribbled-down notes. My writings began with the very day that the storms came to devastate Da's crops in the last year of our Homestead life on the prairie. They told my tale in scattershot fashion all the way up to the night that Al and me had dinner with Tillian Graveley's snooty parents.

I was sure that, no matter how roughly written these notes were, and how ill-educated they showed me to be, they would surely be of interest to the Dean, in whose study I was starting to feel so comfortable.

Once I finished explaining about the notes I'd made, he put down his cup of tea with a loud clunk. 'Good heavens, no.'

'No?' I gasped. I put down my own tea that he'd poured for me. It had nasty bits in it.

He chuckled. 'Do you really think, my dear, that a person such as I have time to go picking through the illiterate, hand-written memoirs of a girl like you? A girl from the wilderness?'

'B-but,' I said. 'I thought you were interested in my life?'

'Indeed I am,' he said, standing up and fiddling with his collar and cravat. 'As an example, or a type. An historical phenomenon. But that doesn't mean that I would find any great value in your written outpourings and the things you saw fit to scrawl down. Or, God forbid, your *feelings*. Oh no, indeed. I need a much more objective and scientific methodology.'

'Methodology?' I asked.

The next thing I knew I was being led out of that cosily bookish room, back into the institutional corridor. Shifty-looking academics in gowns and hollow-eyed students slouched about on missions of their own. Each of them acknowledged the Dean respectfully with heads lowered as he bumbled past. He had me by the hand and was digging his ink-stained nails into the flesh of my palm. I was too amazed by everything to protest.

Then we were out of the building and crossing the grassy quad. It was chillier now and pinkish snow was starting to tumble out of the sky.

'Where are you taking me?'

'Where all the equipment is kept,' he said, and his voice was a whole lot less genial away from his office. His grip was vice-like.

'Dean Swiftnick,' said a familiar and very welcome voice. 'How nice to see you again.'

I looked up in relief to see Peter standing there with Karl in his arms.

'Do I know you?' snapped the academic, trying to shove past.

'A few years ago, you had me thrown out of your department,' Peter said. 'Remember? I was once one of your most promising students.'

The Dean looked up into Peter's handsome face and scowled. 'Oh yes. Caused quite a disgrace, as I recall. We had to report you to the Authorities.'

'I was glad to leave this dump. Now I want to know what you're doing to my friend.'

Dean Swiftnick darted a glance at me. 'You're her friend, are you?'

'She said you invited her to help with your research.'

He sighed. 'Well, yes. In a manner of speaking.' He looked about, obviously uncomfortable at being outside, beyond the protection of the departmental security guards.

'Look, can we have this conversation inside? I'm taking her to the Remembering Room…'

Peter came with us across the quadrangle. 'Are you OK?' he asked, sidling close. I told him yes, but really I wished that I could change my mind and just leave.

At the glass entrance to the new building Dean Swiftnick turned on Peter. 'Things have changed since you were here. This is a highly scientific sterile premises.'

Peter shrugged. 'So?'

'So you must leave that … animal tied up outside the main entrance. That is the rule.'

Peter hugged Karl to his chest. 'He's not well.'

'He's a dog,' snapped the Dean.

'No, he's not,' said Peter in a reasonable tone. 'Though he's not a cat either, mind. We aren't exactly sure what Karl is, but I'm all he's got. And I don't think I want to leave him out here.'

'Suit yourself,' said the Dean. 'Then the pair of you ambiguous creatures must remain outside whilst I take Lora into the Remembering Room.'

I wasn't at all happy about the way this man was telling us all what to do. I decided to speak up. 'Look, forget this. I'm going home. I don't even want you to have my story any more…'

His face turned livid and he seized my arm. 'You will do as you are commanded, young woman!'

'Oh yeah?' I shouted. 'How are you gonna make me do that?'

We were drawing the attention of several hungry-looking students.

Dean Swiftnick licked his lips like he could taste something absolutely delicious. 'I know who has your Servo-Furnishing. Your treasured sunbed. I could make them wipe his memory and identity completely clean...' He snapped his fingers loudly. 'Just like that.'

'Who?' I said. 'Who has him?'

'We do,' he snarled. 'This university. We took him away from under your nose. His buried recollections are even more important than your own, young woman.'

'You've really got Toaster?'

'Yes,' he said, knowing he had won. 'And we will drain him of all information and then sell him to the Antique Hunters, if you don't do precisely what I tell you to. Ah, yes. I see you know all about the Antique Hunters. Now, come along, my dear young woman.' He turned to Peter. 'You may come if you leave your unhygienic mongrel behind. It is up to you.'

The snow was coming down in flurries. Peter looked stricken and torn. Karl let out a pathetic whimper. I decided to make up my friend's mind for him.

'Peter, it's all right. Just wait out here with Karl, if you would. I'll be OK in there. I promise I will.'

'Of course no harm will come to this precious lady,' said Dean Swiftnick, chuckling as he led me into the green glass building. We passed through the electric doors and into the sterile atmosphere of what he told me was their new archive centre. He continued chuckling, very pleased with himself. He had a very high-pitched laugh.

Dean Switftnick led me deeper and deeper into the metal-walled corridors of the archive complex. He hung onto my arm, pulling me along almost hungrily and he didn't say much.

At last we came to a kind of operating theatre labelled 'The Elizabeth Gaskell Memorial Remembering Room'. The old man led me in and told me to lie on a padded couch. All of a sudden I felt incredibly weary. I lay back gratefully and I remembered to ask him how long this would take. I didn't like the thought of Peter and Karl standing out in the weather for too long.

The Dean didn't bother to reply. It was as if I had ceased to be a person to him, now that I was a bona fide object of study. He began untangling yards of wire and attaching electrodes to my arms and head. I couldn't resist. I felt more feeble than I ever had in my life. It came to me that this was why my cup of tea in his office had been gritty. I had been sedated by the Dean. I couldn't cause too much of a fuss because he might harm Toaster. He might siphon his robot mind completely dry and hand him over to those men who would take great pleasure in hunting him across the Martian prairie and blowing him to smithereens…

Now I was drowsy, slipping away…

Dean Swiftnick retreated behind a glass partition where, along with a couple of worried-looking research students, he worked feverishly at a control console. Then his voice came out of a speaker. 'I'll leave you in the capable hands of my research student assistants. They know what to do with you. I bid you farewell, prairie child. I have a lecture that I must give, and a whole lot of very important things to do … *heee heeeeeee heee…*'

I felt very peculiar. It was as if the metal floor was opening up underneath me. No, not beneath my feet. The floor of my mind was dropping away. I squeezed my eyes tight shut and experienced a horrible sensation of suspension. I was teetering above a dark chasm.

Down there, whole worlds were whirling. They were green and blue and crimson and gold.

Sudden, vivid flashes of light came at me through the dark. I could see Martha and George, the golden-eyed burden beasts as they toiled up a sand dune. I saw all my family out in the fields. There was Hannah, only three, wearing a headscarf, trying to help out. I saw Al. He and I were in Adams' Emporium, breathing in the excitement of stealing exotic goods. I watched his tamed lizard bird wheeling gracefully in the air. I could see Grandma and Aunt Ruby, drunk as Jack Rabbits on prairie wine, laughing together at some old, old joke.

And I saw the wilderness, reaching out for thousands of miles in every direction. Here came the Martian Ghosts dancing after us in their long scarves, pricking the shadows with their spiky limbs. Their purple eyes were swirling, dizzy with greed.

At last I saw Sook, my friend, drifting down through the blue night vapours to meet me in secret...

How long all this went on for I didn't know. I was held wriggling above the abyss and still those brightly coloured worlds spun beneath me. They looked like old Earth and Mars and the crimson globe in the churchy room of the queen of lizards. The globe that Toaster once believed held the whole of the City Inside...

Soon I was feeling weaker. The worlds below were exerting a dreadful gravity. I was using my willpower to stay afloat, at the top of my mind, still conscious. But at any moment I could drop into that cauldron of noisy memories and flashing pictures.

Then – with a shock – I woke up.

There was a ripping noise and a sudden sharp pain and a smell like burning chops. I felt what must have been a mild electric shock. Awareness of the bright metal room around me returned all at once, in a flash. Peter was standing there. He looked scared, with a tangle of wires and electrodes in both clenched hands.

'I haven't killed you, have I?'

'I don't think so,' I grinned.

'I thought I should disconnect you,' he said, breathing hard. 'Are you sure you're OK?'

A rush of questions leapt out of me. 'Where's the Dean? How did you get in here? What have you done? You must have ruined his machine…!'

'Never mind that,' he said. 'Do you feel all right?' He helped me off the bench and I swayed dizzily. I suddenly felt sick, deep in my gut, like I used to get if I had to sit in the back of the hovercart for too long.

'I'm OK. Where's the old man?'

'You were in here alone. They left you plugged in. You've been in here for over an hour. I came looking and saw you through the window, there.'

'It was so weird, Peter. Like someone was staring straight into my mind…'

'Yeah, well. I've put a stop to it.'

I grabbed his arm. 'Did you leave Karl outside?'

He nodded quickly. 'We have to get back to him. The snow was really coming down hard.'

One of the Dean's assistants came back in behind the glass partition. She gave a panicked cry when she saw I'd been revived. Next thing, alarms were going off and lights were flashing.

'We have to run,' Peter said. 'Are you up to that?'

'Of course!' I was incredibly grateful to him. God knows what would have become of me, hooked up to that Remembering thing.

Panicked academics or lab assistants tried to get in our way, but we pushed them aside and ran for our lives.

They would have drained my mind away to nothing. Like opening a can or juicing an orange. They'd have squished everything useful out of me and thrown the rubbish away.

Department security almost got us as we hurtled across the foyer of the archive building. A man in body armour even pulled out what looked like a gun. Peter pointed a finger at me and shouted, 'You hurt her and there'll be hell to pay. She's a valuable specimen. I must take her to the Dean at once – so stand aside!'

I felt like laughing at Peter's commanding tone. The startled guard and the floss-haired receptionist fell back obediently to let us through. It seemed so easy! To answer so-called authority back with a dose of their own bullying.

Peter cackled and bundled me through the glass doors. Now we just had to pick up Karl and untie his leash and…

Peter stood stock still before the spot where his cat-dog had been tethered. We both stared at the rumpled, hairy blanket, which was now almost wholly covered in wet pink snow.

Karl was gone.

39

Student protesters were arriving to occupy the quad between the glass towers. The whole place was busier, and with a crush of starved bodies all around us, we couldn't look properly for Karl.

'He'll be crushed underfoot,' Peter shouted, looking distraught. 'He won't know what to do, Lora. This is a place he doesn't know, and…'

I examined his lead, which had been left tangled on his blanket. It wasn't chewed or broken. Someone had cut through it with a blade.

Snow was dropping more heavily and we grew desperate in our search. We hunted in the alleyways and shrouded corners, hoping he might have crawled away to shelter.

'He can't even get very far on his own legs,' Peter said. 'You know him. He can barely support himself.'

We tried to get back into the Department of True Life Stories, banging on the plate glass, to ask the receptionist if she had seen anything. It was a long shot and she didn't even appear to notice us. When we banged at other official-looking doors around the square, the people inside turned up their noses at us.

'Oh God, Lora,' Peter said. 'He depended on me for everything. He trusted me absolutely. I was going to look after him forever...'

I tugged on Peter's arm. 'We'll find him.'

'We can't though, can we? We'll never find him. Just look at this place.'

It was fully dark now and the student radicals were building tall fires in metal bins and gathering noisily around them. A feeling of angry discontent and danger was rife in the air. We went up to some of the less-frightening ones and asked about Peter's cat-dog. The students shook their heads and treated us as if we were ridiculous. What did they care about someone's lost pet?

But I knew how much Karl meant to Peter.

'He's all I've got, Lora, on this whole planet. He's the only one I've got to care for.' Tears were streaming down his face and they were starting to freeze.

I thought: we all need someone to love. My tired thoughts were coming in little blips like this. Obvious, perhaps, but they seemed like huge, important thoughts just then. We need someone to depend on us. We need them to need us. In recent times I had had Al to look after, but he was grown now. He was his own man. Without him and Toaster, what would I be in this City Inside? If there was just me to think about would I come unstuck? I think I might lose my mind.

Toaster had both of us to look after, too. I believed he

loved us in his own way. He was someone else dear to us who was missing. I didn't know when or if we'd ever see him again.

It was the day before Christmas Eve in the City Inside and disaster had struck. We had come loose from each other – the few folk I knew and cared about – and now we were lost.

'Karl! Karl!' Peter was shouting, sounding desperate. His voice was just one among many ragged voices calling out in the quadrangle. Others were shouting for freedom of imagination and thought, freedom from dogma and debt. Others were crying for food and somewhere to sleep. But right then nothing seemed to matter as much as the fate of that tangled-up cat-dog belonging to Peter.

It was some hours before he would leave the university buildings. I told him we could return tomorrow and resume the search. It would do Karl no good if we both caught pneumonia tramping about the streets, soaked to the skin and freezing.

'Yes, yes, you're right,' Peter said. He was white-faced with worry.

And, as luck would have it, just as we'd decided to head home we witnessed something very strange indeed.

We left the quad via a side street we'd already explored. It was the route back to the nearest Pipeline station and our way out of Ruskin District. We were both plodding along, numb with exposure to the elements and heartsick with fear.

A shiny carriage stood at the side entrance to the Department of True Life Stories. Lights were dimming inside the building – it was after 10pm by now. The glass doors opened and we heard a familiar, cultivated voice calling good night to the security men. Peter and I shrank into the shadows of the iron fences, crouching in the dirty snow. Here came Dean Swiftnick, hurrying down the steps to his carriage, in a tall hat and a heavy cloak. A driver sat atop the vehicle, flexing his whip in readiness, and the stately green horses were whickering softly, eager to be off, now that their master was here.

Peter and I both saw that he was carrying a small cage containing a dark, lumpy shape. A shape that gave a distinctive mewing woof we both knew very well.

Before we could dash into the street to prevent him, that hateful academic was inside his carriage and crying out to the driver to set off at once. In a jingling and rumbling and clattering of hooves, they were gone – sizzling through the scarlet ice and snow.

Peter and I turned to stare at each other. We could both still hear Karl's pitiful cries. Had he seen us? Had he sensed that we were close by? Perhaps the cat-dog had even caught our scents.

'He's been kidnapped,' Peter said, his voice hoarse. 'That old monster has stolen him away!'

But at least we knew that Karl was relatively safe, I kept saying, as we jumped on the Pipeline home, back to Stockpot District. Swiftnick hadn't harmed him. The old man had stolen him in order to have a hold over Peter and me. He was a wily old devil.

Peter glanced at me as if he was wishing that he and his best friend had never offered to accompany me that day. He covered up that look with a hopeful smile.

When we got back to Stockpot and our tower block he reclaimed his harp from the locker in the empty Downstairs Market. I told him to come to our apartment on Storey 202 to get warmed through and have something to eat. He was silent and shivering as we rode the elevator upstairs.

When we got to the apartment he glanced around appreciatively. 'Look at this place. And the Authorities just gave this to you and your brother?'

I nodded. 'Should I have been more suspicious?'

'I think maybe you should have been.' He moved to the vast greenish window and gazed at the City spread out below. There was a blizzard going on down there. Great flurries of rose-coloured snow were blowing through the canyons.

'You'd best sleep on our sofa,' I said. 'No need for you to trek all the way to your Den tonight.'

He didn't put up much of a fight. He went off to take a hot shower, which he said was a massive luxury. While

I waited for him, I hunted in the kitchen for food that I could quickly heat up. I found everything orderly and spotlessly clean, just as Toaster always left it. I gave myself a swift talking to: there was no use getting overcome with sadness and all that. I needed to think. I needed to be practical. Otherwise I wouldn't be of any help to anyone, would I?

Peter rejoined me wearing a heavy blue jumper and some loose house pants that were big enough and not too girly. I made him coffee in the fancy pot and suggested we have some soup Toaster had left. It wouldn't take long to heat up.

Peter looked at me searchingly as I got on with this. 'They're really after you, aren't they?' he said. 'I look at you, and you're just you. But there's like this net, all around you, and it's closing in. Someone is tightening it...'

I knew he was right. I had felt like that ever since we'd arrived in the City Inside and were given this marvellous place to live. Nothing ever came for free. 'I'm just glad that I've made a good friend here,' I told him.

There was a key scraping in the front door and lots of happy, clattering noise. Al was home, bringing bag-loads of Christmas shopping and a breathless Tillian Graveley in tow. They were both covered in feathery snow and laughing about something.

As he flung off his smart coat Al greeted the ragged Peter like a long-lost friend. I suppose I had mentioned

Peter once or twice in recent weeks. I explained about the missing Karl, prompting sympathetic noises from both Al and his girlfriend.

The dishing up of Toaster's vegetable soup led to another explanation – how Toaster had been taken away. He had been tricked and stolen and was currently in danger.

Tillian looked sceptical and Al gave a nervous laugh. 'Oh, come now, Lora. You're just being paranoid and silly, surely. You know he's had problems with his memory circuits.' I watched Al glance at Tillian for back-up. I felt a flash of anger, realising that they must have discussed me. Al asked, 'Why would the university want to kidnap Grandma's old sunbed…?'

My face burned to hear him dismiss my fears and Toaster himself. Toaster was our oldest and most loyal friend.

'But why would they kidnap a harmless creature like Karl, either?' Peter said, more rudely than I think he meant to. 'They want your sister's memories, that's why. The Uni and Dean Swiftnick are working for the City Authorities, I bet you…'

Exasperated, my brother turned to his girlfriend. She looked amazed, and not very pleased at all. 'Lora,' she said, sternly. 'It sounds to me rather as if you've been hanging around with radicals and anarchists.'

I glared at her. 'I'll hang about with who I want to,

Tillian Graveley. And I'll say and think what I want to, thanks very much.'

She grumbled and muttered at this, delicately finishing her soup. I suddenly thought that we should have been more careful, telling our tales in front of this girl. She was, of course, involved with the Authorities. Her father owned *The City Insider*. Peter and I should have waited till she was gone before saying anything at all.

Al swerved neatly into small talk. 'Where is it you come from, Peter? Where do you live?' He was checking him out, looking at him from top to toe. I realised my brother was turning out to be a snob.

Naturally Peter didn't tell them that he lived at the Den. He was used to keeping that stuff under his hat. He just told Al that he lived in the Eventide District.

'Oh!' Al burst out. 'I must tell you, Lora. Today we were shopping in that very district, where they have the most extravagant Christmas displays. Tillian has been most generous. She's been buying us wonderful presents.'

'That's very kind of her,' I smiled. I started to gather in the used dishes.

'But, listen, Lora. In one particular store I saw the most astonishing thing. I saw the Homestead, Lora! Our Homestead on the prairie! Exact in every way. A child's toy, a play-set ... but it was unbelievable. I saw our lives – everything we thought we'd lost – and they were all in miniature...'

40

Later, when I was alone, I thought about what Al had described. He had talked as if he'd found something unexpected and amusing; something I would find interesting.

But I was starting to feel alarmed.

He and Tillian had been in a lavish toy department. The most famous in all the City Inside. Tillian had told Al, 'I know that the childhood you and Lora had was very poor and deprived. It sounds so harsh, the time that you lived on the prairie…'

And so she had taken him to the fairy grotto that she remembered from her own childhood. It was a fantasyland, crammed with every toy imaginable. Laughing, she described how Al had regressed to childhood in there. His eyes had bugged out and he had wandered around that Christmas wonderland in a daze, peering at space rockets, teddies and gingerbread houses.

And then he had seen the elaborate playset representing our Homestead on the crimson prairies of Mars.

'There were scarlet dunes and neat rows of blue corn. Farmers and green burden beasts all carved beautifully out of wood, working in those fields. And in the middle, a two-storey dolls' house. A rather primitive building, with sides that opened out. I cried to see it, for it was our family home all in meticulous detail, Lora. The family were all at work – three children and a stooped grandmother. They were hauling water from the well and feeding chickens. The bulky Servo-Furnishing was doing some heavy work on the barn. And there was a mother cleaning pots with red sand in the kitchen, and a father at the table. Just like ours. He was looking at a tiny folding map.

'It was all so like us, Lora. I felt all my memories stirring up. Things I had thought I could no longer see or taste or feel. But just standing there in the toy department, where it was all noisy and unreal … I felt like I was floating through the skies above our past and looking down upon us all and how we used to live.'

'But how?' I burst out. 'How is it possible? They don't know us here, do they? They don't know anything about where we came from, or how we lived at the Homestead. They don't really know anything about us…'

Al shrugged and Tillian smiled indulgently at her boyfriend. His eyes were all bright with delightful memories. I felt a horrible chill stealing over me. The Authorities know everything about us, I thought.

After Tillian left, Al went excitedly to bed ('Christmas Eve tomorrow!') and Peter went off to the bathroom. I suspected he was keen to use the shower again, getting the most out of its novelty. He was putting on a very brave face, I knew. He'd been quietly irritated by all our chatter about toyshops and the like. All he could think about was what might be happening to Karl. Was he safe? Was he terrified? Had someone fed him? I patted his arm as if he were the pet, telling him, 'Tomorrow we'll get right back onto the search. We'll get him back.'

His expression told me he was prepared for the worst. Then he said, 'What your brother told you about the wooden toys and the playset in the store – it really freaked you out, didn't it?'

I nodded. 'And I'm not even sure why. It's how we must seem to them, I suppose. Just playthings. Distant, made-up, fantastical creatures.'

He kissed me on the cheek and went off to sleep on the sofa.

Back in my room I lay on my bed and found I was too tired to sleep. My thoughts were so disordered I couldn't clamber back inside my Victorian novel. What I did though, was reach into my bedside cabinet and take out that single piece of paper again, and read the address to myself.

536 / Appt D
Bolingbroke District
900044 NNVX

These few lines kept creeping into my head like the stanza of a poem that had a meaning I couldn't get. They were important somehow, the way they kept suggesting themselves. I slipped the piece of paper, without really thinking about it, into my purse.

The next day was long, frosty and frustrating.

We went back to the Ruskin District and the quad where the students had been agitating the night before. In the icy morning we found everything empty and still. We managed to get ourselves back into the Department of True Life Stories because I guess, to the guards and such, we just looked like any other students. There was nothing particular about our furtive shabbiness to mark us out. When we hurried by her desk, I was aware of the penetrating gaze of the pink-haired receptionist. She didn't stop us, though.

Peter led the way to Dean Swiftnick's office. His memory of the building's layout was good. The corridors were congested with students on the move, and once we'd fought our way through, we found a sign saying he was out on business for the day, and his office hours were cancelled till further notice.

Peter swore and thumped the door. For the first time I actually found myself thinking – are we really going to get his Karl back? And Toaster? Are they both completely lost to us?

I decided that if the Professor wanted my memories that badly, he could have them. He could use his horrible brain drain machine on me again, but only if he returned Karl and Toaster to us.

I knew Peter was hideously disappointed. I knew he had imagined some miraculous reunion with a barking, happy, waggy, trembling Karl, and it hadn't happened. I made up my mind to tell him I would bargain with Swiftnick as soon as we saw him again. And then we ran into someone I recognised at once.

It was Tillian's Da, the nattily dressed Mr Tollund Graveley. He stood out a mile amongst the scruffy students in his immaculate charcoal-grey suit. For a beat he looked astonished to see me, but it took only a moment for him to smooth his reaction over and turn back into his calm, collected self. 'Lora Robinson, my dearest girl. How absolutely extraordinary to come across you in this place.'

I asked him suspiciously, 'Why are you here?'

He flushed at my poor manners. 'My newspaper, *The City Insider*, often liaises with academics from this faculty, using them in a consultative role…'

'Dean Swiftnick,' I said suddenly. 'You're in league with Dean Swiftnick.'

A whole gaggle of noisy students surged past and Peter was drawn away from us. Old man Graveley and I found ourselves pressed against a noticeboard.

I gasped. 'That's how Swiftnick knew I had heard about

the antique hunters. You told me that awful story…' My head was spinning with conspiracies.

The old man was flummoxed, beetling his bushy brows at me. 'I am afraid I have no idea what you mean…'

'Never mind all that,' I snapped. I needed to get Al away from the Graveley family and away from his beloved Tillian. If her father and the Dean were in cahoots then I didn't want my brother anywhere near any of them. But how would he react to that?

Peter was pushing his way through the crowd towards us, like a swimmer against high tide. Mr Graveley leaned over me. 'Actually, Lora my dear, there is indeed something I need to tell you. I think I must take advantage of this extraordinary coincidence of our bumping into one another…'

His breath reeked of some kind of spoiled meat – a mess of horrible offal. I drew back. 'What do you want?'

'Well, it seems that my foolish daughter has done something rather unfortunate.'

I went cold. Was he going to say something was wrong with Al? Something had happened to him? And yet I'd seen him that morning at breakfast. He was happy and fine.

'It seems that, in a quite extraordinary act of indiscretion, my silly daughter has given your brother a particular bundle of papers. Now, these are very important and secret documents printed by the Archive Machine at *The City Insider*…'

I saw what he was after and knew that I had to play dumb. 'Really? I don't think so.'

He bent even closer, with his breath blasting hot on my face. 'You know what I mean. My daughter gave your brother a fancy box, tied up in ribbons, the night the two of you were entertained at our apartment. You are now in possession of that box, and the bundle of papers it contained.'

'Oh, that.' I saw I couldn't deny it any further. 'It was nothing. Just empty pages.'

'I hardly think so. It is the property and copyright of the City University. And I will have it back, my dear.'

I didn't say anything. Just kept staring at him defiantly.

'Extraordinary willfulness,' he whispered. It was as if we two were the only people in the whole building. He carried a feeling of deathly hush with him. 'You really have the most fiercely stubborn personality I have ever encountered. I thought as much when I first met you. I suppose your intransigence is how you managed to escape alive from the ghastly, benighted place that produced you.'

I wanted to punch him.

'We want those papers, Lora. But we will be reasonable. Have the bundle back in its chocolate box, all tied up in ribbons, and I will call on you tonight with Tillian, when she comes to pay her visit to Al. It will be a lovely social call and you will offer me refreshment and hand me back my property.'

Still I didn't say anything. I realised that Peter was standing very close by, observing everything. Mr Graveley's manners were impeccable. He bade us both goodbye, turned smartly on his heel and was gone.

'Who was that creep?' asked Peter. 'What was he saying to you?'

I shook my head. 'I'll explain as we go. I need your help, Peter. You said you could help me find my way across the City...'

'Yes, anywhere.'

'There's somewhere in particular I need to be. This afternoon.'

'The traffic will be busy. It's Christmas Eve.'

That brought me up short. Of course it was. Christmas had snuck up on me. I'd been so concerned with everything else – these mysteries and Disappearances and all – I had nothing ready. No food, no decorations, not even a present for my brother.

I came from a place where everything was so ordered and the seasons' rituals always followed a laid-out pattern of anticipation and preparation. Here in the City things were much more chaotic. Time moved in jerks and jumps and you had to keep up, otherwise you'd be left out.

On the Pipeline train Peter examined the small piece of paper I had tucked into my purse.

'But what will we find at this address, Lora?' he asked. 'What are you hoping will happen?'

I truly didn't know. But if Mr Graveley didn't want me to have this information then I knew it was something – *somewhere* – important. And I intended to find out why.

I sat fretting in the wooden train carriage in the underground tunnel, watching the greenish steam flooding by, hardly aware of my fellow passengers. I felt bad for Peter. I'd let his pursuit of Karl slip by the wayside, caught up in my own search.

We climbed out of our train at last and up innumerable stone staircases and one of those escalators I still couldn't get used to. The tiled station echoed pleasantly with the voices of a choir singing Earth songs I didn't recognise. Snow was blowing down from street level and I thought: Why can't I just enjoy the holiday like everyone else? Why can't I forget my concerns and simply have a nice time?

I could buy a gift for Al. I could forget all the mysterious stuff and just go buy him a present. And what if I bought that prairie playset and all its wooden figures? He could set them out and imagine the world we used to live in. Then, suddenly, that seemed a ridiculous thought and, besides, how much did it cost and how little money did I have? Did I really think the Authorities would keep giving me cash, after I'd run out of Swiftnick's Remembering Room?

What if they took the apartment off me? I was following Peter up the slushy red steps to the busy street above. It hit me that I could be homeless in the New Year, living rough on the cold streets of the City Inside. I'd not even thought of that when I'd escaped from the Dean's memory machine.

We did battle with the oncoming crowds, or were drawn along on their tides through broad thoroughfares where we could barely see the colourful window displays. There was a barrage of exotic smells from street food – sickly sweets, spitting hot fat, Christmas fruit and spices. I even felt a tinge of festive nostalgia at some of those scents as we bustled by.

Peter paused to consult a City map and looked again, frowning, at the piece of card with the address on.

'It's so good of you to help me when you're worried about Karl.'

'We're in this together. We're a team, aren't we?'

I felt he was right and it was our togetherness that was keeping us both calm. With all the festivities ringing brashly about us, I was glad of Peter's dependability. He felt real. I knew he always saw things as they actually were. He knew his way around this strange City and he made me feel safe. We were a team because neither of us fitted in and we both knew it.

He led us away from the main boulevard and all its brightness into a series of twisting back streets, deeper and deeper into the City. We passed more modest, then more down-at-heel stores and dwellings. Metal staircases zigzagged up tenement blocks way above our heads and I realised that thousands of people must live up there behind those humble-looking windows. Most were shuttered against the cold and dark.

We hurried up the steel rungs of fire escapes, careful of the frost and slimy ice. We went up two, three, four storeys. It was all a far cry from the smooth, mirrored bronze of the elevators in the tower where I lived.

Candles flickered and dipped on draughty windowsills as we went by and I saw the vague shapes of inhabitants watching us and shrinking back into the gloom. Peter urged me up to the fifth floor and the particular apartment door we were after.

536 / Appt D

Unlike the doors beside it, the red paint wasn't blistered and the number was on a neat little sign, not written with pen. Someone who lived here took some pride in this humble abode. But the door didn't reveal much more.

Before I could even ask Peter what he thought we should do, he raised his fist and knocked hard, three times.

I held my breath.

A square letterbox, almost at head height, flapped upwards. There was warm light and a waft of delicious baking smells. It took a moment to see a face there. We could see the wrinkled, dark orange skin and the thin, cracked lips, painted a festive scarlet. The teeth were yellow and broken.

A very unfriendly voice came out of the mouth. 'Go away,' it said. 'Whatever you're after, we don't have any of it here. Go and bother someone else. It's Christmas, you know!'

41

'Please madam,' said Peter, so politely. 'My friend here was given this address and it's very important to her.'

I felt unsure and numb, standing out on that fire escape. I was trying not to look down.

'What's that?' demanded the ancient voice. It was so scratchy it was hard to tell if it was a man or a woman. 'Well, let her speak for herself, why don't you? What is it you're after, girl? Why are you knocking on doors where no one wants you? Why are you bothering old folks on Christmas Eve?'

When my voice at last came out, I sounded so young and shaky. 'It was just an idea, that's all. I'm not even sure why we came knocking on your door. We'll go now.' I made a swift gesture to Peter. I was shivering. 'This was a mistake.' I turned back to the flap in the door. 'Goodbye, then.'

The wrinkled face gurned. The old woman was chewing her own lips thoughtfully. It looked like she was powering up to unleash a stream of horrible invective on us. We were going to get berated for wasting her precious time.

Something went clink and fizz in my mind. The echo of a memory.

I remembered another nasty old woman who pursed her lips just like that, and who'd chomp her yellow teeth before she bawled you out.

There was no time to develop the thought any further. Thudding footfalls made the whole fire escape tremble. Someone large, heavy and determined was running up the zigzagging staircases from ground level towards us, coming at speed.

'Ma?' called a gruff voice below us. The man sounded concerned. He had heard our voices and the old woman telling us to go. 'Ma, are you all right?' It was a very resonant voice. A strong and dependable voice.

My breath froze in my throat and my heart was the size of a sack of sand in my chest.

Bang bang bang on the metal rungs, the running man came closer. I looked down and saw the bulk of him. He was swaddled in heavy winter clothes, and wearing a dark hat and muffler.

Everything about him – even glimpsed from this odd vantage point – was instantly familiar.

Peter noticed my strange reaction. He thought I was about to faint and fall over the side. 'Are you all right?'

The old woman's mouth was grinning in ghoulish satisfaction. 'I'm here, Edward! I'm all right, but I'm getting harassed. I've been dragged to the front door by these ruffians!'

She shouted past us, smacking her cracked lips and

gloating. 'My Edward will see you off, you robbers! Try to get inside an old woman's home, would you? Steal her few poor possessions, would you? Edward – help me! I'm here! Come quickly!'

Peter told me, 'I think we'd better go.'

But I couldn't move a muscle.

The bulky man reached the top of the staircase. He towered over us both. He removed his battered hat and rubbed the snow out of his hair and beard. He stared at me and his eyes burnt holes in my face.

'Lora,' the man said.

I could only get out one word in reply.

'Da…!'

Where had he been?

Had he been here all along?

He had been taken away. He had been Disappeared. We had learned to live with that fact. I knew better than to hope to see him again.

We stood staring at each other. Nobody moved.

At last Peter spoke up. 'Lora – do you know this man?'

Da spoke roughly, moving past us to the apartment door. 'Open up,' he told the still-visible mouth in the hatch.

After a few seconds there was the sound of locks and bolts sliding and slamming. Then the door opened, revealing Grandma in the warm hall light. She looked even older and more fragile than when I'd last seen her. She was even more tanned and leathery, too.

'It's Lora, is it?' she cackled. 'I would hardly have known you.'

I didn't move to hug her. I didn't know what to do.

We were led inside. Those wonderful baking aromas enveloped us. Da followed us into the hallway and secured the door.

The old woman took us into a spacious but cluttered living area. Aged Christmas decorations were everywhere: cheap, cheerful and tatty. There was a tinsel fir tree in one corner.

This was the home – incredibly – of my da and my grandma.

Da was staring at me. 'You look older. Even though it's only been a few months. You are the spit of your ma.'

I said, 'You can't be here. Either of you. This isn't possible. It can't be true.'

'We are,' said Grandma, sitting heavily on a faded armchair. Her voice was still harsh and her eyes were shifty. 'You know it's us. Of course it's us. Who else would we be? We never forgot you. Not for a single day. Could it be that you've forgotten us?'

'Of course not!' I said. 'But you both Disappeared. We thought you were dead and gone. That's what we believed…'

Grandma wore a patch where her glass eye had fallen

out. Now that I looked, she had a new cybernetic leg that sparked as she adjusted it.

There was no doubt that they were who they said they were.

I fell into my da's arms and when he hugged me close I thought I would suffocate happily in the feeling of coming home.

'Is Hannah with you?' he asked. 'And your ma?' It was as if every word pained him. 'And what about Al? Are they all here in the City Inside?'

'Al lives with me,' I said, trying to see through my tears. 'The others … I don't know. We were all separated, I don't know where they went, or if they are OK or not. It was terrible, Da. We left the Homestead. We went into the wilderness alone…'

He hugged me closer. 'I know. I know. Don't cry, Lore. I know how difficult it must have been. You did the best you could. We were hoping that one day you would find us and come to be with us…'

We didn't attempt any further explanations or swapping tales. There would be time for that later. We simply gazed at each other.

Da looked like he had aged some since his Disappearance. He was more grizzled and grey, but he was still vigorous and powerfully strong.

Grandma hopped out of her chair and hurried away to bring us mulled wine and some spicy bread. Just the type she used to make at Christmas when I was a little girl.

'You live here,' I said, trying to make it all sink in. 'You actually live here, in this City...'

I was suddenly aware of Peter on the periphery of my vision. I called to him and introduced him to my surviving family members.

I don't remember much about our journey back across the City, late that afternoon. My thoughts were saturated with the heady spiced wine Grandma had made us drink.

Peter came with me. Our plan was simple. We would go home and fetch Al and bring him back to Da and Grandma's apartment. There we would have a family Christmas together. It would be kept a surprise to Al until he got there.

What could be better than that?

'We've got a goose,' Grandma was cackling when we set off. She was smiling by now. 'You fetch that little boy of ours.'

We sat in the Pipeline carriage and Peter touched my hand. 'Are you sure you're all right?'

I was. I truly was. This was the best possible Christmas present. An impossible present. But I was freaked out and my mind was swimming frantically to catch up.

They were alive. They had been transported here, some months ago, so far from the prairie and they had been eking out a living since then. Da was working as a carpenter at a toy workshop. Grandma stayed home most days. She still didn't relish the busy City streets. But they were settled by now in the City Inside. Their horizons had drawn in closer about them.

For these past months they had wondered what had become of the rest of their family. They had petitioned the Authorities and they had begged to know more.

I suddenly thought, Hadn't they seen the newspapers when Al and I came out of the wilderness? Hadn't they followed our story? Why didn't they try to contact us?

There would be time for these questions later. Time for a whole load of catching up.

Peter said, 'They didn't really mean it, did they? About asking me along, too? I'd only get in the way of your family reunion…'

'Nonsense,' I told him. I didn't want him to return alone on Christmas Eve to his Den. I could imagine him sitting in his alcove, without Karl. He said there was always lots going on down there, and maybe he would go to the bars. But I worked to convince him that he was welcome to share Christmas with me and my family.

Me and my family! How long since that had been a real, true thing?

Even so, Peter still didn't look sure. I don't think he was used to being wanted.

42

By the time we got back in Stockpot District and on Storey 202 of my building, it was evening. I knew as soon as Peter and I set foot in the apartment that we had company.

My brother was sitting at the dining-room table, flanked by his girlfriend and her father. All three were beautifully dressed. Tillian was pouring them dainty thimbles of sherry, making herself right at home. They looked like a portrait of folk in olden days.

Glancing at the room I could see that my brother had, in my absence, made an effort at decorating the place. It looked a bit spartan and sad after all the golden tinsel in the home we had just left.

I was bursting to tell him what had happened this afternoon. The miracle.

But I couldn't. Certainly not in front of the sober-suited Mr Graveley and Tillian in her fancy tea-gown.

Peter and I crashed into their sherry-tippling and we just wanted to grab Al, and to hijack him away. He looked at us in some confusion. There was that small frown line between his eyebrows that he always got when he was displeased and wasn't sure what was going on.

Mr Graveley took charge, standing up and smoothly offering me a drink.

'We aren't staying,' I told him. 'We only came to fetch Al. He's coming out with us this evening.'

The old man dismissed this with a wave of his hand. 'Oh, that's impossible, I'm afraid. You've got that quite wrong, my dear Miss Robinson. You see, you will both be spending Christmas Eve at my home, with Mrs Graveley, my daughter and myself.'

'What?!'

Al seemed upset. 'Can I see you privately, Lora?' he said, in a voice he'd never used on me before.

Then we were in my messy bedroom.

I held up my hand. 'Listen. There's something I have to tell you.'

'No, Lora. You listen to me for once. You might not like it, but Tillian's family are being really kind, asking us to spend Christmas with them...'

'No, they're not,' I snapped. 'Her family are in cahoots with the Authorities. I don't trust them an inch. You've got to keep away from them.'

'You can't tell me what to do! Not any more!' he shouted. He raised his voice, sounding like he'd been brainwashed. 'And,' he went on, 'you've got to give that bundle of papers back. Mr Graveley needs them returned. We should never have taken them.'

I shrugged and grabbed them out of my bedside cabinet.

'Whatever. He can have them. I've got what I needed from them.' I dumped the beribboned parcel into his arms. I was losing patience with my brother. Why was he turning into such an idiot?

'What's wrong with you, Lora? Why are you being like this? Why can't you just be happy?'

'Because you're so into that snobby lot?' I asked.

'You can't be happy about any of it, can you?' he yelled. 'About our new life here. You should be grateful to the City Inside. You should be grateful to the Authorities and to men like Tollund Graveley. They have given you everything you need. And how do you repay them? By running out of the Remembering Room and damaging expensive equipment and causing a rumpus. Oh yes, I heard all about that. Everyone involved is most upset. Why can't you be content and obedient, Lora? Why can't you be happier, like me? Why can't you be *grateful*?'

His voice was very high and loud by then. Was this really the Al I'd grown up alongside? The Al who'd questioned every little thing?

I hung my head, biding my time and pretending to feel ashamed. 'I don't know,' I said. 'I wish I could be happier.'

'Is it that boy you've been hanging around with?' he asked. 'That hobo?'

My jaw dropped open. I couldn't believe what he'd called Peter. He'd been so friendly to him when they met.

I pushed past him. 'I never thought you'd grow up snobby like this.'

'Me?' he cried. 'What about you? I'm ashamed of you, Lora. Look at you – shabby and paranoid and horrible! You won't get a proper job and you hang around with … vagabonds and deviants!'

I'd had quite enough of this. I spoke to him in a very quiet, controlled voice. 'This isn't you talking, Al. It's those awful Graveleys speaking through you. I realise that. Now, I'm going to give you a chance. I'm going to tell you something very important and exciting. After that you can decide what you want to do. Whether you want to come with me this evening, or whether you want to accompany the Graveleys to their home in snooty old Darwin District for their Christmas shindig.'

He frowned at me, hugging that parcel to his chest. 'I'm going with Tillian and her father. What have you got to say that will change my mind?'

So I took a deep breath and told him.

And it changed his mind.

'I'm afraid there has been an alteration in my plans,' Al told Tillian when we returned to the dining room.

She rose out of her seat. 'What are you talking about?'

'I can't come with you tonight. I'm going out with Lora.'

The Graveleys stared at us, dumbfounded. 'But,' began Tillian, 'you can't. He can't disobey us, can he, Father?'

Mr Graveley smirked. 'It would be very unseemly.' Then he snatched the parcel out of Al's hands. 'That's mine, is it? Thank you, my dear Alistair.'

I wondered when he would peek inside and discover that every page in the bundle was empty?

'Look, Tillian,' Al told his girlfriend, keen to mollify her. 'I'll see you tomorrow, won't I? We'll be together on Christmas Day.'

'It's not the same,' she said, crestfallen. 'It's our family ritual, Christmas Eve. I thought you would want to be a part of it.'

Al went to pick up his coat and gloves. 'Something very important has come up. Peter – could you please pass my scarf from over there? Thanks!' Al was looking very excited. He could barely contain himself. He hadn't noticed the distress Tillian was in or how her face was suffusing with angry colour.

'As my boyfriend you should do what I want,' she said.

Pulling on his coat and gloves, Al laughed. 'I don't think so, Tillian.'

Then Tillian surprised us all. She stepped forward smartly and slapped my brother in the face.

No one had ever hit Al before. He stood there swaying, as if he didn't know what had happened to him. I think we were all shocked, even Tillian herself. Her father just looked pleased, like he thought all of us young people ought to be soundly slapped into obeying his orders. Old man Graveley started chuckling. It was a horrible noise. Quite high-pitched.

Heee heeeeee heeeee…

A figure flew past me. It was a blur of speed and it took a few seconds before I realised it was Peter. He grabbed Mr Graveley by the furry collar of his fine overcoat and punched him hard in the stomach. Both men fell down at once, all crumpled limbs and lots of shouting. Tillian screeched, leaping backwards. Everyone was yelling, and all the dishes and glassware came crashing down off the dining table along with the cloth.

In the ridiculous, violent struggle Mr Graveley pointed a rigid finger at me. 'I blame you for all of this! You rebellious malcontent! You scheming witch!'

After that I wasn't too sure about the order of events. I just knew that I wasn't going to hang around arguing with these people. And I wasn't about to let them call the Authorities out on Peter for assault and causing an affray. I just bundled my brother and my friend out of the apartment and next thing, we were aboard the elevator and hurtling down to ground level. We were escaping!

Peter was jubilant, though his nose was bleeding where Graveley had thumped him back. Al had a hand over his mouth like he was about to throw up.

Just before we reached ground level he said, 'She actually hit me.'

'She did,' I said. I didn't say any more. Tillian had shown

herself up. Just like her father, she expected to be obeyed in all things. Far as I was concerned, Al was lucky to get this wake-up call.

We hit the Downstairs Market, which was the busiest I'd ever seen it. Peter sighed that he was missing the best night of the year for busking.

'Is it true, Lora?' my brother asked me, taking my hand. 'What you told me up there? You weren't just saying it, were you?'

I grinned at him. 'Every word is true!'

43

We ran through snowy Christmas streets. Running so my lungs were bursting and I could hardly breathe. I wanted to laugh and cry all at the same time. We hadn't run like this since we lived on the prairie. Since we were wild kids, before we were respectable City dwellers.

Peter laughed, seeing us like this. He ran with us, dipping and swerving past the shoppers, the last-minute bargain-chasers. We veered into the gutters to kick the fresh pink snow, and we darted across roads through slow-moving traffic.

We hurtled underground and onto the Pipeline, cutting through the heart of the City. Jingling carols and drummers and buskers assailed us everywhere we went. We ran like our lives depended on it. Like the Graveley family and all the Authorities themselves were coming after us.

When we got to Eventide District, we went by the department store Al had talked about. The one with the famous toy department. This was his idea. He wanted to show me what he had found there.

Of course the toyshop was mobbed. We had to fight to

catch a glimpse of the display. Peter talked to a lady sales assistant, distracting her as I leaned in close.

I could hardly believe what I was seeing.

It was the Homestead in miniature. It was our house, and our past, in every detail.

I wasn't planning on doing this. But next thing I knew I reached out and plucked out the figure that stood by the stove in the kitchen. I liberated the carved wooden mother and slid her into my coat pocket without anyone noticing.

Peter told us, 'It's the big surprise hit of the season. It's the biggest-selling toy in the store. It's all the fashion, apparently...'

'Really?' Al was delighted. But I wasn't so sure. We hurried back out of the toy department, and onto the escalators. Al asked me how much money I had with me. We both emptied our pockets to pool our resources.

'I think we should buy presents for them,' he said. 'For Da and Grandma, I mean. We can't turn up empty-handed, can we?'

'I'm sure they're not expecting anything,' I said. 'Why, until this afternoon I didn't even know they were still alive!'

Nevertheless, Al would have his way and he dithered in the ladieswear and menswear departments, picking over expensive wallets and bags, silk ties and headscarves. I knew Da and Grandma wouldn't want anything from here. They'd find these things too pricey and fancy. Also, we were wasting precious time. It was late by now and the shoppers were starting to thin out as people headed home at last.

'Al,' I told him gently. 'Just leave it. They aren't expecting presents. They just want us. They want to see us.'

He seemed nervous. 'Do you think? I don't know.' He bit his lip. His face still had a mark where Tillian had slapped him. He said, 'I feel a bit scared. What if I don't recognise them? What if they don't recognise me? We could be like strangers to each other...'

'Is that all you're worried about?' I laughed. 'Al – of course you'll know each other! It hasn't been all that long! And besides, they are your blood! Leave those silly, expensive presents. Peter – do you still have that address? Can you remember how to get us there?'

He nodded. 'It isn't far. Bolingbroke District is a few blocks away.'

'Come on, then.'

I convinced Al to put down the stuff he had been grabbing. We left the department store without having made any purchases. Except I had picked something up in there, hadn't I? With my hand in my pocket, I kept a tight grip on that small wooden model of our Ma.

We went back through the network of dark and rubbish-strewn alleys. It was a complicated business finding our way. Not all of the streets were signposted, as if these addresses wished to remain obscure. As if the streets had twisted their shapes about since our visit that very afternoon.

But after some time – and a few wrong turnings – we found the tenement building. Snow was falling heavily and the trip up those metal staircases seemed even more daunting than before. I took a deep breath and led the way. Strangely, Al didn't make a single noise of protest at the scary route. Either it didn't bother him, or he figured that we had come so far already and been through so much, a few slippery iron steps and trembling gantries weren't going to put him off now.

We climbed and climbed and climbed, past dark windows. Behind each door and each set of drawn curtains we knew families were settling down for the night and their own celebrations. And now, at last, the Robinson children were coming home, too.

'I can't believe it,' Al said, his voice very high and young-sounding in the freezing air. 'Thank you, Lora. And thank you, Peter.'

We were on the metal walkway of the fifth storey, at the very top of the building. Here was the red door again, the only one where the paintwork had been kept neat and spruce.

Inside they would be waiting for us. The old dame would be basting the goose in hot fat. Da would be tuning his guitar, perhaps, and later we would sing. We could sing all the old songs again.

I banged hard on the door. 'Da! Grandma! We're here! We're back! Let us in! Happy Christmas! Let us in!'

It took a few moments for the door to be unbolted and opened. It swung inwards and for a split second I thought: what if none of it's true?

What if there was no golden light, no tinsel nor spicy fruitcake smells? No shuffling, cackling Grandma in her apron. No laughing Da?

What if we found the hallway harshly lit and quite bare? And the flat all emptied and gutted? What if it was nothing but a hideous trap, and standing there was Dean Switftnick in his top hat and cape? Policemen with him, wearing black armour and training guns on us…?

Heee heeeee heeee…!

But these were terrible, morbid thoughts. I don't even know why I was imagining such things, when everything had turned out so right.

Perhaps I just couldn't take in the facts and accept the good news yet?

Thankfully, the door opened and the apartment beyond was wonderfully warm and festive. There was music, and laughter – and both Da and Grandma were there waiting for us.

It was one of the best nights ever. That's no exaggeration.

I don't think Al and I had ever eaten so much, and Peter looked amazed by all the food that Grandma brought out of that tiny kitchen. The old lady had been working like crazy all day. She had revived all her old skills and knowhow, and she had baked like she hadn't done in years. There were pies and squashy cakes loaded with cream, and this was even before she brought out the baked ham and the roasted goose.

'Slow down, Ma!' Da laughed. 'You'll make them burst! Have you cooked all our holiday food at once?'

'All of it!' she grinned. 'I've cooked everything that we had in the cupboards and the cold store! We've got to feed these kids up! Look at how skinny they've got! Just look at them!'

It was especially nice for me, the way they took Peter in and made him feel like a part of the family. His eyes bugged out at everything. He shook Da's hand very manfully, and complimented Grandma on her new Christmas frock, even though her apron covered most of it. Peter even joined in – uncertainly at first – when Da got us all singing together. I hoped that Peter could put aside his worries about Karl, just for tonight.

Al was grinning like a loon all evening. He seemed to forget about the mess he had gotten into with Tillian and the Graveley family and he went straight back into his childhood. He tried to hide that he wept when Grandma folded him into her skinny arms. He had always been her special favourite. He reminded her of her long-lost brother, Thomas – of course, I remembered now how she used to say that all the time. She'd always had a special soft spot for Al. Now they would be inseparable again.

'We thought you'd gone,' Al kept saying. 'We thought you'd gone for good.' He looked at Da too, and Da ruffled his hair fondly.

This was later in the evening, when we'd all eaten our fill and the dishes were cleared away. A fire was burning merrily in the grate and we sat peacefully together by the light of the Christmas tree.

'It must have been very hard for you,' said Da. 'Thinking that we had gone forever.'

I nodded. 'We thought you had been … eaten.'

Grandma gave a squawk of fright. 'Eaten! Oh, my goodness! Who'd eat me? A tough old girl like me? Tougher than the old bird we've just demolished!'

We all laughed at her, but I could still remember what Sook had said about what the Martians did.

'They took you away. You Disappeared. We thought they had eaten you…'

Da was frowning. 'But that's a horrible thing to believe! That's what you've truly thought for all these months?'

I nodded. I was starting to feel a little foolish by now.

Al said, 'We decided we had better leave Our Town and keep moving west. Into the wilderness.'

Da sighed. 'It's always been like that for us. We've always had to keep moving across the prairies. I thought we had to keep away from the Martians. That's why we kept walking into the wilderness…'

'But not any more,' cackled Grandma, looking glad. 'We don't need to keep running anymore.'

She hauled herself to her feet and went off to heat up some milk, she said, so we could have a final drink before we went to sleep. She peeked out into the snowy gully between the tall buildings and declared it best if we stayed the night. We weren't going to complain about that. She told us to fetch the spare coverlets and pillows from the airing cupboard and we could make a small camp in the living room and sleep under the tree.

While Al and Peter went to deal with the bedclothes, Da held me back for a moment. 'I know you did your best, Lore. You did the best you could to save everyone.'

'I did, Da. I really tried.'

He said, 'I believe they're still out there, you know. Your Ma and your sister, Hannah. Even that kronky old Toaster and mad Ruby. And we'll find them, I promise. We'll bring them here to be with us.'

'Good,' I said. 'But I still don't understand how you came to be here. Did the Martian Ghosts bring you to the City Inside?' I could hear Grandma singing happily in her tiny kitchen, boiling the milk. I could hear the boys messing around in the hallway, bringing duvets and things.

'Christmas next year, we all will be together,' Da said quietly. 'I promise you.'

I could tell that, for some reason, he wasn't going to answer all my questions tonight.

'And you're happy to be here, in the City?' I said. 'You don't want to return to the prairie?'

He surprised me then. 'Things are better here, Lora. Don't you think so?'

'I – I'm not sure…'

'Oh yes,' he rubbed his beard thoughtfully. 'Here, we've got the help and support of people who know far more than we do. Clever people, who've been on this planet much longer than we have. I think back to the living we scratched out of the ground before in our old lives and it seems so pitiful. We didn't even know this grand, wonderful City was here!'

He smiled broadly and kissed me on the cheek. The conversation was over, I could tell.

I was pretty surprised and all, by Da's attitude. If there was one man who'd been happy in those wide-open Martian spaces, then it was him. I never thought to see him content in a tiny, cosy flat like this. But I guess people change. The stuff that happens to them forces them to change.

'You'll see, Lore,' he winked at me. 'This is a great City. A good place for us to live.'

Then the boys were coming in with all the bedclothes to make our overnight den, and Grandma was bringing a tray of steaming mugs.

She grinned, nodding at the clock above the mantle. 'Look! It'll soon be Christmas Day!'

44

I woke before all the others.

It wasn't quite dawn.

I sat up in the festive living room under the dark shape of the Christmas tree and watched them sleeping, Al and Peter breathing contentedly. Grandma and Da were in their own rooms. The apartment was very still. The clock on the mantle ticked very softly.

I found myself looking through a gap in the thin curtains. Starlight, Earth light and a Mother of Pearl glow. I got up and drew closer, hugging my duvet to me.

One of the stars was slowly expanding. It grew into a large ball of blue light.

It was falling out of the sky, coming closer across the tall tenement roofs. Somehow I knew the light was coming directly to me.

My family and friends slumbered on as I went to stand at the window to meet this light halfway.

I thought it might be a fairy, or a genie, come to grant me wishes. I thought it might be a Christmas angel. Or a ghost.

Something marvellous, magical.

And so it was.

It was Sook.

She slid out of the sky onto the fifth-storey gantry with ease, her scaled wings folding up neatly behind her. She looked so gorgeous and perfect. I opened the window for her and in she came, noiselessly, bringing a scattering of snow. I fell into her arms and she chuckled at me.

'I found you again, Lora.'

'You were looking for me?'

'Of course.'

'You just left us here, in this City. And then you went away again.'

'Yes,' she smiled. 'That is my job. I bring you to the City. Just as I brought your father, your grandmother, and all the others.'

'W – what?'

She didn't say any more just yet. Next thing, she drew me out of the apartment.

I felt a heart-stopping pang at leaving the others behind, but I had no choice. We were standing on the roof on Christmas morning, just before dawn. It was freezing and we were flying, plunging into the frosty skies over the proud towers of Eventide District. Sook had her arms tightly about me and the whole pale, pink sky was starting to come alive. The Christmas morning light was like golden sheets of flame whirling about us.

I saw that this District was on the eastern flank of the

City Inside, where the horizon started to curve upwards into the sphere of sky. Now we were soaring back into the centre, streaking past green glass towers and sapphire steeples. I'd never seen the City look so beautiful before.

Sook kept on chuckling. She was delighted I was with her again. Her whole body shook with joy and her sheer delight in flying and holding me like this.

I recognised some of the City below us. Certain districts and distinctive buildings. I even thought I glimpsed our own tower block in Stockpot.

Soon it looked like the very centre of the City was beneath us. There were the university buildings and the grey stone of the library. Here was the smooth green dome of the Planetarium. It was in the very heart of the City Inside and now I looked all around me, I saw how huge that City was. Two hundred and fifty years in the making. All that life, teeming within.

Sook said, 'I once told you that the friendships between humans and Martians were very important.'

'You did,' I said. My teeth were chattering. My breath was coming out in long plumes.

'I brought you here because of our friendship, Lora. You must believe that.'

'Sook,' I said. 'Are there Martians here, in this City? I think I've seen them … I think I've heard their laughter…'

'They are here, Lora,' Sook told me. 'The Martians and their strange children rule this City in secret.'

I felt a horrid sensation, like small, cold hands squeezing my heart. 'Are they going to take us over?'

'We are already here. Human and Martian lives are inextricably linked in the City Inside.'

'Da says you're wrong, Sook. He says the Martians don't eat human flesh…'

'Oh, but they do, Lora. The Martians are always very hungry.'

'Well then, what am I to do?'

Sook slowed to a graceful halt above the curved rooftops. She gripped me hard about the waist, and kissed me once on the lips.

'You are going to save your people and this City, Lora. And I swear I promise to help you.'

Before I could say anything, Sook lifted us back into the skies.

I was too breathless to speak, as we took flight across the sheer, fantastic blue of Christmas morning on Mars.

Acknowledgements

Thanks to Penny Thomas and Janet Thomas and everyone at Firefly, and to Patricia Duncker.

Paul Magrs grew up in Newton Aycliffe, County Durham and went to the University of Lancaster. He was a Senior Lecturer in English Literature and Creative Writing at UEA, running their famous MA course, and then at MMU in Manchester. Now he writes full time, at home in Levenshulme, where he lives with his partner Jeremy Hoad. He's written many children's and YA titles, including five *Doctor Who* novels with BBC Books, *Strange Boy, Exchange* and *Diary of a Doctor Who Addict*.